C000186446

© 2017 Tegan Maher

Dedication

First, to Dustin, for always being there and always being you. Love you always!

To Heather Horrocks and Danielle Garrett—for being exactly who you are, and for sharing your lives, your knowledge, and your friendship. Your generous spirits inspire me.

To my baby sister Jennifer, just because of everything.

Chapter 1

Using the hem of my apron, I pulled the last batch of blueberry turnovers out of the oven and slid them onto the counter to cool. They were an even, golden brown, and a quick poke with a fork assured me the crust was light and flaky.

Perfect. The customers at Brew4U, my best friend and cousin Raeann's coffee shop, were going to eat them up. And that was good, because right now every few bucks mattered.

Speaking of money—I glanced at the clock on the microwave, and that cold, I'm-gonna-be-late feeling swept over me. As always, time had gotten away from me while I was baking; I only had about fifteen minutes to get to work. Panicked, I turned the oven off with a wave of my hand, then bolted into the laundry room and pulled my server's apron and work shirt out of the dryer. I changed into the tank top on my way through the living room, grabbed my purse, and bolted out the front door.

And nearly face-planted when I tripped over our miniature donkey, Max, who was napping at the bottom of the steps.

"Watch it, you big clod," he snapped. "Maybe I shall kick *you* in the head the next time you're napping." He yawned widely, taking most of the intimidation factor out of the threat.

"If I were sleeping at the bottom of the steps, I'd expect to get kicked in the head," I said over my shoulder as I recovered and headed toward Bessie, my faded blue, shabby-chic 1984 F-150. Yes, shabby-chic is code for "POS." Don't judge me; it's paid for.

And yes, the donkey talks, but we'll get to that a little later. Trust me—after you meet him, you'll be glad for the delay.

I slid into the truck, yelping and lifting my hips when the backs of my thighs hit the searing-hot cracked leather seat. I pushed my apron under my legs and settled back gingerly, then, with an encouraging pat to the dashboard, I cranked the key. Bessie coughed and wheezed a little, but surprised me yet again when she caught and roared to life. Another check in the win column for the day. I backed out of the yard and headed down the driveway to the main road, admiring the late-morning view.

Even with my window down, the temperature inside the truck was just this side of hellfire, so I reached across the seat and cranked the passenger window down, too. Midsummer in southern Georgia was brutal. The AC in the truck had gone out a few months back and, unfortunately, fixing it didn't even make the top twenty on the laundry list of priorities that demanded a chunk of my check.

Still, as I rumbled out of the yard and drove past the horses grazing in the pasture, I figured I didn't have a whole lot to complain about in the scheme of things. No matter how many times I traveled our mile-long driveway, I never got tired of it. Ancient oak trees draped with Spanish moss lined both sides, forming a canopy of leaves and limbs, and small patches of sunlight dappled the shaded road.

I breathed a sigh of relief as I entered the tunnel of shade and the interior of the truck finally dropped below the melting point of flesh.

Just as I turned onto the main road, I spotted a couple of deer out of the corner of my eye. When I tapped the brakes in case they decided to run out in front of me, the pedal felt spongy. Since my house sat on an overlook outside of town, much of my drive was a steady, winding descent; brakes weren't exactly optional, so I tested them again.

I was coming up on the first of several hairpin turns, so when the pedal went clear to the floor, so did my heart. Cold fingers of panic raced down my spine as I stomped on it again, then a third time, to no avail. The truck picked up speed, and as I bounced and rattled toward my demise over potholes that now felt like craters, I had only one thought: How on earth was Raeann going to finish raising my hellion of a little sister without strangling her or hexing her into a convent?

You heard right—I said "hex." We're witches, which you'd think would have come in handy right about then. You'd be right, except I was too freaked out—and busy trying not to die—to pull any magic together.

SWEET MURDER

I managed to make it around the first curve, but there was another one a quarter-mile ahead. If I dropped off the road there, I would careen about three hundred yards down a steep slope and fly over a cliff into a granite quarry — assuming I didn't meet my maker by smashing headlong into a tree before then.

Adrenaline flooded my body, and I felt like I was wearing boxing gloves as I did my best to wrangle the truck into the turn. I was almost home free when the passenger-side tire dropped off the steep berm, blew with a tremendous bang, and jerked the truck off the road.

After that, it was all over but the crashing.

The truck plowed through the brush at the edge of the road and kept rumbling right on over the edge. My skull *thunked* off the doorframe and the forward momentum shoved my knees into the dash—in the '80s, seatbelts weren't quite what they are now. The sound of rocks and bushes scraping the undercarriage harmonized perfectly with the terror raking over my nerves.

My head whipped forward and cracked on the steering wheel, and my seatbelt finally caught. I came so close to a giant oak that it ripped my mirror off and flung it into the truck. I scrunched my eyes shut and threw my arms up to defend my face from the incoming debris.

Then, just when I'd resigned myself to a bone-crushing demise, the truck lurched to an abrupt stop.

For a few seconds, I was afraid to open my eyes, then I was afraid not to. Metal groaned and I reached forward with shaking hands to shut the truck off. I poked my head out the window to see what had stopped my descent to certain death—or at least extreme agony and disfigurement—and saw that a little maple tree about eight inches thick was wedged between my rear bumper and the body of the truck.

Bessie slid a bit, so I didn't waste any more time. I opened the door and jumped from the cab, releasing a sigh of epic proportions as I landed relatively unscathed in the soft grass. I grabbed my purse from the floorboard and just left the door hanging open, scared the movement would send the truck the rest of the way over the hill. The last thing I needed was to completely lose my transportation, and there was no way I had enough magical mojo right then to pull it back up the hill. That trick would have been a stretch on my best day, and this definitely wasn't that.

I bent over with my palms on my knees, waiting for my body to stop shaking enough to make the trek back toward the road. Once I had a modicum of control over my limbs, I walked up the hill a bit and collapsed onto a butt-sized rock, staring in disbelief at the sight of my beast of a truck dangling halfway down the hill from that one scrawny little maple tree. Something trickled down the side of my face and when I touched my eyebrow, my fingers came away sticky with blood. I hadn't even felt the pain until right then.

I put my head between my knees and thanked the universe for giving me a pass, and sent a grateful push of energy to the little tree. When my hands stopped shaking and my head cleared enough to allow me to think beyond surviving, I reached for my phone and scrolled through my contacts until I found the number for Skeeter's Garage and Appliances.

Don't let the name fool you; he meets all three of my gold-star requirements: he's good, he's honest, and he's cheap.

After three rings, Skeeter himself answered. I'd never been so happy to hear his cheerful twang. I gave him the 411 on what had just happened and told him where I was, grateful for once that I live in a small town where the only directions required were "the curve right above Old Man Bailey's quarry on the way to my place."

I ended the call and had turned to scramble the rest of the way up the hill when the feeling of being watched made the hairs on my nape stand up. I searched the trees and caught a glimpse of sunlight reflecting off something a hundred yards or so up the hill on the other side of the road. My gaze darted toward the glint and I scanned the spot for any other sign of movement, but all stayed still. I decided to stay right where I was, figuring it would be a whole lot harder for some ax-wielding serial killer to drag me up the hill than to just shove me in a van if I was standing conveniently by the road.

Yes, I'm a capable witch, and I live in BFE, Georgia, where the odds of a random serial killer just happening by were about the same as going to Walmart without seeing at least one hairy butt crack. But I wasn't feeling particularly rational at that point.

Pulling as much defensive magic into my hands as I could manage in my frazzled state, just in case, I leaned on a pecan tree and hoped Skeeter would hold true to his promise to get there in "two shakes of a coon's tail" before my paranoia got the better of me.

Little did I know then that just because you're paranoid doesn't mean you're wrong.

Chapter 2

It only took Skeeter about ten minutes to get there, and when he looked over the hill, he gave a low whistle. "Holy sh—moly, Noelle. You must be doin' somethin' right cause there's no way that little ole tree shoulda stopped that truck like that. You sure you're okay? I can take you home or the hospital instead."

He looked me over head to toe, but in a non-creepy way. Skeet and I had grown up together and I was sort of the little sister he never had; just ask Billy Johnson, the guy who got handsy with me at my freshman homecoming.

I nodded as I wiped the blood off my face with the mostly clean bandana he offered. "Yeah, I'm all right. I just cracked my forehead on the steering wheel or something. I'm probably gonna be sore as all get-out tomorrow, but I think I can walk it off. I can't afford to miss my shift, especially now."

We both knew what "now" meant; I'd recently inherited my farm when my aunt Adelaide had passed, and thanks to our no-good crook of a sheriff, the county "inheritance" taxes had taken every dime I had and then some. I was barely scraping in enough cash to cover groceries and lights for my sister and the myriad of critters we had.

Shaking his head in disgust, he motioned to his tow truck. "I know how you feel. I just had to pay taxes on the shop and barely came away with my scalp. Hop in. I'll give you a ride to town then swing by and pick up one of the guys to come back and help me haul your truck up."

Taking one last glance over the hill, I pulled out my cell and took a picture; this was gonna be one for the records. I also scanned the woods one more time, even though the feeling of being watched was gone.

By the time we made it back to town, my nerves had settled and I'd convinced myself it had been the trauma and my imagination, enhanced by the psycho-slasher flick Rae and I had watched on Lifetime the night before.

I didn't want to admit it, but I was already getting sore. I dug through my bag for Advil as I called my boss, Bobbie Sue, and told her what had happened and that I was on my way.

After several rapid-fire, mother-hen questions, she informed me in no uncertain terms I wasn't working that night. "You just dang near died, and you're gonna feel like somebody took a baseball bat to you in another couple of hours. Go home, take a hot bath, and call me if you need anything. You sure your head don't need stitches? Maybe you should go to the ER, make sure you ain't got a concussion."

Though I appreciated her concern, I assured her that I was fine and tried to convince her I could work. She wouldn't budge. Since my afternoon had just opened up, I asked Skeeter to drop me at Brew4U. Keyhole Lake's gossip circle worked better than any PA system and the coffee shop was one of the two hot spots, so Raeann would hear about my wreck within the hour if she hadn't already. I needed to stop and let her see for herself that I was okay before she heard about it second-hand.

When Skeeter rolled to a stop in front of Rae's, I reached across and gave him a hug.

"Thanks a ton, Skeet. I don't know what I'd do without you."

He hugged me back and I smiled at the scent of Old Spice and motor oil that was uniquely him. "Don't you give it no nevermind, Noe. You know I've got your back. I'll drag that ole workhorse of yours up that hill and set her to rights in no time. Don't you worry."

My smile turned to a cringe as I slid out of his truck and tried to straighten up. I felt like my muscles had locked into place while I'd been sitting there.

Skeet waited for me to make it to the door of Brew4U before he rolled away. With a final wave, I pulled the door open. The happy jingle of the bell above the door and the whoosh of cold air against my skin almost made me cry with relief as I made my way to the black faux-marble counter and leaned against it.

I must have looked worse than I thought because when Raeann saw me, the color drained from her face. Her mama and my mama were sisters, and we'd been best friends our entire lives. We were more sisters than, well, most sisters. We'd learned magic together and were so inseparable growing up that she had her own room at the farm. She had an incredible knack for herbology, which was why her coffees were so good. She seemed to know exactly what blend was right for every circumstance and was quickly making a name for herself and her little coffee shop in both magical and mundane circles.

She rushed toward me and pulled out two seats at the coffee bar, then reached out and pushed my hair back from my forehead to look at my brow.

"What on earth happened to you? You look like you got hit by a truck."

I gave her a wry half-smile as I caught a glimpse of myself in the mirror behind the bar. She wasn't wrong. The cut on my forehead was crusted with blood, and my cheek was streaked with it too, along with dirt and mud. My hair had mostly escaped its ponytail and was a frizzy mess. My jeans were dirty from where I'd fallen a couple of times walking up the hill, and my fingernails were caked with dirt. No wonder the few patrons in the shop were staring at me; I looked like a deranged zombie.

Instead of sitting down, I hobbled toward the bathroom, motioning to Raeann. "Funny you should put it that way—because a truck is exactly what did this to me. Come with me. I'll explain while I try to make myself look like something that didn't crawl straight out of a grave."

She reached for a clean bar towel and the first aid kit, then followed me. "Roy, keep an eye on the front for me, will ya?"

Roy, a spry, eternally happy little old farmer, had become a regular since his sons had taken over most of the day-to-day work of his farm. He and my mom and Aunt Addy had grown up together. Back when we were kids, we use to swim in his pond and eat peaches from the trees that surrounded it for lunch. Now, more often than not, you'd find him and Jimi—another old timer—playing chess and arguing politics at Brew4U in the early afternoon.

"Sure thing, sweetheart," he said. "You take care of our girl."

In the bathroom, she pushed me onto the toilet so she could reach my forehead better, then pulled her sable hair into a ponytail so she could see to work. At five-one, she was still barely taller than me, even though I was sitting. She wet the rag and slapped my hand away when I tried to take it from her, then started carefully dabbing at the cut.

"Now spill," she demanded, concern reflected in her hazel eyes as she gently cleaned my cut.

I shrugged. "There's not really much to tell. The brakes went out on my truck, and I missed the turn above the quarry and went over the hill into Old Man Bailey's field. Thankfully my bumper caught on a maple tree about halfway down."

She rinsed the rag and began to scrub at the uninjured part of my eyebrow, then wiped my cheek clean before washing her hands and reaching for the first aid kit.

"I told you that piece of crap was gonna get you killed some day," she said, frowning. "I know you're broke, but you need to trade it for something that's not thirty years old and held together with chicken wire and baler's twine." She dabbed a blob of her secret-recipe neon-green healing ointment onto the cut before slapping a butterfly bandage over it.

"It's no big deal. I'm fine." My words sounded defensive even to me. "It's my own fault for ignoring Skeeter when he told me to bring it by so he could check them out. Though I have to admit, I thought I was a goner." That glint of sunlight off something shiny flashed through my head again, but I didn't want to mention it. Raeann worried about me enough, and it was probably nothing, anyway.

"I snapped a pic of it," I said and pulled it up on my phone.

Her eyes about bugged out of her head. "Holy crow, Noelle. You aren't joking! How the heck did that little tree stop your tank? Never mind—it doesn't matter. I'm just glad it did." She typically shared my aversion to physical displays of affection, but now she scooped me into a hug. "You're not allowed to die, you hear me? I don't know what I'd do without you."

Her voice was muffled by my hair, but I could hear the fear. I hugged her back. Truthfully, I was just as rattled as she was, though there was no way I'd admit it. I held onto her for a minute, fighting back tears as the last of the adrenaline drained from my body.

Finally, I pushed back from her, wiped the corners of my eyes, and stuffed everything back into her first aid kit. "I'm spent for the day. Can you give me a lift home? I have a batch of pastries ready to bring over, and it doesn't look like I'm going to be able to deliver them. Thankfully they were too hot to bring earlier, or they'd all be piled in the floorboard of my truck right now."

"Of course, sweetie! Just let me tell Angel I'm leaving." Angel, whose mother was the town librarian, was a teenager who helped Rae part-time.

"She took a sandwich and coffee over to her mama at the library, but she should be back. We're past the lunch rush, so she'll be fine."

Sure enough, Angel was wiping down tables and joking with Roy and Jimi, and fine with holding down the fort.

Raeann and I drove in comfortable silence for a while. My mind wandered as I gazed out the window, flashbacks of the crash colliding with worry about how I was going to pay to fix the truck. I was startled out of my reverie when she pulled the car off the edge of the road and stopped at the curve where I'd gone over.

The edge of the road was all muddy where Skeeter had dragged my truck back up, and the hill going down to the maple tree was scarred with ruts. The white flesh of the little maple shone through gashes on its dark bark where the bumper of my truck had chewed into it. I sent another burst of healing energy to it now that I was a little stronger.

Raeann viewed it all in disbelief and hugged me again.

As I surveyed the scene, every second of the crash ran through my head in Technicolor, and I shivered. "It looks so much worse now that I'm looking at it standing still."

She huffed. "I bet it does. I didn't realize it was this bad, but I should have figured from the beating you took." She turned back toward the car. "C'mon. Let's get you home."

When we pulled up in front of my house, my kid sister Shelby's car was in the drive. I limped up the steps and crossed the porch to the front door, looking forward to climbing into my pajamas and sipping a glass of wine or three.

Max, napping on the porch as usual, cracked one eye open and smacked his lips a couple of times. "Good luck."

I paused with my foot on the top step. "What on earth are you talking about?"

He gestured toward the front door with his nose. "Let's just say it's a good thing you don't have the temperament of a sixteenth-century Irish witch."

I raised a brow, confused.

Max, or Maximillian Beauregard Lancaster III, had been born a lesser British noble in the sixteenth century. He'd drawn the eye—then the ire—of an Irish witch, who'd turned him into what she believed to be a more honest representation of his true self. Through a series of odd events, we were stuck with him, but he was part of the family in his own twisted way.

He waggled his ears toward the door and dropped his muzzle back to the ground. "Just don't say I didn't warn you. Or perhaps I was supposed to warn her ..." He donkey-shrugged, then climbed to his feet and wandered around the side of the porch, no doubt in search of food.

I heaved a sigh and pulled the screen door open. I don't know what I was expecting to see when I walked in, but it definitely wasn't my sixteen-year-old sister making out with some punk on the couch. I closed my eyes for a second against the icing on this cake of a day.

She jumped to her feet, running a hand over her hair. Sparks of teenage outrage were flying from her eyes and the boy on the couch jumped up and headed toward the side door.

"Hold up there, trick!" I barked, then regretted it when pain shot through my head. He stopped dead in his tracks and I took a closer look at him. Though he'd no doubt been going for the bad-boy look, he'd overshot the mark by several yards and landed squarely on *greasy loser*.

And unless I missed my guess, he was also past his 18th birthday by a year or two.

His gaze flashed back and forth between me and the door, evaluating his odds.

I narrowed my eyes. "You do realize she's sixteen, right?"

Shelby slammed her hands on her hips, the poster child for self-righteous teenage outrage. "Oh my god, Noelle! What's your problem?" she yelled. "This is my house, too, and I can have guests if I want."

My head was pounding and I was calculating in my head how old I'd be when I got out of prison for killing her or her guest—or both of them. Instead, I pulled a deep breath in through my nose and spooled up for one of the knock-down, drag-outs that had become our new norm.

She stopped mid-tirade when my appearance finally registered. Her rage turned to shocked concern. "What happened to you? Are you okay?"

She rushed over to get a better look, while the greasy groper made his escape out the back door and hopped his bicycle back to Loser Town.

I rolled my eyes at his cowardice, but that just caused another pain to shoot through my head. "I'm all right," I sighed, letting just a little bit of Scarlett O'Hara drama seep into my tone. "I just almost died, is all."

Yeah, sue me. I wasn't above playing on her pity as payback for her shenanigans while she thought I was working to pay the bills. My satisfaction didn't last long though, once she scooped me into a fierce hug and burst into tears. Ugh. Teenage hormones.

I relented and hugged her back, because lately her love/hate feelings for me hadn't leaned toward love much. The road to finding balance after Addy died had been a bumpy one.

"Seriously, I'm fine," I told her when she pulled back and examined my face more closely. "It wasn't a big deal."

Raeann looked at me like I'd lost my mind, and snatched my phone out of my pocket. She pulled up the pic and flashed it at Shelby while relating what had really happened. I blew out a breath and headed to the kitchen, where I pulled out my special blend of lavender and chamomile tea laced with just a bit of willow bark. Rae had made it and I figured it was the perfect thing to calm my nerves and soothe the dull aches already creeping over my entire body.

Shelby took the blend from me and put the water on to boil, then nudged me toward the table. There would have to be a discussion about her latest rebellion, but I just didn't have it in me to do it right then. Instead, I let her make tea and pushed my fears about her future into the *I'll deal with it later* box in my head.

Shelby's concern carried over, and she opted to spend a rare evening at home, joking and talking with me and Raeann. I'd missed this side of her and wondered what had happened to the easy relationship we used to have. Lately, I couldn't even get her to tell me where she was most of the time.

We'd always been tight; our mom had made our home happy and instilled the importance of family. But Mom had died when I was eleven, and my dad had ditched us with Aunt Adelaide not long after that. Since Addy died, Shelby had been on a tear. She was running with a bad crowd, regularly blew off her curfew, and refused to practice her magic. She was mouthy and incorrigible, and had nearly been suspended from school for repeatedly sassing teachers and skipping class.

Meanwhile, I begged, yelled, grounded, took away car keys, talked 'til I was blue in the face, and made a big deal when she *did* do something right—but nothing worked. I was only seven years older than she was, and just couldn't seem to get a handle on raising a teenager. I was messing her up and had no idea what to do.

So when I got the increasingly rare chance to have fun with her, even if it meant I was sore and miserable and we were just hanging out at home, I grabbed on with both hands.

A couple of hours later, the three of us were making chocolate chip cookies when my phone rang and Skeeter's number showed on caller ID. I swiped to answer.

"Hey, Skeet. I saw you got her up okay. Thanks for that. How much damage is there?"

"Hey, Noelle. Yeah, it was a little tricky, but we managed. There's not much damage—a busted headlight, both mirrors, and the dent where the tree caught it. That's not the problem though."

I could practically see him shifting his weight from one foot to the other and taking off his cap to scratch his head then slapping it back on again. "Spit it out, Skeet. What's up?"

He paused for a couple more seconds, then said, "Well, it was definitely the brake lines, but they didn't fail because they were old. Somebody up and cut 'em, Noelle. Both of them."

I thought back to that glint of sunshine I'd seen and could barely resist the urge to pull all the curtains closed.

"Well, then," I said as Raeann and Shelby stared at me, waiting to hear what was going on. "I guess maybe I oughta call the cops."

"Yeah," he agreed. "I reckon maybe you should. For all the good that'll do."

Chapter 3

I pushed an errant red curl behind my ear, hoisted a full tray of teas onto my shoulder, and headed for my newest table. It was the kick-off day of the annual Fourth of July cookout at Bobbie Sue's Barbecue, and I was getting my butt handed to me.

It seemed like every one of the twenty-six thousand residents of Keyhole Lake had turned out for the various activities we were hosting throughout the day, and I'd have bet even money every single one of them had asked for at least two refills. Considering it was almost a hundred degrees in the shade, I really couldn't blame them, but that didn't make carrying endless trays back and forth suck any less.

Of course, considering I'd crashed over a mountain the day before, sucking was subjective. I was still riding my *I thwarted death* high, and there was still a slight rose-colored tint to my glasses. On the other hand, I felt like somebody had beat the crap out of me with a sock full of quarters, so the blush was wearing off pretty quick.

It was only two o'clock. In three hours, we'd gone through fifty gallons of tea, seventy pounds of pulled pork, and forty pounds of coleslaw. And there were still six hours to go until the fireworks started. We were only serving food until six, but most of the locals took the phrase "all you can eat" as a personal challenge.

Georgians do love their barbecue, especially when it's free.

To be fair, like all good southerners, everybody had brought a covered dish. Four long, white, plastic tables groaned under the weight of fried chicken, potato salads, casseroles of every variety, cornbread, rolls, fruit pies, and a rainbow of jiggling desserts shaped like Bundt pans. Then there were the competition peach pies lined up on a table and labeled with numbers, and—I kid you not—guarded by one of Keyhole Lake's Citizen Watch volunteers. They'd be judged by the mayor, the sheriff, and the head of the chamber of commerce later in the afternoon but until then, Lester Casto would make sure things stayed on the up-and-up.

Women around here take their pies seriously, and none of them like to lose any sort of competition. So, when you put the two together, it's confectionery carnage just waiting to happen. Hair-pulling and name-calling were almost as traditional as the contest itself, but the mayor had been accidentally creamed by a paper plate full of baked beans and deviled eggs a few years back when the smack-talking got out of hand, so now there was a strict moratorium on speaking during the competition. That didn't prevent silent gestures, but it did curb most of the overt animosity—or at least kept it at the non-verbal, non-violent level.

Fourth of July fell on a Friday that year, so it coincided with Keyhole Lake's annual BBQ competition. People came from all over the state to participate and Bobbie Sue hosted it, so that meant I had another two days to go before I could really slow down. It'd be good money, but I was beginning to wonder if there was enough Advil on the planet to get me through it.

With a smile and a little friendly bantering along the way, I delivered my tray of drinks and took orders for the next rounds as I went. As I worked my way back to the kitchen, I filled my tray with empties and scanned the buffet table to make sure we still had enough meat, slaw, and baked beans to keep the insatiable crowd from rioting.

I bumped the swinging doors that led to the kitchen open with my hip, hollered to Earl—Bobbie Sue's husband and the pit master—that we were about out of slaw, then went back to the storage room to grab more Solo cups. Armed with them and a bulk-store-sized pack of foam plates, I headed back to the madness.

I'd just filled my umpteenth tray of tea and lifted it when somebody called out my name. I cringed as I recognized the entitled, domineering bark of Hank Doolittle—Keyhole Lake's crooked sheriff, self-appointed overlord, and the bane of my existence.

I heaved a sigh and pasted a smile on my face before I turned around to see what fresh hell he'd decided to dump on me today. His presence alone was enough, but it was a sure bet he wouldn't just go for passive torture. Anna Mae, his pretty blonde wife, was getting something from the buffet, so he was sitting at a table alone, beer gut hanging over his jeans and elbows hooked over the back of his chair. He rolled a toothpick back and forth between his fleshy lips in a way that he no doubt thought was sexy. I stifled a disgusted shiver as he openly ogled my boobs and legs.

"Hey, Hank," I sighed, resigned. "What can I get for you?"

"Well now, I'm glad you asked. I understand you've decided to keep the farm." He paused and looked at me like he was picturing me naked. "Nice of Adelaide to leave you that place when she passed. I was going over the county property appraisals and noticed the farm was significantly under-appraised when it went through probate." He paused long enough for that to settle in. "I had Peggy Sue send you a copy of the new appraisal, along with a bill for the remainder of the balance. It's going to be tough to come up with all that on a waitress's salary. Sure would be a shame for it to go on the auction block. My offer to take it off your hands still stands. Course, I'll have to drop the offering price a bit now that I know it may go for taxes."

I narrowed my eyes at him; he and several other parties had made me offers on my property in the months since Aunt Addy died, but I wasn't interested in selling so much as an acre of it. I'd made that abundantly clear, but was apparently going to have to hit him with an axe handle to get it to sink into his thick, good-for-nothin' skull. "Hank Doolittle, you know good and well those inheritance taxes were already double what my place is worth, but I paid 'em fair and square. I'm not selling out to you or anybody else."

Hank just smirked at me and stuffed a huge forkful of pulled pork into his mouth. Since I'd used up my weekly portion of luck by not dying the day before, I supposed it was gluttonous of me to hope he choked.

Speaking around the food, he said, "I'm sure sorry you feel that way, Noelle. I heard you filed a report about some brake trouble yesterday. May want to take better care of that truck, being all independent the way you are. It would be a shame if something happened to you."

He swallowed and his tongue darted out to lick his lips. Despite his efforts, a blob of sauce still clung to the corner of his mouth.

"I'm also concerned about how you're having a hard time keeping Shelby in hand. She's just runnin' wild all over the county while you're working all these hours. Just the other night, my deputy caught her and some other kids partying down at the quarry. Dangerous down there." He paused and tilted his head. "I'd hate to see her get hurt."

A hot bolt of rage shot through me, and the teas on my tray started to vibrate.

Breathe, Noelle. The last thing I needed was for my temper to get the better of me. I was already under close scrutiny by the Council of Witches because of Shelby's unique situation and her complete refusal to even attempt to walk the chalk. I didn't need trouble with local cops too—especially this one. Still, I couldn't resist closing my fist at my side, imagining it was his windpipe in my hand.

He gasped and choked. Careful to keep the smile on my face, I balanced my tray and leaned a little closer to him so that he was the only one who could hear me. "If I were you, Hank, I'd be careful who I went around threatening. One of these days, you're gonna bite off more than you can chew."

I opened my hand, releasing the spell, and slapped him on the back as Anna Mae approached. He glared at me, confused and gasping. There had been rumors going around Keyhole about our family for so many years that it was pretty much a given everybody thought I was a witch. Most of 'em just didn't know for sure they were right.

Loathing tinged with a touch of fear glittered in Hank's rat-like eyes. Anna Mae sat down across from him and smiled at me, oblivious to what was going on.

I smiled back.

"Hey, Noelle!" she said. "How you doin' sugar? I haven't seen you for ages. How are things out at the farm? I sure was sorry to hear about Ms. Adelaide passing, but I was glad to hear she left the place to you. You deserve it, and it'll be good for Shelby to be able to stay in the house."

I had no idea why such a truly good person as Anna Mae stayed with the likes of Hank. It was no secret there was no love lost between the two of them, but I supposed she had her reasons. I set a couple of fresh teas on the table and straightened, carefully stepping away from Hank and re-balancing the tray so the remainder of the teas were centered.

"Thank you, Anna Mae. Aunt Addy was a good woman. The world's a little dimmer with her gone. Now, if you'll excuse me, I've got a lot of thirsty folks to tend to. You have a great time." I meant it, too.

I nodded curtly at Hank, barely able to keep the repulsion off my face, then headed toward the next table to replace empty cups with full ones.

As I walked away, I heard him tell Anna Mae, "You forgot the extra slaw. Go get it, and get some sauce while you're up."

I gritted my teeth, but shook my head and kept walking. If I turned around and saw the hang-dog look I knew she was wearing, I'd be tempted to finish what I'd started.

Turned out, I didn't have to.

I'd only taken a few steps when Hank began to choke again. Since it wasn't my doing this time, I didn't pay it much attention—but then it just went on and on. I turned and Hank was tugging at the collar of his too-tight polo shirt and sweating profusely. That wasn't really anything new for Hank because he was always sweaty, but his skin had a scarlet cast that definitely didn't look healthy. He was groping clumsily for his tea.

I thought he was actually choking—how ironic—and moved toward his table to do what I could to keep him from dying on my shift, whether I wanted to or not. He managed to pick up the cup and drank like he hadn't had a drink in days. He sucked down half the icy-cold goodness, pouring the other half down his shirt and soaking the navy polyester blend stretched over his beer gut. The empty cup clattered to the table as he tried to stand, then he sat back down again with a solid thump. The folding chair squealed in protest as all three hundred pounds of him collapsed on it at once.

Hank tried to say something, then looked at his hand as if it were an alien appendage. His eyes were wide and bloodshot, and darted back and forth as he reached for Anna Mae's tea, then they rolled back in his head as it lolled back. It hung suspended for a minute, then tipped forward, gaining momentum until he face-planted with a wet splat right in his coleslaw. His one visible, sightless eye was still bulging out of his head and drool bubbled from his slack lips as rivulets of mayonnaise-based dressing dripped off his bulbous nose.

Absolute silence reigned for the span of a couple heartbeats, then Anna Mae began to scream, and the entire place erupted into chaos. Behind me,

I heard one of the tables of food collapse as somebody who was rushing to see what had happened crashed into it. I turned just in time to see casserole dishes, bowls full of dip, and a variety of aluminum-foil-covered bowls and plates slide in slow motion to the ground in a massive heap of fried foods, bacon-laced delicacies, and sticky, fruity fillings.

One beautifully molded green gelatin creation stuffed with pineapple chunks rolled toward me and bounced twice before plopping to a jiggling stop in a pool of tea a couple of feet from my shoes. I'm ashamed—sort of—to admit the first thing that flashed through my head was that I was going to be cleaning up pies, casseroles, and bean salads for half an hour when all was said and done.

Gathering my wits about me, I tried to remember my CPR training. I pointed to Jesse Lee Simms and told him to call 911, then about threw my back out when I pulled Hank off the chair and to the ground. He landed with a thud and I began a preliminary assessment to see if he was really dead or if he'd just eaten himself into a food coma. No breathing, no heartbeat—not that I was sure he even had a heart.

I sighed as everybody around me continued to panic; it was gonna be me or nobody. I couldn't just walk away and start pouring the champagne—well, I could but it might come off as tacky. I had to try to save his worthless ass.

The thought of actually putting my mouth on his made me want to vomit, partly because he was foul, and partly because I knew some of the places where that mouth had been. Eww. I shivered, repulsed by what I was about to do.

Then, just as I mentally pulled up my big-girl panties and reached for his nose, a hand landed on my shoulder and stopped me from leaning over Hank. I closed my eyes and gave thanks for the divine intervention. I might also have stupidly promised to avoid ice cream and sarcasm for a year in payment for the reprieve, but the exact phrasing was sketchy afterwards.

Anyway, I looked up into the Caribbean-green eyes of a man wearing a deputy's uniform and a nametag that identified him as *Woods*.

Frankly, between those eyes, the solid muscles straining against his uniform shirt, and the fact that he'd just saved me from placing my lips on Hank Doolittle's, I didn't care what his name was; he was a god among men in my book. He motioned for me to step aside as two paramedics moved into the canopied area with a stretcher.

They must have already been there in case anything went wrong at the celebration, because there was no way they'd made it from across town in under two minutes, especially since it was Hank. He wasn't exactly a fan favorite at the fire station, because he'd charged old Mrs. Huddlestein the full fire fee when a few of them had helped rescue her cat from her roof.

Anna Mae was still howling and dabbing at her eyes, but the skeptic in me wondered how much of it was anguish and how much of it was hysterical laughter that she'd been so blessed on such a gorgeous day. Most everybody knew Hank stepped out on her regularly, and after nearly twenty years of marriage, that had to grind. Apparently, yesterday had been my day to get lucky, and today was hers.

I stood up and wiped my sweaty palm on the front of my bean-and-slaw-encrusted apron and shoved that stupid curl behind my ear again. I swear, I was about ready to lop it off. I'd gotten the knees of my jeans wet when I'd kneeled beside Hank, and there was something sticky all over my hand. Gross. Since there was nothing left for me to do, I headed to the back to get a bus tub to start cleaning up the mess, nearly going bottoms-up when I stepped on the ring of green Jell-O now turning to goo in the sun.

"What in the name of blue blazes are they doing to me?" Hank's panic-stricken voice sounded from behind me and I squeezed my eyes shut. I took a deep breath and turned around, dread and irritation warring within me.

Sure enough, Hank—or more precisely Hank's ghost—was trying to no avail to push people away from his body. When his hands kept running through people, he stopped and looked at his hands, then up at me.

Hoping against hope that he didn't realize I could see him, I turned back toward the kitchen.

"Noelle Flynn, you tell them to stop whatever it is they're doing and help me get back in my body or I swear you'll live to regret it. I'll ..."

At that point, the ground around him began to bubble—honest-to-God boil—and black tendrils of sooty smoke curled up around his ankles and wound around his calves. He began to scream and hurl threats at me, but the strange mist had encompassed him and was dragging him down into the earth.

His eyes were wide with terror and he reached for me, but he was hateful right to the end; he wasn't begging for my help, he was screaming invectives at me. The writhing smoke curled up his arm—the only part of him still above ground—and pulled him the rest of the way under.

The soil stopped churning as Hank's fingers disappeared; the sounds of confused, excited voices that had been dim just seconds ago returned to full volume, and things were back to normal. Or at least as normal as they could be when people were filling plates with barbecue and tapping their toes to the sound of "Dueling Banjos" while a fat, dead guy was being loaded into an ambulance twenty feet from the all-you-can-eat table.

Chapter 4

When I made it to the kitchen, I braced myself against a stainless-steel table and took a couple of deep breaths. Honestly, I felt a little guilty for my apathy towards Hank's fate, but I reckoned it was one of those rare times when I got to witness Karma in action.

I was surprised to see that Bobbie Sue and Earl were still hard at work. The sound from the dishwasher drowned out all other noise as Bobbie chopped cabbage and Earl sliced a brisket. Apparently, they hadn't heard the brouhaha that had gone on out in the tent. I stood staring at them, trying to decide how to tell them that the most hated man in three counties was being stuffed into an ambulance, dead as a hammer, at their carefully planned Fourth of July party.

Before I could decide on the best approach, the dishwasher kicked off and they noticed me at the same time. Without giving it any real thought, I blurted, "Hank Doolittle just keeled over dead in his coleslaw."

Bobbie Sue and Earl just stared at me for a few seconds, knives held in mid-air, and Sarah, the other waitress, slid her forgotten tray full of teabags and refilled ketchup bottles down on the counter beside her. Finally, my unflappable boss raised her brows. "Huh," she said before she resumed chopping the cabbage. "Do I need to bring out a fresh bin of slaw, then?"

I blinked twice then shook my head. I'd like to say she was just in shock because such a terrible thing had happened, but she wasn't. Hank was just truly that big of an ass.

Before I really had time to comfort Bobbie Sue in her time of obvious distress, there was a tap on one of the swinging doors. It pushed open before I could respond, and Deputy Woods took a step inside, peering at us expectantly with those sea-green eyes—though I had no idea what it was he expected.

Before Earl could shake a meat cleaver at him for entering sacred space, I asked, "Yes, Deputy? Is there something we can do for you?"

He didn't seem to know what to do when he realized we weren't particularly shattered because the sheriff had just fallen over dead within fifty feet of that very door. If he was expecting to find us clutching each other amidst a shower of heartbroken tears, he'd probably have had better luck telling us they revived him.

He cleared his throat and arranged his face into some semblance of professionalism. "I need to talk to the owners, please."

Bobbie Sue held up a chef's knife. "That would be me, Deputy. Give me one second and I'll meet you out there." She pointed the knife in the direction of the door, then resumed cutting up the rest of the cabbage.

The deputy took another uninvited step into the kitchen and opened his mouth to say something.

I waited for the cleaver to drop, because the man had just stepped further into the inner sanctum after literally being shown the door, but Bobbie Sue just cocked a brow and told him a bit more firmly, "I said I'll be right out."

He finally caught on, and his ears turned a bit red at the obvious dismissal. I couldn't tell if it was from irritation or embarrassment but he snapped his mouth shut, pivoted on his heel, and left the kitchen.

Bobbie Sue covered the tub of cabbage and wiped her hands on a nearby bar towel, shaking her head. "The boy obviously had no raisin', bless his heart. It's not his fault. If he sticks around here, we'll teach him some manners." Bobbie Sue was nothing if not kind.

The ambulance had already pulled away and flies were starting to swarm over the spilled food when we walked out of the kitchen and headed toward the deputy. He was leaning against a table looking over the backyard at the crowd, shaking his head about something.

Food from the knocked-over table was oozing in all directions, and the floor was littered with plastic plates and utensils. The bluegrass band had started up again outside. People were still filling their plates with meat, slaw, and the potluck dishes remaining on the three tables left standing. They were even being polite enough not to walk through the mess, though that could have just been because most of them were wearing flip-flops.

When we approached, the deputy held out his hand, first to Bobbie Sue, then to me. "Deputy Hunter Woods."

It took a minute for the name to sink in, and I slammed my mouth shut to prevent an immature giggle from bursting forth. I behaved myself because it wouldn't be polite to make fun of his name, especially after he'd saved me from a postmortem lip-lock with Hank. It also helped that he was hot with a capital H, and I was in the middle of a dry spell. Unfortunately, that happens when you live in a small town; the only thing shallower than the gene pool is the dating pool.

After the introductions were made, he glanced back out at the laughing crowd, furrowing his brow. Bobbie Sue cocked her head and looked at him appraisingly. "Well, what did you expect? That everybody would abandon the Fourth of July celebration just because Hank Doolittle kicked the bucket? Apparently you have no idea how good Earl's barbecue actually is, and you sure didn't know Hank. Shoot, for many of the people out there, his unexpected passin' is cause for even more celebration."

He stared at her, then took his hat off and ran his fingers through his dark hair before slapping it back on. "I've never seen anything like this, though. A man died right over there less than a half-hour ago. I at least expected people to show a little bit of emotion or respect. He was the sheriff and a long-standing member of this community, right?"

Bobbie Sue snorted. "Shee-it. If you're waiting for people to get all teary-eyed over Hank droppin' dead, you might as well pull up a chair and get comfortable. He was crooked as a dog's leg and mean as a snake. He abused his power, and was a bully and a blow-hard. The only thing that surprises any of us is that it took this long for his meanness to catch up with him."

She was straightening the containers on one of the remaining food tables, moving the empties to the back and tucking foil around the rest to keep out any flying picnic crashers. "Did he choke to death, or did that shriveled up ticker of his finally give up the ghost? Lord knows he stuffed so much bacon and donuts into his pie-hole, it's a wonder it didn't happen years ago."

Hunter looked uncomfortably at the ground and shifted his weight from foot to foot. "He definitely didn't choke. We're taking some additional steps just to make sure he died from natural causes. It's just standard procedure until we know for sure."

"What additional steps, exactly, and why?" I asked, bending over to pick up a pie spatula and some paper plates that had fallen off the table.

"We'll just need to talk to people. Ask some questions. And we'll run some tests on his plate of food just make sure it wasn't something he might have eaten." He was making a point to look anywhere but at us. "But I'm sure that's not the case," he hastened to add.

Bobbie Sue's face turned crimson when she realized what he meant. She stepped forward and put her finger in his face. "Don't you even dare imply anything was wrong with my food. In twenty-five years, we've never had so much as a bellyache for any reason other than eatin' too much, and if you start spreading word we flat out killed somebody, you and me"—she waggled her finger between them—"are gonna have a problem! 'Sides, you don't just drop dead from food poisoning five minutes after you eat." She waved a pair of salad tongs she'd picked up off the ground at him and scowled. "Not that there's even a remote chance that was what kilt him."

With a final glower that would have wilted plastic flowers, she stomped back toward the kitchen and through the double doors, slamming them open so hard they bounced off the walls.

For a few seconds, it felt like all the oxygen had been sucked from the area, but, being used to Bobbie Sue's temper, I wasn't fazed.

Hunter pinched his lips together and drew his eyebrows together. "She certainly seems to have some anger issues, and she made it clear she didn't like the sheriff. Have they had any recent dealings? And did she just threaten me?"

I stopped cleaning off the table, narrowed my eyes at him, and squared my shoulders. "Apparently you haven't been listening. *Nobody* liked Hank, so you can't use that as motive, else you'll have the whole town locked up. You may be new to these parts, but I'm here to tell you Bobbie Sue Banks is one of the best-hearted people in this town."

I waved the pie spatula I'd picked up around the tent and toward the crowd. "Look around you—she's eating the cost for all this because times are hard and she wants the entire town to enjoy the holiday. And that's not all she does for this town, either. She may have a temper, but she's not the poisonin' type. Trust me—if she wanted Hank dead, she woulda shot him and been done with it." I paused to suck in a breath. "And if she was threatening you, you'd know it."

He must have realized he'd stepped in it again because he held his hand up. "Take it easy. I'm not implying anything. I'm just asking standard questions. Like I said, at this point, we're assuming it was a heart attack. He was certainly a prime candidate and that's what it looked like to me. I'm just covering the bases. This is the last place he ate—"

I cleared my throat and raised a brow.

He started over. "I mean, there's a small chance this may end up being a crime scene and you were the last to serve him, so it's logical to question you."

Yeah, because pointing the finger at me was so much better. Although it probably wouldn't have bothered me so much if I hadn't half-killed him a minute before something else finished him off.

He took a deep breath and started over. "Look, I don't think anything. I just have to do the paperwork on it and I want to do it right. I've only been here for a couple of months, so I'm not really in the loop yet. I'm investigating because honestly, nobody else stepped up." He scrubbed a hand over his face. "I'm usually much better at communicating but we apparently got off on the wrong foot. Let's start over."

He seemed relieved when I relaxed and sank into a chair, motioning for him to do the same. I curled my toes and rolled my ankles. Wow, did that feel good. I'd been running non-stop since nine that morning and my feet were killing me. A soft breeze blew through the tent and cooled some of the sweat on the back of my neck. I was so caught up in the reprieve that I lost track of what he was saying for a minute. When I tuned back in, he was asking me for my version of events.

Since he seemed more interested in how Hank died rather than any speculation on my part, I started with what I saw—how he was red and pulling at his collar—then talked him through every detail I could remember right up until he saved me from making the ultimate oral sacrifice in an attempt to save Hank's miserable hide.

"Thanks for that, by the way. There just isn't enough mouthwash. I'd have likely been dead within a week from whatever was crawling around in there. Then you'd be lookin' into two fatalities instead of one."

Hunter smiled at the joke for a split second before remembering himself. His teeth were impossibly white and he looked absolutely delectable. Heat curled in my belly but I scowled and pushed it aside.

"It sounds like you didn't care much for the sheriff," he said, "but I'm beginning to understand nobody did. Can you think of anybody who would kill him?"

I snorted. What a loaded question. I gave it some thought, trying to remember anything out of the ordinary that had to do with Hank, and nothing more obnoxious than usual came to mind. Sadly, what he'd said to me that afternoon was nothing out of the ordinary for Hank. He was a pimple in the armpit of society.

I thought back to our interaction, and a tendril of doubt crept through my mind. Surely that was a coincidence. I'd dropped the spell and walked away; what happened had nothing to do with me.

Still, I didn't think it was strictly necessary to mention the fact he'd been threatening me ninety seconds before he kicked the bucket. Some information you just didn't volunteer.

"Honestly, I think it would be easier to tell you who *didn't* want to do harm to Hank, if there is anybody. He's far and away the most disliked person I've ever met. He would have taken candy from babies and smacked the groceries out of the hands of little old ladies if he was sure he wouldn't get caught. For that matter, I'm sure there were times he did."

I racked my brain for a few seconds longer but shook my head. "It's not that nobody wanted him dead," I said. "I just don't know of a single person who thought Hank was worth the time it would take to kill him. Of course, I'm not exactly at the hub of the gossip mill."

I paused, hesitant to point him to where he actually would find the latest gossip, but decided the girls could more than hold their own against him. And it wasn't like it was a secret.

"You may want to check with the ladies at the Clip N Curl. If they don't know it, it didn't happen."

He wrote that down on his notepad. "Did he have any friends? I know the department has a bowling league he played on. Any particular guys he hangs out with?"

"Hank didn't really have any friends and even the guys on the league only tolerated his cheating and showboating because they had no choice. He had a couple of lesser bullies that he kept around to stroke his ego and provide muscle when he didn't want to get his hands dirty. I guess if you count that as *friends*, you want to talk to Butch Davies and Ronnie Dean."

"Okay, thank you Miss Flynn. May I get your number in case I have any more questions?"

"Please, call me Noelle." I rattled off my phone number. "And if you need anything, I've lived here all my life. Things are done a little different here than what you're likely used to. People tend to circle the wagons when it comes to strangers, at least until you're not a stranger anymore."

He quirked his lips in a manner that was a mix of indulgent and condescending. "This isn't my first rodeo, Noelle. I've been doing this for a while in Indianapolis." He turned toward the back lot where everybody was gathered, presumably to question more people. "Thanks for the offer, though. I'll call if I need anything else. Like I said, this is all just a precaution, anyway."

I glared at him as he swaggered away toward the crowd. He might have had experience with crime in Indiana, but he was about to experience a trial-by-fire initiation into the workings of the Good Ol' Boys Club here in Georgia. He was in way over his head and didn't even know it yet, but damned if I was going to feel sorry for him now. He'd figure it out.

I curled my toes one more time before I had to stand up, then felt the wad of cash in my apron pocket. I smiled. Hank was dead, I'd made some money, and I'd met a hot guy. If it weren't for the mountain of deviled eggs, macaroni salad, and tater tot casserole I had to clean up, I'd have been positively gleeful at the way the day was going.

As it was, I turned back toward the melting, fly-covered pile of food on the floor and heaved a sigh. My Advil was wearing off, and soreness was creeping in. By the time I'd righted the table and dragged the trashcan over, I was spent. I glared at the mess then glanced over my shoulder, exhaustion and irritation prevailing over caution.

The coast was clear for the moment so I cast a quick glamour around the tent so it looked empty, then flicked my wrist toward the mess. If not for the dishes in the goo, it would have been easier to just heave it all toward the trashcan, but that wasn't how this worked. I had to salvage as many dishes as I could, or else half the town would have a hissy because I tossed Great Aunt Sally's eyesore of a pie plate.

I kept one eye on the crowd while I concentrated on moving all the non-disposable dishes from the muck to a waiting bus tub. After that, it only took me two fingers and ten seconds to move the rest to the industrial-sized garbage can, where I dropped it in with a sloppy splat.

I released the glamour and checked the tea canisters, glad to see they were still relatively full, then set about restocking plastic silverware and napkins. I had the whole tent straightened up to *good enough* in about fifteen minutes.

I dried my forehead on my sleeve and took a long drink of tea, mulling over the last couple of hours. I'd mostly blocked out the vision of Hank being sucked to his crappily-ever-after and was focused more on the here and now. Like Bobbie Sue, I was sure that Hank's heart had finally lost its battle with mass quantities of saturated fat.

Still, the deputy's line of questioning made me think. Again, guilt and doubt niggled at me about what I'd done, but I dismissed it again as an overactive conscience. However, if somebody else killed Hank, then that was a whole new can of worms. *Why* somebody would kill him was a no-brainer. Pick one reason from a hundred.

The only real mystery, if it turned out somebody punched his card for him, was figuring out who'd finally worked up the gumption to put him out of our misery.

Looking back, I really should have thought a little harder about that part.

Chapter 5

Earlier in the night, Skeeter had brought my truck over to me. I'd filed a report about the brakes with one of the deputies the day before, but I was mostly given half-hearted platitudes and a line of bull that led me to believe my report would never see the light of day.

It was almost nine-thirty by the time everybody cleared out from the festivities. We'd started cleaning up when the fireworks began, so by the time they were over, the only thing left to do was pick up the trash on the lawn.

Even Bobbie Sue, the never-ending bottle of energy, was whipped. She took one look at the mess and collapsed onto a chair. "I just have to sit down for a minute before we finish up. I'm beat. You girls have to be, too."

Sarah looked as ragged as I felt. She was a young single mom with an adorable little boy named Sean. She'd gotten mixed up with a real tool who'd left like his hair was on fire five seconds after she told him she was pregnant. To top it off, her uncle had disappeared right before Christmas, so she'd taken in his four-year-old daughter. Now she was working her tail off trying to make ends meet while raising two kids and taking classes at the community college.

I looked around to make sure we were alone, then wiggled my pointer finger to turn out the lights and extinguish the tiki torches, leaving only the moon and the glowing neon signs to see by. I muttered a few words, and in short order the yard was clear and the cans were full. I didn't have the energy to empty the cans, magically or otherwise, but the rough part was done. I dropped back into a chair beside Bobbie Sue.

I don't let just anybody in on my secret, but Bobbie Sue and Earl have known my family since before I was born, and I'd worked with Sarah for almost four years. In fact, she had some psychic talents of her own, though they were pretty much all passive. Magic ran thick through more than one Keyhole Lake family, though many wrote it off as gossip or tall tales.

Bobbie Sue sighed and put her arm around me, leaning her head on my shoulder. "Bless your little heart, Noelle. Now, let's go home."

Sarah and I split the tips folks had left in the jar rather than handed to us, and I headed toward my truck. I'm not gonna lie and say I wasn't nervous about driving again, but it had been parked in plain sight since Skeeter dropped it off. Plus Hank had practically admitted he'd been the one to cut them, and he'd been taking a permanent nap since before my truck left the garage.

I climbed in and just enjoyed being off my feet for a minute before I reached down and twisted the key. Bessie didn't groan quite as much as usual when she turned over, and I made a mental note to thank Skeeter for showing her a little extra love. I gave the brakes a few test pumps as I drove down the street—just to assure myself they worked—then turned out of town toward home.

Ten minutes later, I turned onto the driveway. Even in the dark, I could imagine the green pastures that stretched beyond the pristine white fences on either side of the road. I couldn't help but marvel that all that property, and the antebellum house and ten-stall barn at the end of the drive—along with the responsibility for their upkeep—belonged to me. I felt equal parts love and terror. Whatever happened, good or bad, was my responsibility.

Shelby and I had moved in with our Aunt Adelaide and Uncle Calvin when I was twelve years old, right after we'd lost our mother. My dad was beside himself. He barely knew how to deal with his own grief, let alone how to soothe two young girls. My sister was only four, so the concept of death wasn't so defined for her yet. I, on the other hand, was already dealing with newly acquired magic and the angst that came with pre-teen hormones.

Dad had dropped us off at the farm one day and never returned. Addy and Cal didn't miss a beat; they waited a week, then went to our old house, loaded up our stuff, and moved us in. That was that. In the following years, I spent much of my alone time in the barn grooming, cleaning stalls, and talking out my problems with my little paint mare, Brandy. Uncle Cal passed when I was 16, and it broke my heart, but we managed to get by. When Addy had passed a few months back, I was devastated.

I continued running the farm because somebody had to, and it was a good way for me to feel close to her. About a week after her funeral, her attorney came to the farm to formally notify me that she'd left me everything.

What the attorney didn't know was Addy had already told me herself a couple of days before he did. Imagine my surprise when, during one of my stall-cleaning crying jags a few days after she died, I turned around and saw her standing in the doorway to the stall. She'd passed up the opportunity to move on and had decided to stay around, at least for a while, because she was afraid to leave us behind. I couldn't have been happier. Well, except since she could no longer hold a pitchfork, she hovered over me, pointing out spots I missed.

I bumped along the pothole-ridden drive and was surprised to find a deputy's cruiser sitting in my driveway. Surprise turned to panic when I thought about why a cop would be at my house so late at night. Was Shelby in trouble? Lord, what had she done now? Had something happened to her?

My mind raced as I ran up my front steps and across the porch. By the time I made it inside, I'd worked myself into such a tizzy that it didn't even occur to me that if something had happened to my sister, the deputy would have been sitting outside waiting for me.

I slid into the kitchen with my heart pounding to find Deputy Hotstuff Jerkface sitting at my kitchen table drinking iced tea with Raeann and Shelby. Addy, invisible to him, was hovering over a spot near the stove watching but looking relaxed. From the easy way Hunter was speaking, I assumed nobody I cared about had lost life or limb and I wasn't in imminent danger of going to jail.

Once I realized that, I stopped mid-stride and waited for my heart to drop out of my throat and back into its normal spot. Shelby was laughing at something Raeann said, so she must not be in trouble, either. I cleared my throat and four sets of eyes swung my direction.

"Hey, Noelle," Raeann said. "We didn't hear you come in. I figured you'd be at least another hour or so. I was just telling the deputy here that he may want to go back down to Bobbie Sue's to talk to you." She got up from the table and pulled a pint jar out of the one of the oak cabinets beside the fridge, then poured me a glass of tea.

I sank into one of the soft kitchen chairs and ran my hand over the gleaming pine of the farm table, brushing off imaginary crumbs while I tried to figure out why he'd want to talk to me again. At that point, I honestly didn't have the energy to care. I took a long pull from the tea and rolled my shoulders, letting some of the stress of the day melt away.

"Don't worry, honey," Addy told me as she floated behind him. "He ain't here to arrest anybody. He just has a few questions. Answer, but don't offer anything additional." She paused and arched a meaningful brow at me, like she knew what I'd done. I swear, the woman took the phrase *eyes in the back of her head* to a whole new level. "Be nice. He's an outsider and don't know any better."

I was worn to the bone, and his highhandedness earlier hadn't exactly given me the warm-and-fuzzies, despite Addy's words. I just wanted to find out what he wanted so he'd leave and I could take a shower. I let out a long-suffering sigh and turned to him.

"So, I'm here. What can I do for you? I'm exhausted, sore, and can't imagine what else you'd need that I didn't include in my statement from earlier."

Raeann and Shelby looked perplexed at my rude tone, but I was too tired and irritated to care.

Hunter, at least, had the good grace to look abashed. "Look, I think I may have been a little condescending earlier."

I cocked a brow at him. "You think?"

He cleared his throat and continued. "Yes. I'm sorry. It was a really ... odd day for me, and I was having trouble wrapping my head around the situation. I still am, frankly. The reason I'm here is because I was going through the sheriff's office and found a police report wadded up in his trash can. I have no idea how it ended up in there and figured I'd ask you about it. It was one you filed yesterday about your truck."

I huffed and shook my head. Of course he threw it away. "Are you asking me why I filed it, or why it was in his trash can?"

Hunter looked a bit off-kilter, which was rapidly becoming his standard expression. "Well, both I guess."

Shelby's eyes glittered with anger, outraged for me. "That no-good sack of crap just threw away the report?" She turned to Hunter. "Somebody cut her brake lines and tried to kill her yesterday. Her truck crashed over the hill on her way to work and if it hadn't been for a bunch of luck and a tiny little maple tree, she'd be dead."

"But why would he throw it away? That should have been a priority." He looked so serious that I felt bad for him. He was obviously one of the good guys, but he was in way over his head. He might as well have been on another planet.

Addy scowled and shook her head. "I told you it wouldn't do no good to go to the cops. They're crooked as a barrel of fish hooks." She rubbed her chin. "He don't get it yet, girls. You're gonna have to spell it out for him."

I heaved a sigh and nodded. The faster he got it through his thick head that he wasn't in Northern Normalville anymore, the faster he'd leave so I could take off my pants and bra. "Look. Keyhole Lake isn't anything like Indianapolis. We have less crime, but things just don't work the same here. Sheriffs tend to have a lot of power and nobody to keep them in check, really. So if they're good people, they're good sheriffs. If they're asshats who think the sun rises just to hear 'em crow, then they're going to be arm-twisting bullies like Hank was."

I got up to refill my glass. "But, to answer your question, Hank and I didn't see eye to eye. I have no idea why he threw my report away. Maybe it was because he didn't like me. Heck, maybe he was the one who cut them to begin with. It sounds about like something he'd do. He wanted this farm."

Raeann, who had sat back down beside me, added, "She doesn't mean he did it himself. Hank was too lazy—and too fat—to pull that off. He would have had somebody else do it."

Hunter's brows shot up. "Are you seriously suggesting the *sheriff* tried to kill you to get your farm? Why would he think he'd get it even if you did die?"

I shrugged. "You're asking me to look into the head of a dyed-in-the-wool good ol' boy and sift you out a logical answer. I have no idea. Maybe he thought he could scare me into selling. Maybe he figured if I died, he'd be able to get it because Shelby's a minor. Who knows. Maybe he just didn't feel like investigating it. All I know is I filed a report."

I still didn't feel the need to come clean about my last conversation with Hank. I figured it couldn't do any good, but it sure would make me look guilty. Then the tax bit of the conversation popped into my head. That was going to be on paper. "I should probably tell you that when Hank got there today, he made it a point to mention there'd been an 'error' with the property appraisal when this house was in probate and that I owed more taxes on it."

I used air quotes, which made him raise his brows. "What do you mean, 'error?'" He tossed the air quotes back at me.

"I mean Aunt Adelaide left me enough money to cover the first round of taxes, which were already inflated. She wasn't rich, but she did have some money tucked away. Luckily, so did I. Hank knew I'm barely making ends meet and that the taxes cleaned me out. I can't pay another cent, even to hire an outside appraiser. He'd get the chance to buy the farm on the courthouse steps for the taxes when I defaulted."

While he digested that, I looked around my kitchen and drew strength from the happiness it gave me. Addy had remodeled it a year or so before, and while she'd kept the antique oak cabinets and large farm table, she'd replaced the old Formica counters with gleaming gray marble and installed a new farm sink and stainless-steel appliances. She'd pulled up the peeling linoleum and had the original wood floors refinished. The memories of helping her plan it were just as comforting as the warmth that seeped from the walls of an old house that had been filled with nothing but love.

"Who did you file the report with? Did you talk to Hank, or was it one of the deputies?"

Raeann answered. "I went with her. It was that snot-nosed little punk nephew of his. Gerald. That kid's cut from the same cloth as his uncle, but he has no spine and couldn't pour piss out of a boot without diagrammed instructions. He does have a mean streak a mile wide, but he's more the type to kick puppies rather than take on a full-sized dog."

Hunter looked confused. "I knew when I moved here I'd have to get used to some things, but I didn't realize it would go beyond language quirks and unhealthy levels of fried food and sugar. This place is like stepping back into the '60s."

I shook my head and patted him on the shoulder as I got up to refill my tea. "Like James McBride said, 'beneath the smiles and southern hospitality and politeness, there are a lot of guns, liquor, and secrets.' Welcome to

Keyhole Lake. If you're fixin' to rock the boat, I sure do hope you know how to swim."

Chapter 6

Hunter asked us a few more questions about Hank and the town, then stood to leave.

"Look Noelle, I'm really sorry I was such a jerk earlier. It's just that I have honestly never seen anything like this in my life. It's almost like I've stepped into the Twilight Zone. And I've seen some weird things since I got here, too. That doesn't help." His gaze was thoughtful and I had to wonder what weird things he was referring to. "You're one of the few people I've met who seems moderately normal."

I could barely suppress a grin as I looked around. My ghostly aunt was checking out his butt, along with my witchy bestie and little sister, and my talking donkey was snoozing on a giant dog bed by the fireplace. Yup, that's me: Miss Normal.

He looked around one more time, then cleared his throat. "If I have any more questions, I'll be in touch. And you need to stay in town, at least for a few days. No offense, but you had motive and opportunity."

Addy scowled and smacked him on the back of the head, but her hand passed right through his skull. He shivered and looked behind him, his eyebrows drawn together.

I bit my lip to keep from smiling. "If you need me, I'm not hard to find. I'm at one of three places: here, Bobbie Sue's, or Brew4U."

He nodded, then moved toward the door.

When I pushed it shut behind him, Raeann and Shelby looked at each other and giggled.

"What?"

"What do you mean, what? We caught him looking at your butt when you stood up in there," Raeann teased, shoving my shoulder.

"Yeah, because he seems like a guy who'd be attracted to a woman he thinks may have killed somebody," I said as I headed toward my bedroom to change out of my crusty, barbecue-and-sweat-scented clothes. I only made it about three steps before somebody knocked on the door. My first thought was that Hunter had decided to just up and arrest me and get it over with, but Shelby peered out the peephole and groaned.

"It's Camille. Can we just pretend we didn't hear her knock?" Camille was Shelby's caseworker from the Magical Oversight Committee, a sub-branch of the Witch's Council meant to monitor young witches, or witches who had problems assimilating.

"I heard that." Camille's voice was muffled but her irritation was plain. "And no, you can't. I'm not exactly the person you want to be rude to tonight, young lady."

I raised my brows. "Something you need to tell me, Sister?"

Shelby rolled her eyes but not before I caught a glimpse of guilt. As soon as she opened the door, Camille strode in like she owned the place, sucking all the joy right out of the room.

She gave me the once over, right down her nose. "I suppose you don't know what's going on ... *again.*"

As much as her condescending tone toasted my buns, it burned even more that she was right. My cheeks flamed and I glared daggers at Shelby. "No. I worked all day and dealt with the sheriff dropping dead at my table. I was a little busy."

"While you were serving death on a plate and glasses full of sugar water to hundreds of overweight rednecks, your little sister here wasn't paying attention to her surroundings and accidentally exposed herself to a strange mundane."

Despite what most people thought, letting somebody in on your own secret was pretty much a personal decision as long as you respected the rights of other witches to remain in the closet if he or she wanted.

However, that only extended so far. If you weren't discreet and responsible or couldn't control your magic, they took the power and the decision away from you for your own good, and for the safety of both other witches and humans. It was no joke. You couldn't just go running down a crowded beach throwing light balls instead of beach balls if you wanted to stay a functioning witch.

I pressed my lips together and pinned Shelby with my *I'm-waiting* look. She squirmed under the pressure, but finally gave in.

"Fine. I was down at the lake, back in the cove, and had a miserable migraine. I felt like I was going to explode, but I was afraid to try anything here because I didn't want to accidentally blow up the barn or something. I thought if I just tried to let a little bit of magic out, there where it seemed safe, then maybe it would ease up a little." She looked at her feet.

For the first time, Camille looked less like a hangman showing up for duty. She knew how much Shelby struggled, but she couldn't just let it go. "And?"

Shelby cast a quick glance at me, then looked back at her feet and mumbled, "And some boy came up behind me while I had some skipping stones suspended in mid-air, zipping them one at a time across the water." She begged us with her eyes to understand. "I didn't mean anything by it. I just wanted the headache to let up!"

"Shelby—" I started to tell her she knew better, but Camille interrupted me.

"This is the last time, Shelby. I have to take action. You exposed magic to a strange human for cripes' sake! What if he'd come ten minutes earlier when you were blowing up bigger rocks to make those skipping stones? You could be excommunicated and stripped of your powers!"

Shelby squared her shoulders and sneered as only a teenager can. "You know what? Take them. Please! They're nothing but trouble to me, anyway." The crystal fruit bowl on the entry table exploded and the lights flickered as she ran to her room and slammed the door shut behind her.

Time was suspended for the span of several heartbeats, all of us absorbing the shock of what she'd said. Being excommunicated was bad, but voluntarily surrendering your powers ... it was like cutting off a limb. Worse, even.

"She didn't mean that, Camille," I breathed, watching her face carefully. Her expression was neutral, but I could see her jaw muscle flexing.

She took a deep breath. "I know I'm hard on you, Noelle, but I'm not sure how much longer I can hold off the council." She turned to Addy. "I know you're here for them, but that's not enough. If you still had your magic, I'd sign her off to you to train, but you don't. And Noelle is too busy trying to put food on the table to provide proper guidance, assuming she even had the experience to do so."

Rae said, "I can—"

"No, you can't," Camille said, holding up her hand before Rae even finished her thought. "No matter what you were going to say, there's nothing you can do to make this situation better."

Addy, on the other hand, was handling it as she did everything: head-on. "The council knows good and well what the circumstances are here. Their purpose—"

"We're well aware of our purpose, Adelaide!" Camille snapped.

Addy continued as if she hadn't spoken. "Their purpose is not only to maintain order, but also to provide resources for witches in need. Shelby is about as *in need* as it gets."

"Are you done?" Camille asked. "Because if so, I have a proposal." She glanced from me to Addy, and even to Rae. She ran her tongue across her teeth and took a deep breath. "It's going to take all of us, but I'm willing to invest the time if you are. And if Shelby is."

We all three nodded. Addy crossed her arms. "I'm listenin'—cuz heaven knows we've run out if ideas. And she didn't mean that. Or even if she did now, she would regret it on down the road."

Camille nodded and for the first time, I saw compassion in her eyes. Wonder of wonders. In the year she'd been working with us, I'd never known her to be anything other than hard-nosed.

On that note, she said, "We have to figure out what's wrong with her, then we have to fix it and train with her every day to get her up to par."

Raeann's hackles rose and she jumped to Shelby's defense. "There's nothing wrong with her. She's just—"

Camille held up her hand. "There *is* something wrong with her. She shouldn't be having these problems controlling her powers. I've been working with her for a year, when she bothers to show up for her lessons. She's erratic to the point of being dangerous—mostly because when she lets loose, she does stuff like that." She motioned toward the candy dish, or the crystal shards that remained of it. "But that was an accident. She can't always call it up, and she certainly can't stop it. I've seen this with weaker witches, but not with ones as powerful as Flynn witches. She has power in spades, but if she can't control herself we'll have to bind her, if for no other reason than to protect her from herself."

My heart ached for my little sister. I didn't get it. She'd come into her powers at eleven, an average age. They usually started manifesting at around the same time as puberty, but she hadn't grown into them. They'd never really become a part of her like they should have. Camille was right; it didn't make any sense.

I bit my lip and forged ahead. "So what do you propose?"

She waved her hand. "I think she needs to be tested."

Addy's expression was thunderous. "Over my dead body will those old termagants crawl around inside her head!"

Camille raised a brow and looked at her.

"It's an expression," Addy scowled. "You know what I mean."

"I do, actually. And I'll have you know that I am one of those *termagants*, as you so eloquently put it. I can do the testing myself, so it'll be as non-invasive as I can make it."

I'd heard bad things about the so-called testing the council did, but I was getting desperate. Not only was she in danger of running afoul of them, she was miserable.

"Can we be there?"

Camille paused. "Yes. I think it may even be best if we do it here. But, depending upon what we find, the solution may not be ... palatable." She looked between us, trying to gauge our thoughts. "If we can solve it, then we can work toward a solution. If we can't figure it out, we'll have to bind her."

Addy was pacing back and forth a few feet off the ground. "And if we say no?"

"Then I'll have no choice but to bind her anyway. The council is pushing hard for that already. I have to give them something."

Wow. There was no option at all.

Camille stood up. "Look, take tonight to think about it. Let her calm down, then discuss it with her. I'll be back tomorrow night for your decision."

The three of us remained frozen in place, consumed by worry. Camille made it to the door, but paused with her hand on the knob. "I want what's best for her too, you know," she said softly. "Things haven't been easy for her. Or for you, either, Noelle. I'm willing to help if you'll let me."

I blinked once and nodded at her as she stepped out into the night, pulling the door closed behind her.

As soon as the door clicked shut, Rae and Addy started talking at once. I was trying to keep track of what they were saying when Shelby cleared her throat behind us.

"I'm going to do it."

Addy crossed her arms. "You'll do no such thing, young lady. We'll find a way—"

Shelby held up her hand. "This *is* the way. We all know she's right. There's something wrong with me. Y'all think I'm lazy, or I'm just not giving it my all, but I am. Do you think I *want* to have headaches all the time? To not be able to do something as simple as turn on a light without worrying about blowing all the bulbs, or—almost worse yet—having nothing happen at all?" She looked from one of us to the other, her gaze tortured and imploring. "I'm a witch. I want to be able to use my gifts, but I'm not even sure what they are! If there's a chance she can figure it out, then I'm doing it."

My heart broke for her. When she put it that way, I couldn't deny she was right. "Okay, then. When Camille comes back tomorrow night, we'll arrange it. We'll all be right there with you."

I went over and pulled her into a hug.

"We'll get you straightened out, kiddo," Rae said, and Addy and I agreed. Though when I met their eyes, they were as worried as I was.

Chapter 7

As exhausted as I'd been when I'd gotten home, the visit from Camille kept me from sleeping. I baked my way through four different batches of pastries before I felt remotely tired, then I slept like crap. Fortunately, I didn't have to work the next morning, so I managed to catch a couple of hours before I had to get up.

I'd scheduled a hair appointment a few days ago, before the fiasco with Hank. I thought about Coralee and the crew that would be waiting for me and considered canceling it. Since I was there when he bit the big one, they were going to descend on me like wolves. My hair was out of control though, and the thought of leaning back in the chair while Coralee washed it with her coconut-scented shampoo and massaged my scalp with her salon-perfect nails was too much to resist. I could just close my eyes and tune them out. Okay, that was a little optimistic, but still. Totally worth it.

I got dressed and headed toward town. It was a beautiful day; white, fluffy clouds dotted the sky and the horses were grazing in the pastures, tails swishing, as I drove down the drive and onto the main road. As I approached the crash site, I shuddered. I could still feel the bumps and hear the rocks and brush scraping the undercarriage when I went over. The feeling only lasted long enough for me to get past the site though, then the peace of the morning reclaimed me.

I was worried about Shelby, but at least now we had a plan. I didn't like it, but she was right. We didn't have any other option, and it would be fantastic if Camille could untangle whatever it was that had her magic all mangled. I wanted to believe everything was okay, but there was a seed of doubt growing in my head. What if there was more at play than teenage stubbornness or growing pains?

I made a pit stop at Brew4U to grab a coffee and drop off the pastries I'd made the night before. There were several couples sitting at tables and chatting, but there wasn't a line at the moment.

Raeann was leaning on the counter beside Jake, a guy she'd met at local bungee-jumping event a few months back. She wasn't usually unstable, but I was pretty sure she was a few donuts shy of a dozen for jumping off a perfectly functional bridge. A couple of years before, she'd made up a bucket list of crazy things she wanted to do, and bungee jumping was on it. I convinced her to put it last, since she wanted to do everything else *before* she died.

Even when she started ticking off the small stuff, I held out hope that she'd give up on the idea of wrapping a rubber band around herself and jumping off a bridge, but no such luck.

When the big day came, I went with her for moral support—and to try to talk her out of it. It was all I could do not to lock her in the car when I saw exactly how high it was. Who willingly jumps off a bridge, or anything else that high up?

Still, she'd been talking about it for weeks, and I tried to push aside my anxiety and be excited along with her. When it was actually her turn, I thought I was going to pass out. I held my breath as she stepped up on the platform and let them hook her up. She stepped to the edge, closed her eyes, and jumped. I didn't breathe again until I finally saw her hit the bottom of the band and bounce back up like one of those red balls in the paddle game.

Jake had been the one to unhook her and congratulate her, and they hit it off right away, going so far as to exchange phone numbers right then and there.

She'd wanted to jump again but I'd dug in my heels. "No way am I going to watch you do that again. You've tempted fate enough for one day; we're leaving while you're in one piece. I'm pretty sure your brain musta popped out when you got jerked at the bottom, but I'll come back for it later."

I'd wrestled her away from the hot guy and the bridge and dragged her back to her car, where I stuffed her in the passenger seat. I engaged the baby locks as soon as I was in because she was gazing all goo-goo eyed at the guy—or the bridge, I'm not sure whether it was one or both—as I started the engine.

The entire drive home, she alternated between chattering about the thrill of the jump and the heat level of the guy. She'd always been a sucker for the Black-Irish look, and he had it in spades. Between his carefully mussed raven hair and crystalline eyes, she hadn't stood a chance.

I'd cringed inside and took the latter with a grain of salt. Raeann had the absolute worst luck with men. Her first real boyfriend, Billy Evans, had dumped her on prom night to go with the head cheerleader—whom I promptly beat the daylights out of. My friend was scrappy and loyal, but when it came to taking up for herself, she was a doormat, so somebody had to do it.

I'd thoroughly enjoyed yanking out handfuls of the cheerleader's perfectly teased blond hair, and when a "costume failure" revealed just how hard her push-up bra had to work, every girl in the school grinned with glee. Of course, it was no surprise to most of the guys, except maybe Billy. I even got a good foot to the nuts in on him when he tried to break us up before I was finished with her, so I considered it a two-fer.

Aunt Addy was against fighting in general, but even she gave me a pass on that one.

Since then, Rae'd had a string of guys who looked promising until their shine wore off—and it always did, usually in some spectacular way. I held out hope for this guy though; he'd been around much longer than any of the others, with no sign of mental illness or bankruptcy, moral or financial.

He held the door open for me as I carried in boxes of goodies, then Raeann took them from me and proceeded to arrange them in the glass case beside the register.

"Good lord. How much baking did you do last night after I left? There's enough here to feed an army!"

"Well, I couldn't really sleep and figured with the competition today, you'd need extra. There won't be any desserts available outside of the pie-eating contests."

Apparently, I'd made the right decision. Before she even had them all in the case, a family of five came in and started pointing out their choices, and another group of women came in, perusing the pastries as they waited in line.

I walked behind the counter to the espresso machine and made myself a large mint mocha latte, one of my specials. I pulled an extra shot of espresso into it because I figured I'd need the energy to keep up with the chatter at the salon. Those women could fill up a hot-air balloon on a regular day; I shuddered to think about the gossip high they were riding since Hank met his maker by face-planting in his coleslaw.

I dropped a couple ice cubes into my cup of caffeine because my brain was demanding instant gratification, then took a sip and headed toward the door, bumping Rae with my hip as I passed behind her.

"Gotta run. My appointment's in ten minutes and Belle's probably already counting them down." Belle was the former owner and current resident ghost at the Clip N Curl, and she stood firm on appointments even though she'd been dead for twenty years. She said a lady should be fashionably late for dinner or a ball, but never for a hair appointment.

Raeann gave me a quick hug and Jake waved before jumping behind the counter to help, and said, "There are still openings in our skydiving group if you decide to live a little."

I grinned and wiggled my fingers over my shoulder. "I've decided to live a lot instead of a little, so skydiving is out for me." He laughed, and Rae looked at him like the sun rose and set on him. I tossed out a quick wish to the universe for his wellbeing. He seemed to be a good guy, so I didn't want to have to hurt him if he broke Raeann's heart.

Chapter 8

When I reached the Clip N Curl, three women I'd never seen before were filtering out with fresh hairstyles held firmly in place with at least half a can of Aqua Net. I held the door for them, then stepped inside. The owner, Coralee—a willowy bottle-blonde with big '80s hair—was just finishing up with another woman I'd never seen before. I stifled a cough as I walked through the cloud of hairspray.

"Hey, sugar!" she said with a bobby pin between her lips. "I'll be right with ya. I see you already have coffee. I made some brownies. They're over there in the corner; help yourself."

Coralee was known for two things: her magic scissors and her brownies. They're perfectly fudgy on the inside and crispy on the outside, and she adds something that lends a slightly exotic, decadent flavor. I've tried to duplicate them but, even with my magic, haven't been able to come close. When I asked her for the recipe, she simply smiled and said it was an old secret family recipe. The whole *I'd-have-to-kill-ya* spiel. I bit into one and groaned aloud.

The rest of the Clip N Curl crew was sitting at the nail tables whispering loudly amongst themselves. They were zeroed in on me like well-coiffed vultures waiting for the road to clear. Perfectly manicured fingers waved excitedly at me. I rolled my eyes. The gossip mill was already churning steadily, just waiting for me to add the morning grist. I briefly considered walking out the door just to see if they'd follow and drag me back in.

Like any small town, the beauty salon was the place to go if you wanted to know anything about anybody. If I didn't remember what I'd done yesterday, I could just go there. Even if they didn't know for sure, they have enough eyes around town that they could piece together some version of events.

They were harmless for the most part, though sometimes I wished I had nearly as much fun as they thought I did. To their credit, they quickly set things straight if they got it wrong, but it's usually a whole lot easier to let the cat out of the bag than it is to stuff it back in.

For instance, they were the reason Jane Ellen Peterson got word that her husband Sam was stepping out on her with some red-headed hussy (their words) at the local pub, the Cheshire Cat. Jane Ellen showed up ten minutes later and almost shot him—she's nothing if not fair; he was, after all, the one doing her wrong—before the poor man could explain that he was meeting with the woman to design a surprise addition to their double-wide for her birthday. She'd been complaining forever that she wanted a mudroom because the three men in her house kept mussing up her kitchen floor.

She'd quickly dropped her .45 back in her purse and proceeded to cry and kiss him, then scooched into the booth beside the lady and began telling her exactly what she wanted. The ladies at the salon had some egg on their faces, but proclaimed no harm was done. Sam didn't quite see it that way, seeing as how he almost got shot, then ended up paying twice what he would have by the time Jane Ellen finished adding her two cents to the project.

It was a really nice mudroom, though.

There was only one unbreakable rule about gossip in the salon; you never aired the town's dirty laundry in front of a stranger. That was partly because it looked bad, and partly because Belle wouldn't have been able to fully participate. That gave me a few minutes to come up with some answers while I pretended to look through a hairstyle book from 1989. I could barely keep from laughing as Belle pestered Coralee about the hairstyle she'd chosen for the woman.

"It makes her face look fat."

She wasn't wrong, but Coralee just pursed her lips and glared at her. It wasn't like she could answer her since the stranger couldn't see or hear the flamboyant ghost. That's another rule—we have our ghosts, and they mostly choose to show themselves to locals, but never to strangers. Belle and the others could ghost-shame with the best of them in order to keep the newly departed in check. The last thing we needed was Ghost Hunters showing up in town.

It wasn't long before Coralee finished up with the lady and cashed her out. As soon as the door swung shut, they were on me like white on rice.

Coralee immediately asked for details. "Is it true he landed in his coleslaw? And I heard you almost gave him CPR." She slammed her hands on her hips and glared at me. "Noelle Grace Flynn! What were you thinkin'? You know some of the places that mouth's been. How could you even consider such a thing? Besides, why on earth would you even *want* to resuscitate him?"

I didn't have much of a defense because I'd wondered the exact same thing as it was happening. In retrospect, I had no idea why I'd even given saving him a passing thought. I pursed my mouth to the side and shrugged, then tried to answer the questions in order as I climbed into the chair. "Yeah, he landed in his slaw. He had sauce dripping down his cheek and off the end of his nose. If he hadn't been dead, it would have been funny. Well, it kinda still was. As far as why I considered saving him, I don't know. I guess I just thought it was the proper thing to do."

"Oh, sweetie." She wrapped the cape around me and stuffed the cotton around the edges. "Bless your little heart. You're such a good girl, but you have to remember that the proper thing to do in a situation like that is respect that the Good Lord does things for a reason." The other women nodded, solemn.

Belle hovered closer. "What did he look like when he kicked the bucket? Did he suffer? As mean as he was, I hope he suffered." She was a true southern woman; if she couldn't be the one to deliver somebody's just desserts, she trusted that Karma would.

Still, this wasn't a question I'd prepared for. I thought of the black mist but decided to keep that part to myself. The rest was common knowledge. "Well, his face was all red and he looked like he was sorta suffocating and choking at the same time, so I guess he suffered a little bit. But it didn't last long." They looked so disappointed that I added, "But I'm sure that wherever he went, he's getting what's coming to him."

Belle huffed. Apparently that wasn't the answer she was hoping for. She looked so down in the mouth that I almost assured her I witnessed his black soul being dragged under for processing. Almost. Letting on that I saw somebody get their judgment, or whatever it was, was a can of worms I wasn't going to open.

"Well," she said, "I guess a little bit of suffering is better than none at all, though I lost the pool by six months."

I looked around the group, confused. "Pool?"

Coralee had the good grace to blush. "Yeah," she mumbled as she made a big deal of making sure my cape was straight. "We sorta had a pool goin' for how long it would take Hank to kick the bucket. You had to choose a method—natural causes or murder—and you had to pick a time frame."

Roberta, a rotund woman who headed up the ladies' church auxiliary, piped up. "It's between me and Coralee now, depending on how he died, though we were both off on the date by almost a year. Coralee went with natural causes and I bet on murder. I'm pretty sure I won. From what I hear, that don't sound like no heart attack or stroke I ever heard of."

Coralee scowled. "You don't know that yet. Official cause of death ain't back yet. I still have a shot."

I just sat there in stunned silence, then narrowed my eyes at them. "Do y'all have pools on anything else? Like on anything about me?"

They all shifted uncomfortably, refusing to look me in the eye. Marge, who ran the hardware store with her husband Bob, answered. "Well, yes. But it's nothing bad," she rushed to say. "We have a pool going to see how long it'll take you to catch the eye of that new deputy. The timeline's a lot tighter than it was for Hank. And there's only one choice—how long it'll take for the official first date. We're fairly certain the rest will just fall into place."

She looked a bit put out. "We had a shipment of goods come in at the store the day they made the pool, so I was the last to choose. All the dates I would have picked were already taken." She glared at the women around her.

I was still stuck on the bet itself. The details didn't matter. "What? No! He's a jerk, and you're all going to lose. He's been in town for like five minutes and sees me as a murder suspect! Why would you even think of pairing us?"

None of them looked even remotely embarrassed, so I just huffed. Arguing with these ladies was like talking to a post.

Coralee said, "He seems like such a nice boy, and you're just beautiful. He may be your soul mate, sugar."

I couldn't believe I was doing it, but I turned the conversation back to Hank as Coralee tilted me back and laid the towel between my neck and the sink. I groaned aloud when she began to massage the shampoo into my scalp with her acrylic nails after she soaked my head with the sprayer.

I just enjoyed the pampering while she scrubbed and rinsed, but when she wrapped the towel around my hair and leaned my chair back up, I continued. "So, y'all saw it coming. The way Hank shoveled down donuts and chicken fingers from the 7-Eleven, I can see why you'd think he'd keel over from a heart attack—but I'm curious why you'd think there was a chance he'd be murdered. He made it this long without somebody offin' him."

As Coralee combed out my hair and started snipping, Belle replied, "Puh-lease! That man was enough to make a saint swear. He put a burr up the butt of half the people in this town. It only stood to reason he'd eventually grab the wrong tiger by the tail."

Roberta nodded. "It's true. It's why I went with murder. Why, just last month, he was in the hardware store with the inspectors, sayin' he was worried about public safety. He cited Marge and Bob for having axes hangin' on the wall. Said they could fall and kill someone." She snorted. "Them axes been hangin' there since the shop was built."

I looked to Marge for confirmation and she nodded like a bobble-head doll. "It's true. That was about the fifth violation they found and Bob told Hank if he kept it up, he'd be the one the axe fell on. By the time it was all said and done, we had almost three thousand dollars in fines and—get this—he told Bob he was lucky he wasn't arresting him for threatening a police officer."

Hank was a shyster for sure, but I couldn't understand why he'd target the hardware store. I asked as much.

Coralee snorted. "That jackass Butch Davies wants to put a huntin' supply store in there. He's approached Bob a few times, hinting that it's time for them to retire, and that he'd be glad to take the space off their hands. He and Marge turned him down every time, so we figure he asked Hank to give 'em a push."

Marge, who usually looks like somebody's cheery grandmother, was glowering. "I wanted to give *him* a push. Off a cliff."

I raised a brow. I'd heard Marge say plenty of less-than-charitable things about people, but I'd never heard her wish somebody dead, let alone express the desire to do it herself.

Belle looked at me with an I-told-you-so expression on her face. "See? If he can drive Marge to violence, it's a no-brainer he'd eventually bite off more than he could chew with somebody less ... Christian."

Her words made me think of the conversation I'd had with Hank right before he died. I'd said those exact words to him, and meant them. Suddenly I understood exactly why murder was in the pool.

Coralee's scissors flew around my head as she pulled up strands of hair and clipped off the dead ends. "Then there's that sweet man who ran the little cafe next door. Hank didn't like him cuz he batted for our team, if you know what I mean, so he and his stooges made it so uncomfortable for him that he packed up and left town.

"In the four months he was there, his car was spray-painted twice, his front window was broken, and then the final straw was when the sheriff trumped up the charge that he was using real amaretto in his Irish coffees instead of just the creamers. When the inspectors got there, an empty bottle mysteriously turned up in the dumpster and the poor man was faced with fines out the wazoo for selling liquor without a license. Hank was *good enough* to offer to set aside the fines if he'd close up shop and leave."

Roberta stared into space, wistful. "He made the best fried baloney sandwiches. He used extra meat and put those kosher dill slices on it, along with his own thick-cut homemade chips. They were so crisp that they didn't get soggy from the grease in the meat, and his honey-mustard sauce was to die for."

Belle crossed her arms and *hmph*ed. "All that fluffy, free-love stuff was after my time, but I figure if a man can cook a decent fried baloney sandwich, what he does in his own house behind closed doors is none of my business."

I agreed, then relayed what Hank had said to me right before he died.

Coralee shook her head and squirted a baseball-sized glob of mousse in her hand. She worked it through my hair, scrunching as she went. "That's just a start. Imagine all the wives he hit on and the men he threatened. And that's not even considering poor Anna Mae. Why, nobody would have blamed her a bit if she stepped up and put one through his heart, the way he ran around on her with that trashy Cheri Lynn Hall."

As she finished blow-drying my hair, the conversation turned to what dish everybody was going to take over to Anna Mae's that night. The funeral hadn't been scheduled yet, but since she was all alone, the girls were holding a little get-together to help get her through it.

Personally, I thought they should be planning her a party rather than cooking up tuna casserole.

Chapter 9

Once I paid Coralee and left the shop, I checked my phone. No missed calls or texts. It was only ten. I didn't have to be to work until one, and I didn't feel like going home but I really didn't have anything else to do. I tossed my empty coffee cup and decided that after being run through the wringer at the salon, I could do with some more caffeine.

The cheery little bell above the door at Brew4U chimed when I walked in. The place was almost empty after the morning rush, and Raeann was wiping down the tables getting ready for the lunch crowd. I was shocked to see that in the hour and a half I'd been gone, nearly half the pastries I'd brought had sold.

"Holy cow!" I exclaimed, pointing at the case. "I'm glad I made extra!"

Raeann finished the last table and headed toward the counter. "I know, right? When you brought all those in, I figured for sure we'd end up taking half of them over to donate to the Little League, but now I'm afraid we'll run out."

"I froze a few batches of blueberry and raspberry popovers and bear claws a couple of days ago as backup. I'll run up to the house and get them. Do you need anything else while I'm out?"

"No, I'm good, but it's a good thing you have those. I ordered double the espresso I usually do, just in case, and we're gonna need it. We've made some serious cash today, and it's only ten!"

I thought back to what Hank had told me about the property taxes and was grateful that it was going to be a good weekend. I was going to need every penny I could make. Even though he was dead, I had no doubt the debt would linger. "Okay. I'll just wait to get another coffee when I get back," I told her.

She dug into her purse and pulled out her keys. "Take my car. The AC works and you can just pop the stuff in the trunk."

Not that I didn't love my truck, but the thought of riding in a cool car I knew was going to get me there and back was appealing. I caught the keys she tossed to me, and headed out the door.

I was fastening my seatbelt when I looked across the street. My sister was standing on the sidewalk laughing with a boy who was sitting on some sort of motorcycle that looked crazy fast. I smiled; it was good to see her laughing with a boy who appeared to be a vast improvement over her most recent choices.

Then she pulled a helmet onto her head and swung her leg over the bike.

So much for the smiley, warm feelings I'd just had. Before I could even get out of the car to yell at her, she'd wrapped her arms around him and they pulled away from the curb. I yelled at her telepathically but got no response. Either she didn't hear me or was ignoring me. Even though I knew she wouldn't get it until she—hopefully—arrived in one piece wherever they were going, I pulled my phone from my purse and texted her.

Nice motorcycle. I'm going to kill you if you live through it.

I stabbed send and tossed my phone back on the seat, ready to do murder. I briefly considered chasing them down, but the last thing I wanted was to distract the kid, or worse yet, make him go faster to get away from me. No, I'd wait until both of her feet were safely planted on firm ground before I strangled her.

It only took thirty minutes to get to the house, grab the pastries, and get back to the shop, but my blood was boiling. Just as I pulled back into Rae's spot by the shop, my phone chimed.

S: Stop! It's no big deal. He's the guy from the lake who saw me ... you know.

I heaved a sigh. Lovely.

N: We'll discuss it when I get home tonight. You better be there. And he better not be.

S: Whatev

I closed my eyes and pulled in a few deep breaths. She was okay—that was the important thing. I pushed it to the back of my mind and headed back into Brew4U.

In the brief time I'd been gone, the early lunch crowd had started to drift in. In addition to coffee and pastries, Rae had a limited lunch menu that included a few sandwiches, a soup of the day, and a couple of salads. I carried in the boxes of goodies and slipped behind the counter.

Raeann and Angel were busy with customers so I dropped her keys back in her purse after I filled the pastry case, and made myself an iced mocha latte to go. I gave her a thumbs-up on my way out the door, and she winked while she was taking an order.

The shop had only been open for a few months, but things were going well for her. Between her magical coffee, my enchanted pastries, and a huge dose of her bewitching personality—see what I did there?—the place was a resounding success. She'd gone to UGA with me, and while I earned my degree in criminal justice then tied on a server's apron, she earned hers in business management and opened her own business. At least one of us stayed the course.

My phone chimed with an incoming text from a number I didn't recognize. I was surprised to see it was Hunter when I opened it up. I wondered briefly how he'd gotten my number, then remembered he'd taken it at Bobbie Sue's.

I remembered what the girls had teased me about last night and felt an irrational fluttering in my belly. I'd met the man exactly twice. The first time he'd insulted me, and the second time—well, the second time he was okay, but not butterfly-worthy. Right?

H: It's Hunter. Thanks for the info last night. Wanna grab a coffee?

Me: I'd love to. At Brew4U now. What do you want? I'll bring you a cup and show you around.

I examined my response before I hit send and decided it sounded too enthusiastic. I erased it and started over.

Me: I have a few minutes to spare. Since I'm already at Brew, what would you like? I'll meet you at your office.

H: Sounds great. A double-shot iced cappuccino, plz.

Me: See you in 10.

I thought briefly about the pool the old hens at the salon had going. My rebellious side kicked in and I had an instinctive urge to text him back and cancel, but I shook it off. Not seeing him just to spite them was ludicrous. He seemed okay if you set aside that whole suspecting-me-of-murder thing, and I wanted to get to know him better. If nothing else, he didn't have any other friends in town and he was obviously having a rough time taking it all in.

I walked back into the shop and made his coffee, then grabbed a couple of bear claws and tossed them in a bag. Raeann glanced at me curiously but I just smiled and signed "later" to her. We'd had a deaf friend in college and both of us had learned sign language. It's a good method of communication whether you can hear or not.

She nodded and I rushed out the door and over to the courthouse, which was where the sheriff's office was located.

I couldn't help but admire the architecture of the old structure. A sweeping white staircase ran across the front, with the corners rounded off so the building was accessible from the sides without walking around to the front. Three stories high and almost half a block wide, it had been built back in the 1800s and was the oldest—and grandest—building in Keyhole Lake. The bricks were made from Georgia clay, and the towering white Greek columns lent an air of austerity to the building.

I entered through the double doors and sighed in relief when the cool air hit me. My sneakers squeaked against the marble floors, and the sound echoed off the cathedral ceiling in the front hall. The town founders, who had designed the courthouse, had obviously intended for it to exude the spirit of justice and grace. I could only imagine how many times they'd spun in their graves in the twenty years Hank had held court there.

I walked to the back of the building and into the section designated for law enforcement. Peggy Sue Dalton, a plump woman with watery blue eyes and dishwater-blond hair that was always piled into a bun, had worked as the receptionist at the sheriff's office since God was a boy. I didn't know if she'd always been sour, or if working for Hank had made her that way.

As always, she was at her desk, but for the first time since I'd known her, she smiled—actually, honest-to-God smiled—when I entered. She was even wearing a flowered dress instead of her usual drab navy ensemble and though her hair was still in a bun, there were a few tendrils framing her face.

Well, then. I guess that answered that.

"Good morning, Peggy Sue. How are you today?" I asked warily, in case it was a trap. The last time I'd been in there was to pay a speeding ticket, and she'd about flayed a layer of hide off me because I was a day late. She'd demanded to know how she was supposed to develop an accurate budget if "people like me" were always late.

"I'm fantastic, Noelle. Better than I've been in years. Your hair looks great! How's Shelby? I sure was sorry to hear about Ms. Adelaide."

Okay, now I was starting to wonder if I'd suddenly figured out the secret ingredient in Coralee's brownies, but everything else looked normal to me.

I took a tentative step forward, as if she were some type of exotic animal that might eat me if I moved too fast. "I'm good, Peggy Sue. Shelby's doing as well as can be expected for a teenager, and thank you about Ms. Adelaide. She was a wonderful woman and we miss her."

Addy hadn't exactly had her ghostly comin' out yet, so it wasn't widely known that she wasn't as gone as most folks thought. It made it tough to remember to discuss her in past tense, though.

"She was, at that. What can I do for you today?"

"I'm here to see Deputy Woods. He's expecting me."

She grinned at me and waggled her eyebrows, which freaked me out more than a little. "He certainly is easy on the eyes, isn't he?" Her look turned speculative and she narrowed her eyes and grinned. "And he's about your age, too."

I bit my tongue and forced a smile, wondering if she'd recently gotten her hair done. "Yeah, I guess he is. Is he in?"

"Sure thing. Just let me buzz him."

Once she announced me, it was only a minute or so before Hunter came out to greet me. We walked back out of the courthouse, down the staircase, and across the street to where the Junior League had sponsored a shady little park, complete with benches and a fountain.

We chose to sit on the edge of the fountain and I handed him his coffee. He glanced at the grease-stained bag a few times and I laughed. "Gee, Deputy. Would you care for a freshly baked bear claw?"

He gave me a lopsided grin. "I thought you'd never ask. I can smell them from here and my mouth's watering. Yes, I would love a freshly baked bear claw, please."

I handed him one, then pulled out my own. "So," I asked before I took a bite. "Hank blessing us with his death aside, what do you think of Keyhole Lake so far?"

He took a swig of coffee to wash down a huge bite of pastry. "I don't know yet. Most of the people here seem decent, but sometimes it seems like people are just humoring me. Everybody's been willing to talk to me, but they're pros at answering a question without actually giving me any information. It's frustrating. I've seen some strange things, too."

I couldn't help but smile. One of the "strange things" he was probably referring to was hovering right behind him, eying the bear claws ravenously. Angus Small, our one and only town drunk—though that's a rude way to put it—had died a few years ago when he passed out in the snow behind a yard Santa in the town square. The day after they found him dead, I was startled to see his ghostly self floating and shimmering in front of the courthouse, singing Christmas carols with the ladies' auxiliary.

He wanted to stick around Keyhole for some reason, even though I'd tried to convince him to go on at least a dozen times. Angus spent his time doing the same thing dead as he did when he was living—hanging out at the park. Only he didn't carry a tall boy in a little brown paper bag now. He'd always been a prankster, and he was original. He'd do things like switch neighbors' laundry. You might hang your sheets out in the morning and come home from work to find your next-door neighbor's fine washables blowing in the breeze in their stead.

He had a good heart, though. At Christmas, he always volunteered to help hang Christmas lights in the square, and even showed up sober most of the time. He was also known to tack down loose steps or do other small jobs to help out the elderly or disabled in town. He never asked for a dime; he'd just notice it and fix it. If you ask me, he was the true spirit of community service, bottle and all.

"Hey, Noelle!" He took a deep sniff of the bear claw in Hunter's hand. "I heard you was there when Hank cashed out. You okay?"

Oddly enough, he was the first person who had asked me that. Like I said, he was a good guy.

I smiled and nodded, then looked pointedly at Hunter.

Angus' eyes lit with comprehension. "Oh. Right. Maybe I'll pop out to the farm later. I haven't talked to Ms. Adelaide in a while, anyway. You take care, okay?"

Before I could respond, he popped out of sight.

Hunter noticed my attention had wandered and snapped his fingers. "Noelle?"

I snapped my attention back to him. "Yeah. Sorry. I just zoned out for a minute." Since he seemed to be having a problem adjusting to basic communication skills, I figured now wasn't the time to tell him Keyhole was one step away from having a "living status" field on our voter registration forms.

I cleared my throat. "Anyway, back to the whole communication thing. You're just going to have to ride it out and settle into things. We're kind of clannish, but manners and honesty are important. So decent people feel obligated to be polite to you and tell you the truth, but that doesn't mean they're going to give you any real information. Men may be abrupt because they don't want to be involved or they don't respect you. So yeah. They're kinda humoring you." I shrugged and finished my coffee. "You're a stranger with a badge. Around here, that's two strikes."

He scowled. "What's so hard about answering a straight-up question with a straight-up answer?"

I grinned. "As soon as people get to know you and trust you, you're gonna regret ever wishing for that."

I glanced across the fountain and groaned. Olivia Anderson—the best friend of the cheerleader who stole Raeann's prom date and one of the most horrid creatures God ever stretched a hide over—was crossing toward us like a gargoyle on a mission. She'd been a bully as a kid and was an obnoxious snob as an adult.

I nodded toward her. "You see that woman approaching us?"

He looked in the direction I'd nodded. "Yeah."

"Beware. Don't let the clothes and manicure fool you," I warned. "She's evil incarnate sent here to suck the joy and life from all living beings. If she had a brain, she'd be dangerous."

I didn't have time to explain further because she was now within hearing distance. I took a deep breath and squared my shoulders as she took the last couple of steps toward us. She was laser-focused on Hunter, but I stepped in front of him.

"Olivia! It's been forever. I just love that dress—the cut takes fifteen pounds off of you!"

Olivia narrowed her eyes but maintained her own sugary-sweet smile as her gaze bounced back and forth between me and Hunter, sizing up the situation. Loathing burned behind her eyes as she raked her gaze over my jean shorts and *Bobbie Sue's BBQ* tank top. She looked like she'd smelled something bad. "Noelle. I see you're as ... you ... as ever." She turned her attention to Hunter and her expression changed to *Hey, honey, I'm single and you're hot.* "Who is this handsome gentleman with you?"

I waved a bored hand toward her. "Deputy Woods, meet Olivia Anderson. She was a year ahead of me in school, at least until the fifth grade." I smirked at her, but she ignored the jibe. "She was a little slow picking things up. Olivia, Hunter Woods."

Smiling coyly at Hunter—gag—she stepped into his bubble and held out her fingertips for an insipid handshake, doing the whole Jackie Kennedy stance at the same time. "It's a pleasure, Deputy Woods."

Hunter took the proffered fingers. "Please, call me Hunter. It's nice to meet you. Noelle and I were just enjoying the shade. Would you care to join us?"

Ugh. He'd invited Satan to join the flock. Hadn't he been listening?

"I'd love to. I'm sure Noelle's done a fine job of bringing you coffee, because that's what she does for a livin', but I'd be happy to provide some company."

I bet she would. I rolled my eyes at her smug expression.

She followed us back to the shade and asked him endless questions about how he'd ended up in Keyhole Lake, blah, blah, blah. She hung on his every word. He realized his error within about two minutes and glanced at me, begging for a lifeline.

"Isn't that just something, about Hank?" she said. "Maybe if he'd been a better person, he wouldn't be dead right now."

Hunter's raised a brow. "Is there something I should know?"

"Oh," she said, seeming taken aback by his tone. "Well, since you're new around here, you probably didn't know Hank well. I'm on the Chamber of Commerce."

I rolled my eyes; there were a grand total of eight chamber members.

"Hank wasn't exactly popular with most people. I'm just sayin' maybe his nastiness finally caught up with him."

Hunter's expression remained neutral. "Unless you know something the coroner doesn't know, Hank died of a heart attack."

"Maybe Olivia bored him to death talking," I said.

She glared at me, then steered the conversation back onto solid ground, but I lost track of what she was saying for a minute because Amos was standing beside her mimicking and then exaggerating everything she did, movement for movement. It was all I could do to keep a straight face. When he pretended to adjust his boobs, I had to cough.

Amos winked at me, then zipped off to watch a carnival guy making balloon animals at the fair. I turned my attention back to what Olivia was saying. She was regaling him with stories about her Mary Kay business. Yawn. He looked like a man stuck in a burning building.

"Well, Olivia," I said as she paused for a breath. "Thanks for sharing, really, but Hunter and I were just about to head over to the BBQ contest and I'd hate for you to be mistaken for one of the hogs. It's been a pleasure as always."

She sucked in a breath through her nose and shot me a look that had turned lesser bitches to stone. I just grinned at her expectantly, waiting for her to either rush me or leave. I was okay with whichever direction she wanted to take it.

She stood up and smiled at him, doing her best to ignore me.

"It was a pleasure to meet you, Hunter," she said with enough saccharin it's a wonder her chemically-whitened teeth didn't fall out. "If you need anything, or would like to have lunch that doesn't come out of a greasy paper bag, just let me know. I'm sure Noelle is busy, what with her waitressing job and mucking stalls and all."

To my surprise, Hunter stepped closer to me. "Thanks, but Noelle's great company. Unlike most people, she doesn't seem to have an agenda."

The death beams she was firing at me as she turned on her heel made me smile. She was leaving, and I'd won again.

I didn't typically do the whole catty thing, but she'd brought out the ugly in me since the second grade. I knew for a fact her toothy smile was fake because I'd chipped her real front tooth when I pushed her off the see-saw for stealing a juice box from a kindergartener.

"I'm guessing you two have history?"

"Oh yeah, we go way back. I'm the reason she needed both therapy *and* braces. Now, let's go see what booths are set up."

He placed his hand on the small of my back as we walked around the fountain and I felt a little thrill. I glanced across the street to the salon and saw the curtains sway. Great. The buy-in probably just went up.

Chapter 10

Most of the vendors were open for business—there was everything from fresh-squeezed lemonade stands to a booth selling t-shirts in a rainbow of colors that had *I pigged out at the Keyhole Lake BBQ Blowout* emblazoned across the front around the face of a smiling pig. Bobbie Sue's logo was screen-printed on the back. Ball caps, visors, and koozies were also available on tables inside the tent.

Ellen Camp ran the booth every year and the only thing that ever changed about her products was the year. She lived by the mantra that if it ain't broke, don't fix it. Apparently she was on the right track, because there were already a dozen tourists perusing the goods and haggling for deals on multiple purchases.

"Since this is your first year, you should get something," I told Hunter, nudging him in the ribs with my elbow.

He shook his head and smiled wryly. "The dichotomy of a smiling pig advertising a BBQ contest is a bit much for me, still. Baby steps."

Ms. Ellen glanced up from the cash register and beamed at us. "Well if it isn't our newest deputy. Pick yourself out a shirt. It's on the house!"

Her face fell when he smiled but shook his head.

"Thanks," he said, "but I was just looking."

I stepped up and told Ellen, "He was actually looking for a koozie."

He shot me a look of utter confusion, but I nudged him forward.

Her face lit up, and she hustled him over to the koozie table. "Pick any color you want!"

He chose an electric blue one and thanked her before leaving the tent. When we were far enough away, he asked, "What was that? It was nice of her to offer, but I really didn't want anything."

66

I shook my head. "It doesn't matter if you wanted it or not. When somebody offers you something, the polite thing to do is accept."

He sighed. "I'm never going to get the hang of this."

"Sure you will. It's kind of a no-brainer. If somebody offers you something like that, it's a gesture of goodwill; sort of like holding out a hand to shake. It's rude to say no. Take it and say thank you. The one piece of advice I should probably give you is that any liquid in a glass jar should be handled with care. Unless you trust the source, don't drink it. Take it because it's a big deal for somebody to share their hooch with you, but dump it down the drain. Some of the shine around here will literally kill you, especially if you're not used to it. Even if it doesn't kill you, it'll make you wish you were dead the next day."

"You're kidding, right? Moonshine's really still a thing?"

"It's definitely still a thing."

As we were choosing our food trucks, Will and Violet Newsome walked by. "Hey, Will, Violet! Have you met our newest deputy yet? He moved here a few months ago. Hunter Woods, this is Will Newsome, doctor to all things with fur, feathers, or scales. Violet is his wife and right-hand woman."

Hunter held out his hand. "Nice to meet you, Will. Violet."

"Pleasure to meet you, too, Deputy," Will said, shaking hands. He was normally an upbeat guy with tons of energy and a ready smile, but right then he looked like he'd been through the wringer. Dark smudges rimmed his eyes, and he was sporting a five o'clock shadow that was well on its way to a beard.

Violet, on the other hand, looked fresh as a spring daisy. She was one of those who had never quite found her place in Keyhole, but she'd always been nice to me, and Will obviously loved her.

I furrowed my brow. "Everything okay, Will?" Honestly, he looked like he'd been on a three-day bender, but I knew him better than that.

"Sure," he said, tipping the corners of his mouth up. "Just been putting in extra hours at the clinic."

Violet said, "You know how it is—some days you're the dog, others you're the hydrant."

Hunter nodded, studying Will. "I know how you feel. Since the sheriff died, everything's been dumped in my lap. I've been going through his records trying to bring myself current but there doesn't seem to be much going on. Peggy Sue's been extremely helpful."

Will, Violet, and I looked at each other. There was plenty going on in this town; Hank just didn't bother to make any files that didn't suit him or, more likely, that would incriminate him. Most real reports that would require effort or wouldn't make him money, he just tossed straight into file thirteen like he did mine. Maybe I should suggest to Hunter that he dig deeper into that garbage can.

"So have you found anything odd?" Will asked. "The sheriff had a lot of ... side interests."

It was a good question, and I knew what Will was getting at. With everything Hank had going on, he had to have some sort of system to keep track of it all.

"Nothing really strange so far."

"Good luck, then." Will paused. "The sheriff wasn't exactly a nice guy, Deputy. Don't be surprised when you find evidence of that. There may come a time when you hold a lot of power over a lot of good people. And I hope you're a better man than he was."

Well, that wasn't cryptic at all. I was just about to ask him what he meant when Violet looked at her watch.

"Will, our next appointment is in twenty minutes." She turned to us. "We just popped up to grab something to take back to the office. It was nice to meet you, Deputy. Noelle, always a pleasure."

We said our goodbyes and they continued on their way.

After he'd gone, Hunter turned to me. "I'm starting to think you weren't exaggerating. Was the sheriff really that bad?"

"No, I've been lying to beat a murder rap."

He scowled at me, but didn't reply. "What was with the cryptic comments?"

"I don't know." I tilted my head and thought about my experiences with Hank—the taxes, the threats, and even the brakes. "Hank was into some shady crap, and if he had to put a head or two in a vice to get something he wanted, he'd squeeze as hard as he had to. It's hard to tell what's going to turn up now that his rock's been kicked over."

The smells of greasy carnival food and barbecue tinged the air with deliciousness, and my stomach rumbled for something more substantial than the bear claw.

There was a makeshift bar set up in the middle, but since both of us were working we skipped it, opting instead for the homemade lemonade the Boy Scout troop was selling.

The choices for BBQ were overwhelming, and I wasn't feeling any kind of smoked or sauced meat. Instead, I opted for a foot-long corndog and fries, and Hunter went to Bobbie Sue's booth and bought a pulled-pork sandwich from Sarah.

We sat at one of the long, family-style picnic tables and were almost finished when Sam and Callie McCauley, a couple who had moved to Keyhole from Tennessee a few years back, plopped down across from us with plates piled high with food. I introduced them and we chatted about the town for a while, and Hunter told them a little bit about himself. It wasn't long before the conversation inevitably turned to Hank.

Callie brought it up first. "So," she said, hesitant but determined to talk about it. "It sure is sad what happened to Hank yesterday."

Sam snorted. "Sad that it took so long for it to happen, you mean. Maybe now we can get some law enforcement around here that, you know, actually respects and enforces the law instead of uses the badge to bully people and rob them blind."

Hunter choked on his lemonade but recovered quickly. I shrugged my shoulder and gave him my best *I-told-you-so* expression.

"Is there a single person in this town who liked the man, or even feels a little bad he's dead?"

I dragged a fry through a glob of ketchup and opted to keep my mouth shut so he could see for himself what others really thought.

Callie blushed and looked at her plate but apparently opted for honesty. "Well, I hate to speak ill of the dead, but no, likely not many. I reckon his backup crew, Butch Davies and Ronnie Dean, are probably sorry. They're kind of out in the wind now that they don't have somebody in a position of power on their side."

Sam nodded and took a swig of his beer. "Oh, and Cheri Lynn Hall is probably going to be pretty upset, but only because she's lost her meal ticket."

Hunter looked at him. "Cheri Lynn Hall?"

I swallowed a bite of corndog and said, "Yeah. She's Hank's mistress. Though that seems a bit classy to describe the relationship. She lives on the outskirts of town in a trailer and dances at Tassels which, as the name implies, is a strip club. It's across the tracks."

Before you laugh, yes, we have a literal "wrong side of the tracks" where the less savory businesses have set up shop. There's Tassels, a couple of adult toy stores, a seedy hotel, a run-down liquor store, a shady all-night truck stop, and a pawnshop.

Hunter took a bite of his sandwich and chewed thoughtfully. "Why do I have a feeling there's more to Hank than I learned during my interview, or from working with him over the last couple months?"

"Probably because there is, but none of it's good." I replied.

Sam and Callie just nodded, and I relayed the dirt I'd picked up at the Clip N Curl yesterday.

Callie piped up. "And we all know Jim Simpson slips him a ton of cash to look the other way so he can keep Tassels and the liquor store open after hours. And that's just the tip of the iceberg." She shrugged. "Far as I'm concerned, the mass amounts of fried food and snack cakes he ate finally paid off. At least for the town."

I glanced at my phone and realized it was almost time for me to relieve Sarah at Bobbie Sue's booth. I popped the last fry in my mouth and stood to leave. "Sam, Callie, it was good to see you again. Hunter—"

His phone rang, interrupting whatever I was going to say, which was probably a good thing. I had no idea what would have been the right thing to say. I wasn't exactly graceful when it came to the whole boy-girl thing.

He looked at the screen and held up a finger. "Excuse me." He slid his finger across the screen to answer. "I have to take this." He answered and an excited voice reverberated through his speaker. Hunter pulled the phone away from his ear and scrambled away from the table for some privacy, but it was too little, too late. The rest of the conversation didn't really matter because everybody within a ten-foot radius heard the first, critical sentence that would most assuredly make the gossip rounds in record time.

The tinny voice had yelled, "It wasn't a heart attack like we thought—somebody up and killed him!"

We all strained to hear the rest of the conversation, but Hunter had moved away from the table and was standing by the garbage can several yards away. He had one finger stuffed in his ear so he could hear; the guy on the other end had apparently lowered his voice, albeit a bit too late.

I was dying to hear what was being said as much as Callie and Sam were, but the information well had dried up and I needed to relieve Sarah. "Well. I guess somebody got tired of waiting for the junk food to do its job," I told them. "Y'all have a good day. It was good seeing you."

They said their goodbyes, then I gathered our trash and headed toward where Hunter was standing. He was still on the phone, so I tossed our empty containers in and touched him on the arm. He looked up.

I smiled and mouthed, "See you later."

He winked and nodded, then turned back to his call. I tried to drown the butterflies that wink stirred up in my belly with a huge gulp of lemonade.

When I made it to Bobbie Sue's booth, Sarah was almost beside herself. "Is it true? Did somebody really off Hank?"

I raised my brows and looked back toward Hunter. He was still on the phone, and there wasn't a single customer at the booth. Sure, the gossip mill turns fast, but seriously? "How in the name of all that's holy do you know that already?"

She snorted as she pulled off her apron and scooped her cash out of the tip jar. "You're kidding, right? There were a half-dozen people standing close enough to hear that. I'm only thirty feet away and that's the type of news everybody wants to be the first to deliver. I've already heard it from three people. What they couldn't tell me was how he died."

"I wish I could tell you. You already know everything I do. Somebody called Hunter and was so excited he was practically yelling. Hunter held the phone out before he realized what was coming, and everybody around him heard it. All the voice said was that somebody killed him."

"Well, I can't say I'm surprised." She picked up a box of to-go food. "Your deputy's got his work cut out for him, though. I can't think of anybody who hasn't wanted to wring Hank's neck at some point. Heck, my uncle Dan is a preacher and Hank tried to charge the church a rental fee when they had youth day camp at the county park last summer. Dan is a real turn-the-other-cheek kinda guy, but even he was ready to punch Hank in the mouth."

I thought back to my college days when I had big dreams of becoming a CSI, and considered everything that had happened in the last couple days. For the first time in my life, I was glad to be wearing an apron instead of a badge.

I DIDN'T LEAVE THE fair until after eleven and was beat when I walked into the house. I was dreading dealing with the motorcycle incident, but it needed to be addressed, and Camille was supposed to come for her answer too.

Shelby was waiting for me in the kitchen when I got there, her elbows on the table and her phone facedown in front of her. Her expression was refreshingly devoid of attitude.

I plunked my purse onto the table and pulled out the chair beside her, curling my tired bare toes against the cool hardwood floor. She looked up at me.

"Has Camille been here yet?"

Shelby raised her brow. "Weirdly enough, I forgot she was supposed to be here tonight. I haven't heard a word from her."

That wasn't so unusual. She seemed to be nocturnal and often stopped by after ten. Maybe she did it because that was the only time we were both sure to be home.

On to the main event, then.

"Shel, today wasn't okay."

Her crestfallen look made me want to turn back time by two minutes and keep my mouth shut, but I couldn't.

"It's not what you think, Noelle. He's a really nice guy. He just moved here a few months ago because his parents died. That's why he was at the deserted section of the lake that day. He asked me to meet him at the fair today and when I saw his bike, I begged him for a ride. He truly didn't want to without your permission, but I talked him into it. He drove all the way back to his place from the fair just to get a helmet for me because he wouldn't let me ride without it. Please, just give him a chance, okay?"

This was a side of Shelby I hadn't seen in a long time. For months, she'd been belligerent and hotheaded, refusing to follow any of the rules we'd established or communicate rationally about anything. Raising a teenager would have been hard enough, but raising one with powerful but unruly elemental magic was ten times worse.

"It's kind of nice to hang out with somebody who knows what I am," she continued. "At least if I slip around him, I won't have to make some stupid explanation up. I can be me, which takes a lot of stress off." The look in her eyes was so earnest my anger melted away.

I couldn't even begin to imagine how frustrating her situation was for her. We're both telepathic—or at least we thought she was—but I was able to build walls as I grew to help me filter out thoughts and control my gift.

She couldn't seem to master it or control it; the only thing she could do was try to block it. She said sometimes it was like everybody in the room was talking to her all at once, then it would cut out and she wouldn't hear anything for days or weeks at a time, even if she tried.

She could often project if she really tried, but reception was iffy.

Addy floated forward and whispered in my ear. "Noelle, I don't like the motorcycle thing, but if you push too hard on this, she's just gonna want him all that much more. Pick your battles and play the long game, sugar. He might even turn out to be good for her."

I was shocked when I heard Shelby's voice in my head for the first time in months and saw her concentrating to push her words through. *Please, Noelle. He's different. At least meet him before you decide.*

I had to admit her request was fair, though I was still skeptical. "Okay. But I *have* to meet him, especially before I decide about the motorcycle."

She squealed again and hugged me so tight I thought she was going to strangle me. "You're going to love him—I just know you are! He wants me to show him around tomorrow. I figured I'd take him to the fair. And we'll take my car instead of his bike, until you can meet him. Can I?"

For the first time in months, my sister was actually trying to get along instead of running her mouth, sneaking around, and being a pain. Maybe having a friend would be good for her, even if I didn't particularly like that the friend was a boy. Her best friend Emma, Camille's daughter, was out of town, and most of her other friends were more like acquaintances.

"Fine. As long as you take your car. And stop in at Brew and at least introduce us properly."

For the second time that night, my little sister hugged me. I'm not typically a hugger, but in this case, it was a hundred times better than the back-sassing, door-slamming behavior that seemed to be her preferred method of communication lately. She was happy, and she wasn't mad at me.

I'd take it.

Chapter 11

When I stumbled into Brew4U at six o'clock the next morning, my head felt like it was packed with cotton. For the first time ever, I wished it was just an everyday job so I could have called off, but it wasn't.

I usually worked a couple of days a week to help Raeann keep her labor costs down. Though the shop was doing well, she had student loans and a small business loan to pay. She insisted I keep every penny we made off the pastries, so I figured it was the least I could do.

Besides, between my job and hers, and the extra time she was spending with Jake these days, we didn't get much quality time together.

She was already there, bright-eyed and bushy-tailed, when I arrived. "Well good morning, sunshine!" she chirped.

I blinked twice to clear the sand from my eyes and contemplated strangling her, but just didn't have the energy. Plus, it wasn't her fault she was one of those freaky morning people, and I'd regret it once I was caffeinated.

"Coffee," I croaked.

"Already gotcha covered," she replied, careful to keep her distance as she shoved the cup down the counter to me. She knew me well.

Because most of the prep work was done in the afternoon at closing time, we didn't have much to do other than turn on the espresso machine, unlock the door, and turn on the neon-pink open sign.

Since she'd already warmed up the espresso machine, I flicked my wrist a couple of times to unlock the door and turn on the sign, then slid the pastry case open. Yawning, I summoned two strawberry-cream-cheese turnovers, dropping one on a napkin in front of her and catching the other mid-air.

She smiled appreciatively and took a bite. "Yum. Breakfast of champions. So what do you think about the whole Hank situation?"

I had, of course, texted her the minute Sarah had walked away the afternoon before, filling her in about Hank and the motorcycle incident, but had been too busy the rest of the evening to call her with the details.

"I think I'm glad I'm not the one responsible for finding the killer. That's gonna be a hot mess for sure. The few people who didn't hate him have lost their muscle now that he's dead, and you can't swing a cat without hitting somebody who's wanted to kill him at one time or another. Heck, I had the urge to choke the life out of him myself just a minute before he checked out. As a matter of fact, I gave him a warning squeeze and told him that one of these days he was gonna mess with the wrong person."

"Well, we know for a fact that besides you, Marge and Bob from the hardware store had motive. So did the guy who owned the cafe next to the Clip N Curl, but he moved away. I suppose Anna Mae would, though you'd think she would have done it already instead of waiting twenty years." She paused, considering who else might have taken issue with Hank. "Then there's any number of people he's railroaded out of cash with his trumped-up speeding charges and inflated property taxes and made-up fines and assessments, though you wouldn't think that would be cause for murder."

"Don't forget the women he was constantly hitting on," I added. "There are bound to be some irate husbands and boyfriends out there. For that matter, the women aren't off the hook, either." I thought about what I'd learned about murder while I was in college—and of course from crime shows. "I wish I would have overheard what killed him. That might have helped us narrow it down a bit. My guess is poison, since nobody strangled or shot him right there in plain sight, but was it a one-time thing, or something he ate in small doses over time?"

Raeann considered that. "Poisoning probably points to a woman. A man would have taken a more direct route."

I hated to think it, but if it was poison, statistics pointed the finger squarely at Anna Mae. "You're probably right. Thankfully, it's somebody else's problem. I, for one, think we should get a fund going to build a statue in honor of the stand-up citizen who did it."

"Amen. How did the whole motorcycle conversation go last night?"

I sighed and relayed the details.

"Bless her heart. I can't imagine how horrible it must be for her. Speaking of, did y'all set a date for Shelby's testing with Camille last night?"

I chased the last bite of my pastry with coffee before answering. "She didn't show up, which is completely not like her. Shelby was upset, because now that she knows there may be a way to find out what's going on with her, she's all about it. I called her, but it went straight to voicemail."

"You could always call the council office."

"No," I said, shaking my head. "I don't know if the offer is official. It seemed a little like she was stepping off the rails with it and I don't want to get her into trouble if that's the case."

"True. She'll turn up. She was probably pulled away on a case and just forgot to call you."

"I sure hope so." Other than Camille, the council members were hardcore when it came to rule-breaking; there were no gray areas. The law was the law, and the punishment was the punishment.

I took the last swallow of my coffee and thought about the great exploding candy dish, and Shelby's screw-up at the lake. The idea of dealing with the council without Camille as a buffer sent chills of fear down my spine.

I WAS RESTOCKING THE pastries an hour or so later when a middle-aged gentleman wearing pressed slacks and a button-down dress shirt walked in. His black shoes gleamed and his watch glittered with diamonds. He definitely wasn't from around here.

I smiled and waved him in, then motioned toward the coffee board and pastry case, rattling off the specials. I washed my hands at the mini sink before heading up to take his order.

He smiled up at me, showing teeth so white they set the standard for the tissue test. He ordered, then sat down at a table in front of the window.

I made his coffee then pulled his banana-nut muffin out of the case, plopped it onto a dessert plate, and took both to him. I gave him the standard *let me know if you need anything* spiel, then turned to walk away. He stopped me before I could. "Do you by chance know where the Flynn farm is?"

"I do," I replied, wondering why he was asking about the farm. "That would be my place. What can I do for you?"

He furrowed his brow, baffled. "My name is Gary Wilkenson. I'm a real estate investor. I spoke with a gentleman at a conference in Atlanta several weeks ago, and he said the property was in a prime location for a gated community and that it was in the preliminary stages of development."

I immediately thought back to my conversation with Hank and my blood began to boil. That was why he'd wanted my place.

"Did this gentleman happen to be a middle-aged, paunchy redneck? Dirty-blond hair, about six feet tall?"

"Well no. In fact, he was quite polished and professional. He was tall, but had dark hair and was in his early thirties, if I had to guess. I'm afraid I lost his business card, but I remembered the name of the farm because my mother's maiden name was Flynn.

"I only talked to him for a few minutes," he continued, "but he was trying to garner financial support for development of the property. I came down to Keyhole Lake to meet some friends for the barbecue competition and figured I'd check it out while I was here."

"I'm glad you didn't waste your time on a special trip then, Mr. Wilkenson, because you were obviously misinformed. My place isn't available."

He looked incredibly disappointed. "Well, if you change your mind, I'll be in town through next Monday. Just call me. It's odd, because I was under the impression the young man was already in possession of the property, or soon would be. He even showed me preliminary contracts and applications for re-zoning and building permits."

"I assure you, it wasn't under my direction. Let me give you my number. If you see this person around town, would you mind calling me?"

"Of course."

I found it hard to believe Hank would work in conjunction with somebody other than his own thugs because he'd have to share the profit, but this was too complex for him. The permits had his fingerprints all over them though, so he was involved on some level. I needed to talk to Hunter about who applied for them.

Chapter 12

I didn't have much time to think about it after that, because the breakfast rush hit. We were busy for a Monday, and the primary topic was, of course, Hank. Everybody speculated on who finally sent him to his maker, but nobody seemed particularly sorry he was gone. As a matter of fact, there was almost a holiday atmosphere in the shop.

By the time ten o'clock rolled around and we finally slid into the slump between breakfast and lunch, Raeann and I had added at least a dozen more names to the *who wanted to kill Hank* list.

The bell over the door chimed, and Violet strolled in and took a table by the front window.

"Hey, Noelle. Raeann. How's business?"

"It's good. Coffee? Are you hungry?" I pointed to the soup and sandwich menu. "Rae made the most amazing chicken salad this morning, with grapes and pecans in it."

"I'm waiting on Will, but we're definitely eating. I've been at the salon while he was doing some routine appointments this morning. How are things going with the farm?"

"Great, actually. We're getting a routine going, though we miss Adelaide." It was hard to pull that off since she was right there, but it was still partially true. She was there in spirit form, but I'd never be able to hug her or eat her blueberry pancakes again.

The thought made me sad, and it must have shown.

"I'm so sorry, Noelle. I didn't mean to bring up bad feelings."

"No, it's okay. Thanks for asking." It occurred to me that before she'd moved here, she'd worked in real estate somehow. Maybe she'd know about this guy.

"Weren't you a real estate agent in Atlanta?"

The question seemed to startle her. "Yeah, but that's kind of outta the blue. What's up?"

I pulled the investor's card out of my pocket. "Do you know this guy? He came in this morning and asked for directions to the farm."

I related the details of the conversation with her as she studied the card.

"That is weird. I don't know him, but I know *of* him. He's one of the biggest investors in Georgia. I only sold houses, so he was way above my pay grade, but to be honest, I can see why your farm would be tempting to him."

I took the card back from her and shoved it into my apron. "Why? I mean, I know why it's valuable to me, but it's in the sticks in a town that's not even on the map unless you zoom clear in. What good is a little horse farm in the middle of nowhere to a big shot like him?"

She laughed and shook her head. "You have to realize they don't see it that way. That's prime real estate they can develop into vacation getaways. People would spend a few million an acre if the right house was on it."

She accepted the coffee Raeann had made, and stirred it, thinking. "To be honest, I'm surprised somebody hasn't already made you an offer on it. You have what? Two hundred-plus acres out there? To get ahold of that much land at once would be an investor's dream, especially if they could buy it in one chunk at current market value. Shoot, they'd probably gladly pay you double or even triple what it's worth as it sits."

My head about exploded as I did the math. She was talking about mind-boggling numbers, but the thought of selling the farm, especially to somebody like that, made me sick to my stomach.

"I've had several offers on it since Adelaide passed, but I've turned them all down. None were anywhere near the amounts you're discussing, but I would have still declined. I know it sounds crazy, but there's not enough money on the planet to buy that place from me."

She sighed and patted me on the hand. "I understand, sugar, but you may want to at least think about it. Anyway, that's who he is." She looked thoughtful. "Are you sure he didn't remember the name of the man he talked to?"

"He said he didn't remember, but he's in town for a few days for the competition and said he'd call me if he saw him."

"Oh. Well, good luck, then," she said absently, picking up her phone.

I stocked the condiment bar, preparing for the lunch push. Just as I was finishing up, Hunter strolled through the door.

"Hey, stranger," I said, disgusting myself with how sappy I knew my smile was. "How's everything going?"

He shook his head. "Apparently, I've been designated the interim sheriff until the council can arrange a special election." He heaved a sigh. "They dumped this entire mess right in the outsider's lap."

"It's not like you didn't see that coming. I'm just surprised his nephew didn't fight for it. Slimy little brown-noser."

"Oh, he did. It took the council about thirty seconds to tell him he was lucky he still had a job, at least for now. Apparently now that Hank's out, they're planning to clean house."

Raeann snorted. "Well, it's about time. I'm sorry it all landed in your lap, though."

Hunter sighed. "Believe me, not as sorry as I am. Can I get a double-shot mocha latte? I have both Anna Mae Doolittle and Cheri Lynn Hall coming to the office in just a few minutes. Anna Mae's picking up Hank's death certificate and personal belongings. I don't know what Ms. Hall wants, but she insisted it had to be today. Anna Mae's coming at ten thirty and Cheri Lynn is coming at eleven."

I gaped at him. "You scheduled the dead guy's *wife* and *girlfriend* to be in the same place at almost the same time? Are you high? What if they run into each other?"

"They won't. I just have a couple of questions for Anna Mae so it won't take long. They've co-existed this long and I don't have time to pander to them. I have interviews all over town this afternoon. Besides, it's at the courthouse. You know, that place where we keep the jail? They won't start anything there."

Raeann just shook her head and handed him his coffee. When he pulled out his wallet, she waved it away. "It's on the house. I hate to charge a man for his final cup of coffee."

He studied her for a minute, then took his cup and headed toward the door, looking at us like *we* were the ones who were nuts.

Once the door shut behind him, I looked at Raeann. "Twenty bucks says Anna Mae takes her."

She pinched her lips shut for a minute, then held out her hand. "You're on. Cheri Lynn swings on that pole all night. She's gotta have the upper body strength of a lumberjack."

We shook just as Shelby strolled in, her new friend in tow. Remembering my promise to give him a chance, I schooled my face into a neutral expression.

He stepped toward me and held his hand out earnestly. "Hey, Ms. Noelle. I'm Cody Newsome. I'm sorry about the other day. I should have asked your permission before I took her for a ride. It won't happen again unless you say it's okay."

His sandy blond bangs fell over his eye as he lowered his head, and I found myself liking him despite the fact he'd nearly given me a heart attack. I took his hand. He had a firm grip and made good eye contact. The expression in his blue eyes was open, and I couldn't find a single trace of duplicity.

Dang it, why did he have to be mannerly? I didn't want to like this kid who almost killed my sister. Okay, so maybe that was a bit of an exaggeration, but still. I felt my resolve crumbling, and when I caught sight of the hopeful look on Shelby's face, I caved.

"Hi Cody. It's nice to meet you. You're Will's nephew, right?"

"Yes, ma'am. I moved down here at the end of the semester last year. Now that school's out, I'm helping Uncle Will out at his clinic."

I thought back to how tired Will had looked and was glad he had some help. Will was good enough at what he did that he could have made much more money in a larger town, but he was a hometown kinda guy and came back to Keyhole Lake as soon as he graduated GSU.

"Cody, this is my friend, cousin, and the owner of this place, Raeann Flynn."

Rae shook his hand. "Do y'all want a Coke?"

Both kids nodded so Rae filled up two to-go cups and handed them over. Shelby went around and pulled a couple of pastries out of the case and took them to one of the cafe tables. Rae and I joined them.

"Do you want to be a vet when you finish school?" I asked Cody as he poked a straw into his cup.

He shrugged. "I'm considering it. I like animals, but I like the idea of helping people, too. I'm not sure which way I'm going to go."

Another plus. Not only did he have a goal, he had a good one.

Raeann smiled. "Take my advice—you may outgrow your love of people, but puppies and kittens will always be cute!"

Laughing, Cody replied, "Yes, ma'am. You're not the first person to tell me that. The more I help Uncle Will, the more I'm leaning toward being a vet. He says if I want, I can come work with him when I graduate. I'm not sure if I want to live in such a small place, though. Not much seems to happen around here."

I put my hand to my heart. "Not much goes on? Are you kidding me? In the past three days, we've had a Fourth of July picnic and party, a BBQ competition and fair, and a murder. What else do you want?"

Still smiling, he said, "Well, a fast food restaurant that stays open past nine might be nice, and I wouldn't mind a movie theater that shows more than three movies at a time."

I couldn't argue with him; I'd thought the same thing when I was his age. For that matter, I still wouldn't mind either of those things, but usually the good outweighed the bad. I couldn't imagine living anywhere else.

"You make good points. Anyway, what are you guys doing today?"

Belatedly, I noticed Shelby was wearing an over-sized tank top she reserved for days at the lake, and the ties to her bikini top were dangling down her back.

Her eyes were sparkling when she said, "Where else should somebody go when it's 90 degrees outside and the sun is shining? I was thinking I could take him over to the lake and show him around, as long as it's okay with you."

If this agreeable, lovable girl was the result of Cody's influence, I might be willing to reconsider the whole motorcycle thing. Maybe.

Then something occurred to me—they were both at the age where hormones raged.

"Is anybody else going?" I asked, trying to appear casual.

Shelby rolled her eyes. "Yes, *Mom*. We're picking up Angelica on the way out of town. Don't worry. We won't be *unchaperoned*."

That hardly made me feel better, because it wasn't that long ago I was a teenager. However, it all came down to trusting her, and it was time to close my eyes and take the step if I wanted our relationship to improve.

"Okay. I was just asking. Do you have snacks? If not, grab some cookies or something out of the case to take with you."

Shelby grinned even wider and gave me a hug, whispering, "Thank you. Don't worry about me; I'll be good. I promise."

That actually set my mind at ease, because she was a lot of things, but a liar wasn't one of them.

I swatted her on the butt and told her, "You better. Have fun and try to be back before dark. We'll grill some burgers at the house this evening. Cody, you're more than welcome, and Angelica can come too if she wants."

While Shelby loaded up on a variety of goodies, Cody started to say something, but a huge ruckus broke out in front of the courthouse. We were a few buildings down but could hear the ear-piercing screeches even at this distance. Raeann and I looked at each other and grinned. Hunter's day had just gone right down the toilet.

Chapter 13

Anna Mae Doolittle and Cheri Lynn Hall were screaming like a couple of banshees at each other right in front of the statue of our town founder and Civil War officer, Major Thadeus Washburn. Fortunately, he was one of the spirits who'd decided to cross over into the light after dying peacefully in his sleep at the ripe old age of ninety-one, so his spirit wasn't there to witness the shame.

Angus and Belle were, though.

We all raced for the front door, shouldering our way through as quickly as we could. No way were we going to miss this catfight. It had been a long time coming; the entire town was amazed it hadn't happened years ago.

Cheri Lynn was blinded by curtains of her own brunette hair, and Anna Mae had a pretty good grip on her. She had Cheri bent at the waist, and I cringed when I realized what was coming next. The enraged widow brought her knee up as hard as she could while she gave a vicious yank down.

I could almost hear Cheri Lynn's nose crunch even from that far away. She howled in pain, and Anna Mae, who was typically a real sweetheart, cursed her with a continuous stream of expletives that would have made a sailor blush.

Like the good citizens we were, we moved toward them just in case things got too ugly. Plus, we couldn't really hear what was being said.

A crowd had already gathered. Coralee and the Clip N Curl bunch were standing there along with a handful of other folks who had been in the immediate vicinity. A box had tumbled over and bowling trophies, Bulldogs memorabilia, and about a dozen pictures of Hank hunting and fishing lay strewn across the sidewalk.

I turned my attention back to the action when the smack talk resumed.

"You'll be outta that trailer by the end of the month or I'll burn it down around you! And you're not getting another red cent, you gold-diggin' tramp!" Anna Mae screeched as she slammed her fist into Cheri Lynn's mouth.

"That trailer's mine and you know it." Cheri Lynn said, wiping her mouth and lowering her shoulder to dive at Anna Mae. "Hank swindled the title from me with taxes he knew would break me! And I more than earned it back since then." Cheri Lynn went for Anna Mae's eyes with her claws.

Ducking and lunging at the same time, Anna Mae tackled her to the ground and gained the top position, pounding her with roundhouses. "You earned it *on* your back. With. My. Husband!" she shrieked. She punctuated each of the last three words with several good, solid head punches.

Cheri Lynn managed to buck her way out from underneath Anna Mae, and another round of hair-pulling ensued.

Hunter burst through the front doors of the courthouse and stopped dead when he saw the two women rolling around in the grass. Other than the odd profane or blasphemous exclamation, their vocalizations had pretty much deteriorated to guttural grunts and high-pitched squeals. Hair was flying just as fast as fists.

He stood there for several seconds, obviously unsure how to proceed. I looked at Raeann, then nodded toward Hunter. "Should we help?"

She looked like she felt sorry for him, but shook her head vehemently. "Absolutely not. I am not steppin' into the middle of *that*," she declared, pointing her chin toward the two women.

Anna Mae had regained the top position, so I huffed and stepped forward, motioning to Hunter.

"Don't just stand there like a lump on a log," I groused. "I'll get Anna Mae and you get Cheri Lynn. We have to get them at the same time, and whatever you do, don't let go once you get ahold of her."

We waded in. I grabbed Anna around the waist and locked my hands in front of her, identifying myself as I did and keeping my head between her shoulder blades to avoid a head-butt. I pulled her back, and as soon as I did, Hunter reached down to grab Cheri Lynn. He pulled her to her feet by her upper arm. She immediately snatched it away and launched herself at Anna

Mae, who ducked. Unfortunately, I didn't, and took a solid punch to my left eye.

I ground my teeth together as stars exploded behind my eyes, and barely resisted the urge to blast her with the worst curse I could think of.

Anna Mae had us covered for the second round, though. She braced herself against me and kicked Cheri Lynn right in the gut when she lunged again, knocking us backward. Hunter managed to grab Cheri a second time, lifting her off her feet with an iron grip around her waist.

Anna Mae stopped struggling as soon as she saw Cheri Lynn was neutralized and I let her go as soon as I felt the energy drain from her. She looked at me and had the good grace to blush as she pushed my hair back from my eye. "I'm sorry sugar. That shoulda been me. I'll buy you lunch this week to make up for it, okay?"

I sighed and nodded, then cut my eyes at Hunter.

"I'm sorry too," he said, looking abashed.

I scowled at him and snapped, "What part of *don't let go* didn't you understand?"

Notably, the only one who didn't apologize was the one who'd thrown the punch. I glared at her, but she looked completely unapologetic.

As a matter of fact, she had the nerve to declare she wanted to press charges, but I'd had enough. "So do I, then."

When she looked at my eye and realized I had her cornered, she snapped her mouth shut, then glowered at me. "Well then, I guess I've changed my mind," she said primly after a few seconds.

"Yeah, I figured you might."

I looked at Anna Mae to see if she was going to complicate things; I didn't figure she would because she'd come out the obvious winner. She took a minute to study the mess she'd made of Cheri Lynn.

Her blouse was in tatters, her lip was split, her nose was bloody, and there were several small but obvious bald spots. She was going to have a raging shiner the next day too.

"I'm good," Anna Mae said, smug.

They took several steps in opposite directions, and I was headed toward Raeann to thank her for her help when Hunter spoke up. "Hold up—nobody's going anywhere! You're both under arrest; you can't just brawl on the courthouse lawn then walk away."

We all turned to look at him, perplexed. "Pardon?" we asked in unison. Battery charges for standard brawls were unusual, unless you were somebody Hank didn't like or wanted to blackmail. Even then, you just had to pay a hundred-dollar fine; you never actually saw a cell. Otherwise, the jail would be filled to overflowing all weekend.

"You heard me." He gestured to both women. "You're both under arrest." He pointed at Cherie Lynn. "And you have *two* charges of battery since you punched Noelle too."

I closed my eyes and pulled a deep breath through my nose before responding, which made my head pound. Raeann was right—Cheri Lynn did have hella upper body strength if her right hook was anything to go by. My eye was throbbing. "Do you really want to drag them back inside together while you file the paperwork and process them? Your backup is mysteriously absent, and you only have one pair of handcuffs. If you absolutely have to, tell 'em to come back at separate times to pay their fines."

Cheri Lynn whined about the fine, but Anna grinned like the cat that ate the cream. "I'll gladly pay a fine. I got my money's worth."

Hunter glanced back and forth between them, his expression vacillating between irritation and defeat. "Fine. You're both free to go. After you clean up this mess. Together. Like civilized people." He gestured to the old bowling trophies and other tasteless treasures scattered around the box that marked the end of Hank's regime. He crossed his arms and stood with his feet shoulder-width apart to supervise the process.

"Now you're using your noggin," I told him. "I'm gonna go ice my eye." I walked away, not caring what else happened. Raeann was waiting for me at the edge of the sidewalk and slipped my hard-won twenty into my hand as we turned back toward Brew4U.

I MADE IT THROUGH THE day, but the area around my eye darkened to a lovely shade of blackish purple as the morning faded into afternoon. All in all though, I made some serious pity tips. It seemed like every table left a little extra.

Finally, three o'clock rolled around. We locked up and Raeann took the drawer and the slips to the back to reconcile. I needed to take inventory because it had been a record Monday, due in part to the last of the barbecue folks, and partly because everybody wanted to see my shiner and get the story straight from the horse's mouth.

While Raeann was in her office, I pulled the blinds, turned off the open sign, and flicked my wrist at the mop and broom.

I'm grouchy and tired, hungry and battered. I command you to clean what's been scattered and splattered.

It wasn't my best rhyme, but it did the trick. I didn't need spells for simple tasks like opening windows or turning on the coffee machine, but bespelling objects was another matter. As the mop and broom jumped to work, I turned back to the shelves to do inventory.

The entire stock of espresso was depleted, and we were almost out of regular coffee too. The cups were almost all empty, and several of the syrups were running low. I raised my brows, surprised. I couldn't wait to hear the numbers for the day.

I made my list and headed to the back, grabbing a clean bus tub on my way. I *thunk*ed the tub onto a box of coffee, then slumped against the doorway to the supply room. I was directing each item on my list into it with my index finger when somebody called my name.

"Noelle? Raeann?" Hunter's head popped around the corner and my heart about leapt out of my chest. As neatly as possible, I sent the last of the in-flight objects into the tub before turning back to him. Fortunately, with the way the room was situated, he was unable to see inside of it from where he stood. Otherwise, I'd have had some 'splainin to do.

"Hunter!" I exclaimed. "What are you doing here? How did you get in? You almost gave me a heart attack!" I was still grasping my chest, willing my pulse to slow. Then I remembered the mop and broom. Had they still been working when I finished doing inventory? I couldn't remember. He didn't look completely freaked out, but it's possible they were at work in the bathrooms where he couldn't see them.

"The door was unlocked. When I came in and you two weren't up front, I got worried. I'm sorry."

He cocked his head to the side and regarded me for a couple of seconds while I tried to figure out a way to make sure the mop and broom were safely settled. "No, it's all good. We're just closing up. I thought I locked the door, but it's good to see you."

I managed to peek around him enough to see the broom and mop leaning innocuously against the doorway to the bathroom. Phew.

I was so intent on making sure there were no magical cleaning tools swirling around the place that I didn't notice how close I was standing to Hunter until he leaned closer and examined my face. His cologne smelled amazing—clean and fresh, with a hint of sandalwood and musk. My mouth went dry when his eyes drifted from my eye to my lips and I found myself leaning closer.

The door to Raeann's office *snick*ed open and the spell was broken. We jumped apart.

"Hey, Hunter! I didn't know you were here." Her eyes flickered to me and apparently caught the guilty flush because she raised her eyebrows for a second before she turned back to him.

"We're already closed, but if you'd like, we can kick the machine back on and make you a coffee."

"No, you don't have to do that. I just stopped by to make sure Noelle was okay after this morning. I feel bad because I let such a small woman get away from me like that. I didn't really think it through; I just assumed my presence would be enough." He paused. "They were really going at it, weren't they?"

"Well, to be fair, Anna Mae's had a rough few days, and Cheri Lynn isn't exactly known for her tact and grace," Raeann responded.

I quirked my mouth. "That's putting it mildly. By the way, what did Cheri Lynn want to talk to you about?"

Hunter rolled his eyes. "You'll never believe it. She claimed Hank swindled her out of her trailer. Apparently it's been in her family for a few generations, but he made her taxes too high for her to pay, then bought it when she defaulted and used that leverage to keep her under his thumb, at least according to her. Of course, I told her she'd have to talk to the executor of his will before I realized who it was. I figured it would be an attorney. Turns out it's Anna Mae. And you saw what happened after that."

"I hate to say we told you so," I said, "But we told you so."

He scowled at me. "Yeah, way to kick a man when he's down."

I shrugged. "I can say pretty much anything I want. I'm the one rockin' the black eye."

I went back to the storage room and grabbed the bus tub. Fortunately, I'd managed to get everything from the list before Hunter almost busted me. It weighed a ton.

Usually, I'd have just magicked it, but I couldn't hardly do that. I grinned to myself—I guess I'd have to do it the old-fashioned way. "Hunter, can you please help me?" I called. What? Don't judge me. I was exhausted, and he owed me at least one favor for the shiner.

Chapter 14

I wanted to grab a nap before the kids got home from the lake, but I had to stop at the grocery store first to buy the ingredients for dinner. By the time I managed to make it home, it was all I could do to put the groceries away before I collapsed on my bed. I fell asleep instantly.

The doorbell woke me and I grabbed my phone to check the time. Holy cow! It was almost six. I'd slept the entire afternoon away. I wiped the drool off the side of my face and ran a hand over my hair on the way to the door. When I pulled it open, Hunter was standing on the other side dressed in jeans and a plain blue t-shirt. He handed me a bottle of wine and had a six-pack of Big Wave in his other hand.

"Hello. I'm sorry," I mumbled, blinking and wiping the sleep from my eyes. "I don't even have the grill started. I guess I didn't realize how tired I was."

He smiled. "That's no problem; I know you've had a rough few days. Tonight you can relax though. You're off tomorrow, right?"

"Yeah," I said as he followed me to the kitchen. "Finally. I love the money but hate the hours. My feet are going to hurt for two days. Just when they start to feel better, it'll be time to go back to work again."

"I know exactly how you feel. When I was a beat cop in Indy, there were days when my biggest pleasure was just sitting down. Anybody who's never worked a job that involves being on their feet for hours at a time just can't fully appreciate the value of a chair."

I laughed as I pulled a beer from the pack for him and put the rest of them in the fridge. "You've got that right. And I think it should be a requirement that everybody's first job be in some sort of service industry. People wouldn't be so cheap or so mean to those of us who do it for a living if they actually had to walk in our shoes."

I popped the top of the wine and poured a glass, only taking time to check the label after I took the first cool sip. It was a Chardonnay from a local winery and was buttery and just sweet enough, with a smoky oak finish. I sighed in bliss.

"Would you like to go sit on the veranda? It's shady, and with the ceiling fans going, it's actually pretty cool. Plus I need to get the grill going. Raeann and Jake were going to come, but Jake had to make a last-minute trip out of town and a pipe burst at Rae's mom's house and she had to go help out. She said she may be over later if the plumber is done in time."

"Plumbing problems suck," he said, following me with beer in hand. "I had a pipe break in Indy and went two days without a kitchen sink before a plumber could come fix it. At least here, that's not an issue."

He looked around as I led him to a couple of stools sitting on either side of my bistro table. "Wow. What a fantastic view."

"Yeah, this is one of my favorite spots to relax." Setting my wineglass down, I pulled the cover off the grill and built a pyramid of instant-light charcoal, then pulled out the grill lighter and fired it up. "There. That should be ready just about the time the kids get home."

"How did you end up living here with your aunt, if you don't mind me asking?"

I climbed onto the stool opposite him and took another sip of wine, looking out over the pastures where the horses were turned out. It wasn't like my past was a secret, but sometimes it still stung a little. "My mom passed when I was twelve, and dad started bringing us out here, mostly because he didn't know what else to do with us, I think. One day he just didn't come back for us. We still don't know where he went." I paused and took a sip of my wine, remembering the tortured look on my father's face as he'd pulled away that day.

"After a few days, Aunt Addy—who was my mom's sister—and Uncle Calvin drove to our house, gathered our stuff, and moved us in with them like it was totally normal."

I smiled at the bittersweet memory. "At the time, it felt like the world was ending, but they did their best to turn it into a new adventure. Addy shared her love of horses with us, and provided a safe haven for us to heal. Uncle Cal was a total marshmallow where we were concerned."

He looked out over the pasture, but I had a feeling he was looking beyond that. "It's horrible you lost your parents so young, but at least you had somebody who loved you to offer you a home. That's more than many kids get. They must have been special people."

Unbeknownst to him, Addy was hovering behind him and wiped a tear off her cheek. I offered her a small smile, a silent acknowledgment that I agreed with him. She faded out of sight and I wondered for the hundredth time where it was she went when she did that. She swore she didn't know.

We sat in companionable silence, watching the horses graze as the fluid burned off the charcoal and the corners of the briquettes turned white. The smell made my stomach rumble.

"So were you born and raised in Indy, or did you move there from somewhere else?" I asked as I swirled my wine.

"Actually, I was an Army brat. My dad was Infantry and we lived all over the country, and even spent some time in Australia and Germany. He retired at thirty-nine and we settled down close to his sister, who teaches high school in Indianapolis. I was fifteen."

"Wow. That's an experience not many people can claim. Did you like moving around like that?"

He shrugged. "It had its advantages and disadvantages. I learned not to get too attached to people, but I also think experiencing so many different cultures makes me a better cop and a more well-rounded person."

Grinning, I asked, "So how are you feeling about the Southern culture? Can you compare it to anything?"

"Absolutely not," he declared. "This isn't a different culture; it's a different universe. I don't know if I'll ever adapt."

Max had been sunning himself a few feet down the porch and picked his head up. Fortunately, he kept his mouth shut and only shared his opinion via thought. *Hah! Tell him to imagine being turned into a donkey by an Irish witch, then granted immortality to enjoy it. What a weenie.*

I frowned at him, but he did kinda have a point.

I said, "Nah. It's not that different. Things just move a little slower here, and people get set in their ways. I think it's good to have somebody new in town, especially when that somebody is in a position to do good things." I ran my finger along the rim of my glass and smiled when it hummed.

He took a swig from his beer and gazed out over the pasture. "I don't know. I know so many people can't be wrong, but it's just astounding to me to believe anywhere is so insular that things like what Hank was doing can still happen."

I shrugged. "The devil you know, I guess. Things were coming to a head, though. He was getting a little too big for his britches and people were getting tired of it. Even those who'd bowed to him for years. Honestly, if you ask me, it was just a matter of time."

Addy popped back in and listened for a couple of minutes, then did a float-around, checking him out. "Girl, you better hang onto this one. He's got 'good man' written all over him. And check out those shoulders! I always did love a man with shoulders."

I about choked on my wine when she zipped around behind him and squeezed his left bicep.

He rubbed it and drew his brows together but didn't say anything.

"You okay?" I prompted.

"Yeah, just ... nothing."

"Nothing?"

"Yeah. Well, no. Not nothing. But you'll think I'm crazy. Since I moved here, I get these weird feelings, like cold air on my skin, and I catch things moving out of the corner of my eye. I'm sure I'm just jumping at shadows," he finished.

"Addy always said people only see what the parameters of their minds allow them to."

"What does that even mean?" he asked, as Addy reached out to touch him again.

I glared at her, but quickly smiled when he turned back to me. She just crossed her arms and grinned. "Fine, I'll go back in the house," she said. "I don't wanna spook him. He really does seem like a nice boy and it's slim pickin's for you around here."

I raised my eyebrows and turned my attention back to Hunter. "I think it means you need to keep an open mind. Sometimes things really are exactly as they seem, but it's outside your realm of experience or you have preconceived notions, so you shy away from a perfectly logical, rational explanation."

Yeah, that didn't make me sound like a freak at all. But I was starting to like him and wanted to test the waters. After all, I was a witch, so if he wasn't open to the so-called paranormal, then I didn't want to get emotionally invested. The problem was, how and when do you tell somebody you're a witch?

The kids arrived just then and spared me the trouble of trying to explain further. I figured I'd just let him chew on that much to start with.

Shelby rushed across the yard with Cody following close behind her, flip-flops slapping against the wood of the porch as they thundered into the house.

"Hey, Sister! Hey, Hunter!" Shelby called over her shoulder. "When's dinner?"

I glanced over at the charcoal—it was ready. "Gimme about a half-hour," I yelled back.

"If you want to stay here and enjoy the view, it'll only take me a few minutes to get stuff ready inside," I told Hunter.

He finished his beer and stood to follow me. "Nah, I'll keep you company. I'm ready for another beer, anyway."

Max thought, *Bring me a couple of fingers of my scotch when you come back, please.*

He was kidding, right?

Yeah, sure, because he wouldn't think it was strange at all for me to bust out the Glenlivet and pour my mini donkey a couple of shots.

Spoilsport, he grumbled.

Be grateful Earl threw in a bottle because, for whatever reason, he likes you. There wasn't any fine scotch money left after the electric bill was deducted from the royal coffers.

He snorted. *What good does it do for him to give it to me if you hoard it inside?*

Sometimes I had to agree that the witch was dead-on with her choice of forms. *It's not like you have thumbs, anyway.*

I glanced at him, and he was glowering at me. *That was just uncalled for.*

I pretended I didn't hear him as the screen slapped shut behind us. We made our way into the kitchen and I motioned toward the table. "Have a seat."

I opened the fridge door and handed him another beer, then rummaged around for all the ingredients for burgers and dogs. Before I started patting out the burgers, I poured myself another glass of wine.

"Where did you go to college?" I asked, plopping the hamburger into a bowl and adding seasonings and a packet of onion soup mix.

"Believe it or not, UCLA. I was accepted to several schools on a full football scholarship but chose there because, well, it was Los Angeles." He shook his head and shrugged. "It wasn't for me. I mean, I had a great time in school, but I didn't want to be a cop there. I missed my family, so I moved back to Indy."

"Why didn't you go into the military like your dad?" I asked as I squished the burger between my fingers.

He smiled, showing both dimples. "That was exactly the reason I chose LA. I loved my dad but he was military to the core. I wanted to get away from the structure and the rules, not sign myself up for another four years of it. Maybe if I hadn't gotten the football scholarship I would have."

He took another pull of his beer then washed his hands and started slicing a tomato. "So what about you? Have you ever wanted to leave here?"

"Oh, I did leave. I went to UGA and earned my undergrad in criminal justice, with my sights set on being a forensic tech or maybe a cop. Then I discovered I missed the farm and moved back. You can, of course, imagine why I chose to be a waitress rather than a cop here."

"Well," he said, taking a big bite of crow. "Now I really feel like a jerk about what I said the day the sheriff died. You have the same degree I do."

"Yeah, how 'bout those preconceived notions, again?"

Chapter 15

As soon as the cheeseburgers and dogs were done, I brought out the fixin's and called to the kids, who were playing a game of cornhole in the backyard. After everybody was situated with plates piled high with food, we sat down around the larger patio table and dug in. After a few minutes of companionable eating, I asked Cody what he thought of Keyhole Lake.

"It's not as bad as I thought it would be. It was harder to get around in the city, especially on a motorcycle, because other drivers don't pay attention. I don't have that problem here, and there are lots of good back roads and thinking spots where I can go when I need to get away."

He looked down at his plate and my heart went out to him. I knew what it was like to lose your parents and understood the flood of emotions he was experiencing. At least I had been fortunate enough to be able to stay in my hometown. This poor kid had not only lost his parents, but his entire support system of friends too.

"Well, there's a great little cabin by the lake that hardly anybody remembers anymore. I wouldn't recommend going in the cabin itself because it's falling in, but it has a dock that's great for sitting, dipping your feet in the water, and just letting your mind soak in the peace of the place. I used to ride my horse there, but there's a small access road to it that's more of a path now. A car couldn't navigate it, but you could probably make it there on your bike."

I gave him directions and he thanked me. "I hope it works as well for you as it does for me. Now, are you enjoying working at the clinic with Will? We ran into him and Violet at the fair the other day and he looked exhausted. He said you guys have been putting in some crazy hours there."

Cody looked at me quizzically. "Things have actually been pretty slow at the clinic, so I'm not sure why he'd say that. I have noticed he's distracted and isn't sleeping much though. Sometimes I wonder if part of that is me, but he assures me I'm actually good for him."

He paused to take a bite of cheeseburger and looked thoughtful. "I think that maybe he and Aunt Violet are having some problems; I heard them arguing yesterday. She says she wants to move back to the city and that Uncle Will would make a ton of money if they lived in Atlanta, but he doesn't want to leave grandma and grandpa, or his clients here." Will's parents were Bob and Marge, the owners of the hardware store, and they'd always been close.

"It would be awful if he left," Shelby exclaimed. "Doc Will is amazing. I can't even imagine somebody taking his place!"

"Well, I don't think you have anything to worry about, because as far as I know, he has no plans to leave. Thus, the arguing." He looked a little guilty as he glanced around the table. "Oh man, please don't say anything to anybody about them fighting, okay? If word gets around, they'll know it was me."

"No worries, Cody," I assured him. "What happens here stays here."

Yeah, Max muttered from his place at my feet. *Especially since we may end up counting on him to return the favor if he thinks too much about floating rocks.*

Truer words.

"Thank you!" Cody sighed, relieved. "I'm worried about Uncle Will too. I volunteered to help with Pop Warner football before he started looking so ragged, and now I kinda wish I hadn't. We're planning a guys-only camping trip this weekend and I think it'll do him good. It's just going to be us, Grandpa, and Mike, one of my friends." He paused and shook his head, smiling. "A year ago, I would have never said this, but I'm really looking forward to it. Hunter, maybe you could come, too. Do you like fishing?"

"Actually, I love fishing, but I doubt I'll be able to take the weekend off with everything that's going on at work."

Cody nodded, and that wayward hank of hair fell over his eye again. "I totally get it. Well, maybe you can make it up for a few hours. I'll ask Will, but I'm sure it won't be a problem."

I smiled at the thought of Hunter in a fishing hat and hip-waders, holding a stringer of fish. I just couldn't picture it, but I took my own advice and left my mind open. Who knows; the city boy might have been a Boy Scout.

"Sorry if I sound nosy, but how do you and Violet get along?" She and Will had met while they were in college and though she was nice, she never struck me as somebody who would be willing to leave the city life to live in a Podunk town.

We'd had lunch a few times because she was on the board for Pets United, a charity for abandoned and abused animals. Will started the program several years ago when pet overpopulation became a problem in the county and we raise money to help pay for medicines and shots. Will donated his time to spay and neuter the animals, and the organization worked to find foster homes and then permanent ones for the pets.

I was active in the group and though I didn't have a ton of money, I was great at fund-raising and often fostered any horses, mules, or donkeys that came in. Violet had a ton of contacts both here and in Atlanta and though she was a bit reserved, we had a good enough time when we got together. Margaritas work wonders for opening up just about anybody, but even half-lit she was still sort of stiff.

Cody finished chewing a mouthful of burger before answering. "We get along okay. We don't really interact that much, but when we do, like at meals and stuff, she's nice to me."

The topic seemed to make him a bit uncomfortable, and I was grateful when Hunter asked, "So I hear you have a motorcycle. What kind is it?"

"It's nothing much. Just a '95 CBR 600. My dad and I bought it wrecked and worked on it in our garage until it was rideable."

"Sweet," Hunter enthused. "I have a 2014 GSXR 600. We'll have to ride some day; I've barely had it out of the garage since I moved here."

"That would be great! I've found some sweet back roads around here I'd be glad to show you."

"You're on, then. I have a feeling I'm going to need some wind time by the time this case is over."

Shelby turned to me. "Speaking of his bike, can I ride with him now that you've met him?"

I was still hesitant.

Max's voice popped into my head. *Stop being a killjoy. It's not like refusing her has worked out so well for you so far. Mayhap a change in strategy is in order. And are you going to eat the rest of that potato salad?*

I scowled at him. You have no idea how irritating it is to get child-rearing advice from a donkey, especially one whose definition of responsible was a whole lot looser than mine. It was even worse when he was right.

"Fine," I finally told her, setting my plate down so that Max could have the potato salad, "but there are conditions. First, no riding after dark. Second, you always have to wear a helmet. And finally, under no circumstances are you to speed or go on the freeway with her, Cody."

They bobbed their heads and said, "Agreed." Shelby was smiling from ear to ear and it made me feel good. I just prayed I didn't live to regret it.

"Oh yeah, and Cody? If she gets hurt on that thing, I'll skin you alive!"

He bowed his head. "Understood, ma'am. I'd never do anything to risk her safety."

Hunter said, "Hey, I've got a great idea. Noelle, you're nervous about her riding. Why don't we all go on a short ride tomorrow evening, and you can see for yourself how Cody drives?"

"I don't know ...," I said.

"C'mon Noelle! It'll be fun!" Shelby said, her eyes shining.

She looked so happy that I had to agree, though my mouth was dry as a bone when I did.

We finished up dinner, and since I'd used paper plates, clean-up was a breeze. Hunter started to leave, citing that he had to get back to the investigation, but when I asked him if he had any leads, he admitted it was at a standstill while he waited for a couple search warrants to come through. Since that wouldn't be until tomorrow, I convinced him to stay for a while. I couldn't get him to tell me what the warrants were for but I trusted the well-oiled wheel of the rumor mill to fill me in tomorrow.

He and I paired off against Shelby and Cody for a game of cornhole and my sister narrowed her eyes at me when my aim improved considerably after they'd gained several points on us. Hunter commented on it, too.

"Wow, I guess it just takes you a few throws to get warmed up. At first, you were barely hitting the board, and now you're sinking them like a pro."

Shelby glared at me. "Yeah, it's amazing how her aim just *magically* improves when you guys get behind."

I smiled sweetly at her. "All it takes is a little focus."

She scowled, because that was what I always told her when she was practicing spells.

Max, who had been scavenging leftovers around the table, perked his ears when Shelby mentioned magic. He trotted over when Shelby threw. Her bag landed on the edge of the hole just beside her other one, and he meandered up to me and butted his head against my leg. When he did, his tail "accidentally" swept her bags into the hole. *No cheating,* he thought.

"That doesn't count!" I protested, ignoring Max. Shelby and Cody insisted on counting both bags, citing "acts of nature." I couldn't really argue because a few of my shots hadn't exactly been natural, so I let it slide and played the rest of the game on my own merit, which meant they beat the pants off us.

By the time the game was over, it was almost dark and I still had baking to do. Hunter headed home, but Cody stuck around to watch a movie with Shelby. I was really starting to like the kid, and hoped he'd be a good influence on my little sister.

Chapter 16

For the next hour, I lost myself in baking. The act of mixing the ingredients and rolling out the doughs was better therapy than any shrink, and it was a good way to let off some magical steam.

Though I can perform other spells such as the mop and broom thing with ease, I'm a kitchen witch at heart. I can feel my magic roll from my body into the doughs and batters, giving them just a little boost of love and magic.

That night, I had to make brownies, berry turnovers, and cinnamon rolls. Those were my best sellers. I prepared all the ingredients then fell into the rhythm of creating.

While I was mixing and kneading, I let my mind wander over the events of the last several days. Things just weren't making sense. Not the part about somebody killing Hank; that made total sense.

But the real estate guy had me flummoxed. Who would have contacted him? With nothing but the barest physical description to go on, there was no way I could figure that out, assuming I even knew him.

Then there was Will. We'd gone out a couple of times in high school, but we'd been such good friends that we decided to leave it that way. We didn't hang out as much since he'd gotten married, but he was still my friend and he really hadn't looked good that last time I'd seen him. According to Cody, his claim that it was just too many hours at the clinic didn't hold water, but if he and Violet were having problems, that would explain a lot.

I made a mental note to have Rae put her special revitalizing potion in his coffee the next time he came in.

I had just finished rolling out the dough for cinnamon rolls when the front door opened and Raeann made her way into the kitchen with a bottle of wine.

"Hey!" I greeted her. "Did you get the mess at your mom's cleared up?"

She wrinkled her nose. "Yeah. It took twice as long to clean up the water as it did for him to actually fix it, but it's done. Want a glass of wine?"

"Actually, there's already a bottle open in the fridge. Hunter brought it for dinner and I think you'll like it."

She didn't waste any time reaching for the bottle and pulling a glass from the cabinet. "It's wine. After the mess I just went through, I'm sure I'll love it." She poured herself a glass and added another splash to mine, then leaned on the kitchen island while I brushed butter over the square of dough and sprinkled it with sugar and cinnamon.

I pulled the edges loose from the counter and rolled it into a log. "It sucks that you didn't make it for dinner tonight. I saved you a burger and a dawg so when you finish swigging that wine like it's Kool Aid, make yourself a plate."

"I am *not* swigging my wine," she objected.

I raised my brows and looked pointedly at her half-empty glass.

"Ok, maybe I'm swigging it a little. But seriously, you know Donny Skinner is the only plumber in town and just being around him makes me feel slimier than cleaning up the actual mess does."

We'd gone to school with Donny, and he was the kid who picked his nose and tried to sneak peaks up your skirt when he thought you weren't looking. Unfortunately, he hadn't changed much since then.

"On second thought, swig away. Still, eat something if you're going to drive home."

I finished rolling the dough and proceeded to slice off the individual cinnamon rolls, placing them on a cookie sheet as I did so.

"So, what's new with you and Jake? Any cool adventures planned in the near future?" Please, Lord, don't let her say bungee jumping.

"You're never gonna guess!" she enthused. "He's scheduled a one-on-one skydiving lesson for me instead of doing it with a big group. I'm so excited!"

I don't know which worried me more: the thought of her jumping from a plane or her bubbly enthusiasm about doing it. I was dead on my feet and really wasn't feeling the love for her risk-taking right then. As a matter of fact, if I could have gotten my hands on Jake, I'd have strangled him.

"You know I've designated you Shelby's guardian in case anything happens to me. If you kill yourself, who else do I have? Plus, there's the fact we've been best friends since we were born. The last thing I want to do is have a three-county scavenger hunt for your pieces. *Please* stop tempting fate."

"But it's such a rush," she countered. "The air in my face, the speed. You'd understand if you'd just try it."

I held my hands up. "There is absolutely no way I'm jumping out of a perfectly good airplane!"

"Well, we'll just have to agree to disagree," she said as she finished her wine and headed to the fridge. "You do realize that I have magic and could stop myself if something went wrong, right?"

"What if you pass out from the bends or something?" That was a thing, right?

I folded a towel over the rolls and popped them into the warm oven to proof.

"You know what your problem is?" she asked, pointing a bottle of ketchup at me. "Your problem is that you're stuck in a rut. You work, you come home. That's it."

"That's not true," I protested. "I volunteer at the shelter and do fundraisers for them."

"Yeah, but that's like, what? Once a month or something? And besides—that's boring. You have zero excitement in your life."

Aunt Adelaide chose that minute to pop in. "She's kinda right, sugar. You used to love going places and doing things. Shoot, you haven't even had a speeding ticket in a couple years, and when was the last time you two went out for a night on the town?"

They were right, but I had Shelby to think of now. Just keeping her out of trouble was a full-time job. We couldn't both be irresponsible, and I said as much.

"Oh honey," Addy said. "You can't stop living just because you have responsibilities. You have to have fun, too. That's what life is all about."

Max raised his head from his bed in the corner. "Exactly. I see more action than you do, even in this form." He waggled his wooly eyebrows. "There are a few advantages to being knee-height."

"Yeah, and look where that attitude landed you! And ... eww!"

With a derisive *humph*, he stood up and circled like a cat, then lay back down with his back to me.

I knew they were right, and with the extra money I was making from the pastries lately, I could afford to do something at least once a week. The more I thought about it, the better it sounded. Then I remembered the extra taxes and sighed.

Raeann smirked. "See, I'm not the only one who thinks you've turned into a fuddy-duddy."

Scowling, Addy's transparent body shimmered and she wagged a finger. "You're no better, young lady. You're just the opposite. Didn't I teach you not to run with scissors? First bridges, now airplanes. What's *wrong* with you? If I were alive, I'd go upside your head with somethin'!"

She disappeared in a puff.

Raeann and I paused for a minute, then laughed. "Well, I guess she told us."

The air shimmered above the table, and Aunt Adelaide's face appeared, three times its normal size. "Oh, and Noelle, don't let the handsome hunk of a man get away. He's taken a shine to you. You're not getting any younger." She disappeared again, popping out of sight like a soap bubble.

"And on that Aladdin-like note," Raeann proclaimed as she popped the last of her burger into her mouth, "I have to get home and get to bed if I'm going to be worth a diddly tomorrow."

"Okay. And think about what I said about skydiving, okay? It seriously scares the crap out of me every time you do something like that."

"Fine," she said, giving me a hug on her way out the door. "Come up with something I'll like better and I'll consider it."

She was already out the door before I remembered I *was* doing something risky tomorrow night—I was going on a motorcycle ride. Though on a scale of one to jumping-out-of-an-airplane, that was probably only a solid three.

Chapter 17

After I dropped the pastries off at Brew4U the next morning, I made my way to Bobbie Sue's and began the process of opening. Since it was a weekday, it probably wouldn't be busy except for the couple of hours when people took lunch breaks, so I took my time and did everything by hand. I even had time to call Camille and leave yet another voicemail. I was starting to get seriously worried about her.

My first customers didn't roll through the door until almost noon; by then, I was about twenty minutes past bored out of my mind.

I grabbed a couple of menus and rushed to the table to greet them. A few more people started filtering in and before I knew it, the lunch rush was in full swing. Yay me.

As usual, the flood turned into a trickle around twelve-thirty. I was cleaning the salad area and restocking the tea when the door jangled. Anna Mae was standing at the hostess stand and waved when I looked up.

"Hey, Noelle! How you doin', sugar? I brought Hank's family in for lunch. Anywhere in particular you want us to sit?"

"Nah, just sit anywhere. Teas?"

"You betcha!"

They chose a booth by the window, several seats down from the door. I took their drinks to them and handed them menus.

Hank's dad was a large man, girthy and balding. His eyes sparkled with humor which, to be honest, pleasantly surprised me. I expected an older version of Hank, except maybe sleazier because he'd had a few more decades to practice.

A man dressed in Wranglers, cowboy boots, and a plaid button-up with mother-of-pearl buttons that was about two sizes too small for him was sitting in the booth with Anna. He could have passed for Hank's twin if you added a few years. The slime ball was looking at me like I was the best thing on the menu while doing his best to cop a feel on Anna's knee under the table. She kept shoving it off, and he kept creeping it back on. Definitely Hank's brother.

I wrinkled my nose and had a near-uncontrollable urge to punch him in the throat.

Hank's mother was just the opposite of her husband and son. Whereas Mr. Doolittle was a little rumpled and dressed casually in khaki pants, a button-down white shirt, and well-worn loafers, she was wearing a tailored beige pants ensemble. Her silver hair was perfectly styled in an elegant updo, and her makeup was flawless as she gazed scathingly at her surroundings.

Anna Mae moved her purse so it was between her and Hank 1.2, then introduced me. "Mama and Daddy Doolittle, James, this is Noelle. She was there when Hank ... well, she's a friend of ours."

"Mr. and Mrs. Doolittle, it's a pleasure to meet you. I'm sorry about your son," I lied.

Hank's mother perused me head to toe over the rims of her reading glasses and looked like she'd sunk her perfectly straight, obviously false teeth into a lemon. "Thank you, Nolene. Though it's just like him to go and get himself killed just before we were getting ready to leave on our cruise. He always was inconsiderate like that."

I blinked and tried to keep a neutral expression. Not the response I was expecting. I didn't even bother correcting her on my name because that wasn't even a blip on the radar if you were looking at things wrong with that exchange.

Hank's dad patted her on the hand. "Now, Mama. You know he was just rambunctious. He had a big personality, is all."

Mrs. Doolittle waved her hand dismissively. "Oh, come on. Let's not pretend Hank was anything other than what he was—a selfish, thoughtless bully and a philanderer, though lord almighty knows where he—where either of them—got it." She waved her hand toward her other son. "I suppose boys will be boys," she sighed.

I looked at Anna Mae, unsure what to say. I'd never found myself in such an awkward situation. I mean, it wasn't like I disagreed with the woman that her sons were pigs, but still. Anna just shrugged and smiled, but when I looked closer, it was the same smile she'd worn for the Ms. BBQ Bash beauty pageant in high school. Fake as Aunt Minnie's pearls, and a little maniacal. She was just as out of her depth as I was, except she couldn't escape.

I turned my attention back to Mrs. Doolittle. First Mama, then Aunt Adelaide, had taught me every single rule that applied to any social situation, but I promise you Miss Manners *did not* cover this.

I followed the only rule that was even remotely applicable here: I kept my opinions to myself. "I'm sure you were a wonderful mother, ma'am," I made a fuss over pulling my order pad from my apron.

"So," I ventured, "when's the funeral?"

Anna Mae shook her head, slapping James's hand away again. "We don't know. They haven't released his body yet, but that new deputy said it'll likely be later today."

"Ah, so maybe Friday, then." I said, distracted by Anna Mae's distress. I furrowed my brow at him and pursed my lips. If he thought her leg was so hot, then so be it. I imagined the surface of her jeans to be just the right temperature to fry pancakes, then watched out of the corner of my eye as he laid his hand on her knee again.

He jerked it back so fast he busted his knuckles on the underside of the table, then cradled it in his lap. Anna Mae looked puzzled but relieved and I just smiled at her.

"Absolutely not," Mrs. Doolittle declared, snapping my attention back to the conversation at hand. "Only poor people have funerals during the week. It'll be on Sunday. He's brought the name low enough; we'll at least lay him to rest with some class." If only she knew how little rest he was likely getting.

"The wake will be held at Anna Mae's residence rather than that run-down excuse for a funeral home," she continued. "We'll host a full buffet. He spent his life lordin' it over people around here, so free food's likely the only thing that'll bring anybody around to keep Anna Mae company."

I frowned at the implication; she was right that nobody would show up for Hank, but Anna Mae was a different story. Keyhole's covered-dish brigade had already been to see her once, and Coralee had been keeping her company in the evenings too. Poor Anna Mae had apparently reached the end of her rope. Between the handsy James and the thoughtless, condescending mother-in-law, she looked like she was going to cry, and that burned my bacon.

"That's mighty considerate of you. Anna Mae's well-loved around here, though. If anything, she'll have more of a support system now than she did before Hank died." The woman's beady eyes snapped to mine, but I refused to back down. It was the truth. She'd said as much herself.

"I suppose you're likely right," she said before breaking eye contact and looking down at the menu.

I looked over my shoulder at the empty restaurant like I was busy and asked, "So. Do y'all know what you'd like to eat?"

I quickly took their orders and backed away from the table, feeling horrible for Anna Mae. And I thought *my* family was dysfunctional. A few issues with an unruly teenage witch, a perverted talking donkey, and a dead aunt who still showed up for dinner was downright normal compared to that freak show.

After I'd delivered their food, I retreated to the waitress station to cut lemons. Somebody tapped me on the shoulder and I about jumped out of my skin. I spun around to find Anna Mae standing there. She grabbed my arm so hard her acrylics were leaving marks.

"Noelle, I'm beggin' ya—use some of that Flynn juju to solve this before that woman really does drive me to murder." A denial formed on my lips but she rolled her eyes and gave me the *oh please* look. She poked her thumb in the direction of the table. "You think that back there was crazy? You ain't seen nothin'.

"She's gone through my underwear and thrown away my good ones because she said they weren't proper for a widow. She's ordered new wallpaper with giant mauve roses on it for my living room—my beautiful, eggshell living room, with my eggplant accent wall and all my Home Interior decorations! You gotta get rid of her!" she pleaded.

"Anna Mae, calm down! It's gonna be fine. Hunter will find who did this in no time."

"Be serious," she snapped. "You know as well as I do he's gonna be lookin' at me for it. It's always the wife." I raised an eyebrow at her and she scowled. "You know what I mean. Now please, find who killed Hank before Satan's older sister over there plasters those hideous roses all over my living room!"

She grimaced when Mrs. Doolittle called, "Anna Mae, while you're talkin' to Nolene, would you tell her to be a dear and bring us some of that peach crisp with a scoop of vanilla ice cream? And whatever you want. It's not like you have to worry about those hips anymore."

Anna Mae plastered on her Miss BBQ Bash smile before she turned and called back, "Yes, Mama Doolittle," then hissed, "God Almighty, Noelle, find 'em. Fast."

I shook my head as she walked back to the table. I couldn't wait to tell Raeann about this. Some stuff you just can't make up.

I WAS JUST FINISHING my shift when Raeann sent me a text saying Anna Mae had called it right. They'd just arrested her.

That wasn't a conversation to have in a text, so I just responded that I was on my way to the coffee shop. Since my feet were killing me, I jumped in the truck even though it was only a few blocks away.

I looked at all the quaint little shop windows as I drove through town and wondered which one of them was harboring a murderer. I mean, sure, Hank was a first-rate jerk and I wasn't sorry he was gone, but he'd been riding roughshod over people around there for years and nobody'd done it yet. Why now?

Since it was nearly closing time, there were plenty of spaces in front of Brew. When I walked in, only one couple was lingering over coffee and gazing all starry-eyed at each other.

Raeann was wiping down tables, but stopped what she was doing and motioned toward the hallway that led to the supply closet. As soon as I turned the corner, she grabbed my arm.

"Oh my god, Noelle! Can you believe it? The sheriff's department just hauled Anna Mae in. They searched her house lookin' for whatever killed him I reckon, and found a copy of a life insurance policy in the amount of half a million dollars. They called the company and verified that Anna Mae is the sole beneficiary and that she'd been the one to buy the policy. Two years ago last month—long enough for the two-year contestability period to end."

"No way," I told her, shaking my head. "Anna Mae's not a killer. If she was gonna kill him, she woulda done it years ago, when he first took up with Cheri Lynn or any of the other tramps he's had a go with."

"I agree, but Coralee stopped for coffee and apparently it was like we thought—he was poisoned, and nothin' says *fed-up wife* like poison. To be fair though, she doesn't think Anna Mae did it, either."

"Do you have any idea what kind of poison it was?"

"No. The only people who actually know are Hunter and the coroner. They're keeping it under wraps until they find the killer. Of course, they'll have to release the information to her lawyer, but he won't be here until tomorrow afternoon. The Doolittles are bringing one down from Atlanta because they don't trust anybody from here."

I couldn't honestly say I blamed them. Hank had most of the ones here in his pocket, if rumors were to be believed. Of course, now that he was gone, all bets were off. "What's Anna Mae saying about it?"

"Well, of course she's saying she didn't do it. She says she took the policy out because she figured he'd end up eatin' himself to death eventually, or else somebody else would speed the process up for her."

I quirked an eyebrow and shrugged. "I can't really say as I blame her. If I'd been in her shoes, I probably woulda played those odds, too. She probably shouldn't have said that last part out loud, though."

"No doubt," Raeann agreed. "Oh, and the Doolittles have offered a fifty-thousand-dollar reward to the person who finds the real murderer."

"I met them today. Those people are as messed up as soup sandwiches." I told her about the conversation at the diner. "It says something when even your own mama doesn't like you."

"Well, maybe that's why he was the way he was—mommy issues."

"Yeah. Or maybe he was just a dick."

"True story, regardless."

Chapter 18

I helped her finish closing up, then we went to the diner to grab a bite to eat. The Starlight Diner had opened back in the '50s and hadn't changed much since then, even though the third generation was now running it.

They still had the speckled white Formica tables and bar, and the booths and stools were upholstered with red Naugahyde. James Dean, Vivien Leigh, and Elvis smiled down from numerous pictures, and snapshots of the town through the decades stood witness to how much things had changed, yet managed to remain pretty much the same.

An old-fashioned soda machine squatted on the counter behind the bar, ready to serve up its next coke float, and the comforting smells of bacon and coffee had permeated the walls so they were as permanent as the paint.

The food was affordable, greasy, and delicious, the shakes were thick and rich, and the service was always good. There was a reason they'd stayed in business for almost seventy years.

We chose a booth and flipped open the plastic-covered menus even though we both knew what we wanted.

Becky, the owner's daughter, came and took our orders. While we waited for her to make our shakes, we talked about the real estate investor. Something about that just creeped me out, especially considering somebody'd cut my brake lines just a few days before. That meant there could still be somebody out there who considered me more valuable dead than alive.

"So, who do you think he talked to?" she asked. "Probably a quarter of the male population is tall with dark hair. I mean, that covers Hunter and Jake, even. I don't know that I'd really describe many of the guys in this town as polished though. I mean, our guys are classy, but I'd describe them more as rugged. Polished sounds kinda pansy-ish to me."

"I know. Maybe the guy was working for Hank. I mean, he practically admitted to cutting my brake lines, and he didn't make any bones about wanting the farm. He would have had to rubber-stamp the permits and what not too. I'm not going to borrow trouble."

Raeann rolled her straw paper up into a little ball and fidgeted with her napkin. "I don't know, Noelle. You know he always had his hands in a dozen different shady deals at a time and this feels a little above his pay grade. I think you should tell Hunter about it, at least."

I sighed. "I guess I should. There's not much to tell, but at least if something happens, he'll have a place to start. The guy gave me his business card."

Our food arrived and we were too busy stuffing our faces to say anything else.

After I polished off my cheeseburger and fries, along with every drop of my strawberry-banana shake, I felt like I'd eaten an entire cow. I needed a nap.

"What do you have planned for tonight?" I asked, leaning back in the booth because my jeans were suddenly two sizes too small.

"I have to go check on Mama to make sure her pipes are okay. Jake and I had plans, but he's still out of town, so I planned a mani-pedi movie night with her. Why? What are you doing?"

I loved the way her face lit up when she said Jake's name. He seemed like a great guy, aside from the fact he was trying his best to convince Raeann she could fly.

"Nothing much. I haven't worked with Shelby at all since last week, so I'm gonna spend the evening with her. We still haven't heard back from Camille. At this point, we're just in a holding pattern."

I was still mostly convinced that all she needed to do was learn to focus it, anyway.

"Okay, then. I'll see you tomorrow." She gave me a hug. "And when I do, I expect to hear that you've talked to Hunter about the creepy thing with the farm. You hear me?"

"I hear you," I replied, hugging her back. "I'll go talk to him first thing in the morning."

SHELBY WAS ALREADY home when I got there and was waiting for me in the living room. Aside from the kitchen, it was my favorite room in the house. The floors were a burnished golden pine and the ceilings had bare beams. Pictures of our family throughout the generations lined the neutral walls.

My sister was relaxing in one of two overstuffed, amber recliners, flipping through channels so fast I had no idea how she could read the guide.

I flopped down on the sofa and took a drink of her tea.

She wrinkled her nose when I set it back down. "Gross! Get your own!"

"Why should I? There's a whole glass sitting right here," I teased.

She slapped my hand away when I reached for it again. "C'mon. Let's get the torture over with," she said, pushing to her feet and offering a hand to pull me up. "I know you think I'm just as good as you are if I just focus, but I'm starting to think you're wrong." She looked at me, her eyes soft and sad. "Just don't be disappointed if I don't ever get the hang of this, or if Camille finds something really wrong, okay?"

I hugged her then pushed her to arms' length so I could look her in the eye. "I could never be disappointed in you, you understand? I just know you want this, and I refuse to let you give up. And it kills me, seeing you suffer with those headaches."

Aunt Adelaide popped in and offered her encouragement too.

Shelby smiled and headed toward what we'd dubbed the practice room—an extra downstairs bedroom that now contained objects of various sizes and weights that she was supposed to move from one spot to another. Whether she did it using spell or telepathy was up to her. Personally, I'd started out using spells but had gotten to the point where all I really had to do was will something to move, and it did. I saved the spells for more detailed situations, like with the broom and mop.

The events at the barbecue sparked an idea and I was eager to try it out. I put a hand on her arm. "I thought we'd try something different today. Let's go outside."

She pursed her lips and looked skeptical. "Are you sure about that? What if somebody sees us?"

Addy was as anti-establishment as most folks her age and had long ago placed privacy wards around the entire house and yard. She was good enough that they were undetectable by the council, so we didn't have to worry about them. I didn't understand why it was an issue.

"We'll do what witches do—turn 'em into toads, of course."

I laughed at her disgusted expression. "C'mon. That was funny."

"Yeah. Haha. Seriously, what if somebody comes? What if Cody or Hunter shows up?"

"We'll have Max keep an eye out. I swear you're going to love this!" Usually I was the one who worried about getting caught, so her lack of enthusiasm made me wonder what was up. Finally, the lightbulb came on. She liked Cody. Motivation!

"Look at it this way—if my idea works as well as I think it will, you're going to be a few steps closer to full control. You won't have to worry about little things like, you know, flicking your wrist and knocking over a water glass into Cody's lap."

Slips like that were rare for her, but they had happened. That was one of the reasons I was so determined to get her to master this. Flynn witches were powerful without exception, which made me even more worried. Magic was energy and it had to have an outlet. Otherwise, bad things happened, and the more powerful the witch, the worse the consequences.

I hadn't told her that yet because it would have been kinda like telling somebody her pants are on fire, but not pointing her toward a watering trough. I didn't want to freak her out and make the problem even worse until I could figure out how to fix it. Because of that, I'd worked under the premise that, as much as it killed me, it was better for her to think she might not have enough power. Bass-ackwards logic, I know, but there you have it.

I headed over to the cornhole set and tossed her a set of beanbags.

"I thought we were practicing," she drawled, confused.

"We are. It occurs to me that your problem may be that you don't have enough incentive to focus. We both hate losing and loathe folding laundry. So, whoever loses has to live with that, plus fold the laundry."

She groaned. "That's not fair! You know there's no way I'm going to beat you."

"What do you have to lose? It's your night to fold clothes, anyway. Here's your chance to get out of it."

Her eyes glittered as her competitive nature peeked through. "You're on. Play to twenty-one?"

"Of course. You go first. Max! Will you please make sure nobody sneaks up on us? We're doing a little out-of-the-box training back here."

Do I look like a guard dog to you? I'm taking a nap.

No, I replied. *You look like an ass who lounges around all day and mooches free meals. If I wanted that, I'd just head down to the bar and find myself a husband. Get your big ears up there and earn your keep for once.*

He continued to grumble but pushed to his feet and ambled around front.

Ugh. Why couldn't I have a normal donkey?

Just in case, I cast a glamour that would make the back yard appear empty, then turned back toward the game.

"Okay, Shel. Let's get started."

Shelby wiped her palms on her jeans. Her hands were shaking. That was never a good sign.

"Calm down. It's just a game of cornhole, not a campaign for world domination."

She nodded sharply, took a deep breath, aimed at the board, and tossed. She strained to focus on the bag and I saw it waver, correcting course at the last minute. It was too late, though. The bag landed on the board several inches from the hole.

"Not bad for a warm-up shot," I encouraged. "You landed it on the board."

"I always land it on the board," she grumbled.

"Yeah, well watch this." I aimed, threw, then when I realized I hadn't thrown it hard enough, gave it a little boost. It landed at the edge of the hole.

"You missed on purposed! I'm not going to do this if you're going to let me win," she scowled.

I furrowed my brow. "I didn't miss on purpose. This is just a little harder than I thought it would be. I was only messing around the other night, and truthfully, most of the ones I made were legit. Your turn. Focus on nothing but the bag going in the hole."

She took a minute to aim again, then let the beanbag fly. It was going to be way off—she was going to completely overshoot the board. Suddenly the bag stopped, wobbling almost directly over the hole before it dropped. It landed halfway in the hole, dangling by an edge.

I almost laughed at the shocked expression on her face. When she finally realized what she'd done, she whooped and fist-pumped. "Yes! Beat that," she crowed.

We continued, and she got markedly better the longer we played, though it was still sporadic. I didn't lie when I said we were both competitive, so as the game progressed, so did the smack talk—and her focus.

She was far from perfect and had a couple of complete fails—one of which landed on a tree branch thirty feet in the air—but all in all, it was the most successful practice session we'd had in a long time, and the least stressful by far.

I ended up beating her by six points. She accepted the loss, but was adamant that she'd win when we played again tomorrow. I mentally fist-pumped when she said that. Normally, she did everything in her power to get out of practice, but now she was actually scheduling it herself.

We'd just put the beanbags away when we heard a motorcycle coming up the driveway. Shelby raised her brows and gave me her best 'duh' look. "That's one of the reasons I was so worried about somebody catching us. You forgot, didn't you?" she accused.

I nodded and chewed my bottom lip.

Max chose that minute to wake up but only bothered to open one eye. *Alert. Alert. Somebody's approaching,* he thought in a monotone.

"Thank you Captain Obvious," I snarked. "I'm hiding your scotch. See how you like drinking water with your oats this evening." I was trying to ration his excesses. Between the outrageous cost of hay and grain and rising liquor prices, it was almost impossible to turn a profit on a farm, even with a few boarders.

That's not fair. I did what you told me to do, he complained.

I chose to save my breath and let my actions do my talking; he was proof that mules got their stubborn streaks from the male line.

I eyed the aerodynamic machine rolling up in front of me. Last night, my wine-soaked brain had prompted me to write a check that my sober self now had to cash. Hunter shut the bike off and flipped the kickstand down before pulling off his gloves and helmet.

"You girls ready to ride?" he asked.

I examined the bike like it was an alien being about to rip my head off, then sighed. There was no backing out now, so I pasted on a smile and squeaked, "Sure—I've been looking forward to it all day."

Hunter shook his head and gave me a half-smile. "I promise not to wreck," he vowed, then added, "I don't want to scratch my bike."

I scowled at him, but Shelby giggled and nudged me with her shoulder. "Don't be a baby. You strap yourself to a thousand pounds of dynamite with a brain every time you climb onto a horse. At least a motorcycle isn't going to spook at a deer or balk at a mud puddle."

That actually made sense, except a horse's maximum speed was like thirty miles per hour, and that's a thoroughbred in top racing form. Ours were about as close to that level of fitness as I was.

Addy chose that minute to pop into view and circle around the motorcycle, then Hunter. "Now *this* is what I was talkin' about when I said you needed some excitement! If you back out, I swear I'll sing in your shower for a month."

I rolled my eyes in an attempt to show her she didn't scare me, but the crappy thing was that she'd do it, and her singing voice could peel paint.

We'd no sooner settled onto the porch with icy glasses of tea than Cody came zooming up the driveway. Okay, *zooming* might be a bit over the top, but my baby sister was going to be riding double with him. I considered anything over ten miles an hour reckless driving.

He stopped his bike beside Hunter's and it was then that I noticed each bike had an extra helmet strapped to the seat. I would have preferred full body armor, but I guess you take what you can get.

"Hey, Cody." Shelby rose to greet him. "Tea?"

" Sure."

I tried to put off the inevitable by slowly sipping my drink, but within a couple of minutes, everybody but me had drained their glasses and were heading to the bikes. I found myself wishing I'd had wine instead.

"C'mon, Noelle," Shelby urged. "You're gonna love it; I promise."

I sighed and pushed myself to my feet. Apparently, I was the only non-suicidal one in our little foursome, or for that matter, our entire family.

By the time I buckled my helmet, the guys had started the bikes and Shelby had already climbed on behind Cody. I looked at Hunter's bike, trying to figure out how to get on. Hunter moved his leg and pointed to his foot peg. "Put your left foot here, then swing your right leg over and put both feet on the back pegs. Lock your hands in front of me and squeeze with your knees to hold on. If you need me to slow down, just pat me on the leg."

Okay, easy enough—kinda like mounting a horse. And I had the option to tap out. Good to know. I followed his instructions and found myself pressed tightly to his back. An unexpected tingle of excitement ran through me. As Addy had pointed out, I hadn't had a speeding ticket in *a while*. When I'd been younger, before I had all these responsibilities, there was no such thing as too fast.

"Ready?" Hunter shouted through his helmet over the roar of the bike.

I took a deep breath. "Ready as I'll ever be," I shouted back.

He nodded to Cody and they maneuvered the bikes out of the driveway. Every lurch of the bike made my stomach clench, but after a couple of miles, I started to relax and admire the scenery.

I have to admit, it wasn't as horrible as I'd imagined. As a matter of fact, after I realized none of us were likely to die a fiery death, it was downright fun. It didn't hurt that I was snuggled tight against the back of one of the best-looking men I'd seen in a long time.

Every once in a while, he'd reach back and touch my leg and send me a muffled, "You okay?" Since my arms were around him, I just gave him a thumbs-up. As the ride progressed, the occasional touch turned into more of a caress that sent tingles up my leg. It made me hope for a goodnight kiss.

By the time we pulled back into the driveway, it was starting to get dark. My back was aching a little from sitting in such an awkward position for so long, but it was worth it.

Shelby climbed off Cody's bike and pulled off her helmet. Her face was flushed with pleasure as she walked toward me, smiling from ear to ear. She hip-checked me and said, "See—nobody died or even lost an eye."

I was trying to remain passive, but I couldn't do it; I grinned. "Okay, fine. You were right. Can we do it again?"

I turned to Hunter, who was smiling. I'd never noticed, but he had a dimple on his left cheek. This happy, easy-going person was the man I'd imagined the first day I met him. I laughed when I remembered what I'd thought of him that day. I wanted to see more of this side of him.

"Of course we can. I love riding and it would be great to get out and do it more. Just name the time and place." I rested my hand on the gas tank as he took my helmet from me and hooked it on the bike.

I remembered how his hand had caressed my leg and was glad when the kids walked around back to hang out for a while.

"Maybe this weekend. Cody's going on his fishing trip, but maybe we could go for a ride, just the two of us." I felt my face flush; I wasn't exactly experienced with this whole dating thing, but I knew I wanted to spend more time with him.

"This weekend would be great," he said as he turned to me. We were so close that I could smell his clean, crisp cologne. It reminded me faintly of the ocean. His gaze slipped to my mouth and he brought his hand up to my face and leaned down toward me.

The ringing of his phone broke the spell and he stepped back, pulled it from his pocket, and answered it. He walked away from the bike a bit and turned his back to me. After a few crisp questions, he told the caller, "I'll be there in fifteen. Don't let anybody in."

He gave me a bittersweet smile and reached for his helmet. "I have to go," he said as he pulled it over his face and buckled it. "Somebody ransacked the sheriff's office and Hank's house." His look of passion had turned to one of regret. "Plus, I really can't get involved with you until I put this murder to bed."

My heart dropped a little as he slung his leg over the bike and revved the motor. I didn't realize until after his brake light disappeared from view that I'd forgotten to tell him about the real estate investor.

Chapter 19

By the time I made it to town late the next morning, the gossip mill was churning at record speed. Hunter wasn't taking my calls, so I grabbed a coffee and headed to the salon. I figured I'd just cut out all the middle men and go straight to the hub.

When I entered, Marge was in the manicure chair getting her weekly fill and gums were flapping furiously. They didn't even notice me until I cleared my throat.

"Hey, Noelle," Coralee greeted me. "How you doin', sugar?"

"I'm fine. I just figured I'd stop by and see what y'all thought about the break-ins."

Beating around the bush wasn't necessary with this crowd; they were happy to share their speculations with anybody, especially if there was a chance of gleaning new information. Since I had no doubt I'd been seen with Hunter yesterday, I'd earned my in.

"Honestly, we haven't been able to decide who mighta done it," Marge answered.

"Yeah," Belle continued. "Best we think is it was somebody looking for Hank's little black book. We reckon maybe it was Butch Davies or Ronnie Dean, or both."

Marge snorted. "Only problem with that theory is that they're both worthless as tits on a bull without Hank to tell 'em what to do."

I couldn't argue with that. "Little black book?" I queried.

"Yeah," Coralee replied. "Marge here says he had a book he used to keep track of all the people he was dealing with. He used it to record who'd paid him and who owed him. It's not like he could keep blackmail and extortion files in his office."

Marge nodded so vigorously that it was testament to Coralee's skill that her curlers didn't fall out. "It's true. I saw it one day when he came to collect the money for those trumped-up fines."

"Huh," I said, my mind whirring. "I wonder if Hunter knows about this."

"If he don't, he needs to," Belle said. "I've been tempted to introduce myself a few times, but he don't seem like he'd be real receptive."

"That's probably for the best right now," I agreed, "at least until he settles in. He's already noticed some things—I think Angus has been messing with him a little—but finding out about ghosts and witches right now may send him right off the deep end."

"Well somebody needs to let him know about the book," Coralee stated. "Though even if it was handed to him, that man of yours would still be diggin' through a needle in a haystack to find out who killed Hank. Everybody in the book would be a suspect, and I doubt there's many folks who ain't in the book."

I growled when they referred to him as mine, especially after he rebuffed me last night. "He's not my man. We haven't even been on an official date."

She waved her hand dismissively. "Details, sweetie, details. But back to the book. At least it would give him somewhere to look besides at Anna Mae."

I promised to go talk to him right away, then headed back to Brew4U to tell Raeann what I'd learned.

When I got there, Jake was leaning against the front counter and Raeann was restocking the coffee bar. I headed to the espresso machine. I needed more caffeine, and Hunter could probably use some, too.

"So ... what did you find out? What's the latest speculation?" Jake asked.

I shrugged. "They really don't know much more than we do about who may have done it, but they did mention Hank may have used a little black book to keep track of his alternate business ventures. They figure somebody was looking for that."

"Huh," he said. "Do you think it really exists?"

"Marge from the hardware store claims to have seen it." I added a pump of caramel to my cup and a pump of chocolate to Hunter's. "What do you think, Rae?"

Raeann furrowed her brow. "Well, Marge is a lot of things, but she's not a liar. If she says she saw a little black book, then she did."

"I find it hard to believe he'd keep a book, though. Wouldn't he be running the risk of somebody getting their hands on it?" Jake asked.

"Hank was arrogant enough that he wouldn't even think of something like that." Rae held up her finger. "That's not to say, though, that what Marge saw wasn't just a contact book or something. You know how that crew is—they tend to look for the interesting explanation. That's not always the accurate one."

"True," I agreed as I popped the lid back on my coffee cup. "Still, I'm going over to the sheriff's office to tell Hunter about it."

"Pop in and see Anna Mae while you're there," she said. "She's probably lonely and scared stiff."

"You don't think she killed him?" Jake asked.

I shook my head. "Absolutely not. She doesn't have it in her, though I surely wouldn't blame her if she did."

As an afterthought, I stuffed the cups in a carrier and threw a few pastries in a bag to take with me, too. Just as I reached the door, somebody pulled it open for me.

"Hey, Noelle. Looks like you have your hands full."

It was Will, and he looked much better than he had at the fair. At least he was clean-shaven, and the dark circles were mostly gone from his eyes. He smiled at me.

"Will! You look much better. I was worried about you when I saw you at the fair the other day."

"Yeah, I'm feeling much better. I had a lot on my mind, but managed to work most of it out. Things are looking up again."

"I'm glad to hear it. Whatever it was, I'm glad you managed to work through it. Have a good one."

"You too," he replied as the door swung shut behind him.

It only took me a few minutes to reach the courthouse and when I pushed through the door, Peggy Sue beamed at me. "Hey, Noelle. It's good to see ya again. How are you?"

It would take me a while to get used to this new version of the formerly dour clerk, but I definitely liked it. Today, she was wearing a cheery paisley sundress cut to flatter her ample figure.

"I'm doing just great, Peggy Sue. How about you? Want a pastry? I just made 'em last night."

I was glad now that I'd brought more than a couple, because her eyes lit up as she reached for the bag and peered into it. "I'd love one, thank you." She pulled out a raspberry danish and moaned when she took a bite. "Girl, you have a magic touch."

If only she knew. "I'm glad you like it. Is Hunter in?"

She nodded and motioned me back toward his office. "Oh! Noelle, wait! I have something for you. She set the pastry on top of her coffee cup, then dug through her files and handed me an envelope. I pulled it out and read it, then read it again and looked at her, astonished.

"Peggy Sue, what is this?"

Well," she said, drawing the word out into two syllables, "I was just going through the property appraisals in order to compile the annual budget, and I happened to notice that for some reason, your property was appraised way too high during probate."

She paused. "Oh, who are we kiddin'? Hank told me a week ago to send out an 'amended' appraisal — even though he'd already put the screws to ya the first time around, because he wanted your farm. Now he's dead, and I did exactly what he asked. I sent you an amended appraisal that accurately reflects what you owe," she declared.

"It ain't right what he was doin' to people around here, Noelle. It don't take but half of what people have been payin' to run this town, and the other half was goin' in his pocket. Yours was easy enough to fix. I can't give you the cash back, but assuming there isn't a significant increase in value next year, you paid two years' worth of taxes instead of one. That's the amended receipt."

I didn't know what to say. "Thank you, Peggy Sue. He told me the other day he was charging me more and I've been worried about where I was going to get the money to pay it."

"Well now you don't have to worry about it, sugar. Enjoy that place the way Adelaide intended for you to."

I looked down at the envelope and a huge weight lifted off my shoulders. "I'm gonna keep you in pastries forever, Peggy Sue."

She laughed as I headed toward Hunter's office. "Are you trying to bribe an elected official, Miss Flynn?"

I grinned. "Nope. Just rewarding a darned good person for doing me right when she didn't have to."

I was still smiling when I walked into Hunter's office. For some reason, it was hotter than an Easy-Bake oven in there. He had a window open, the ceiling fan was going, and there was an oscillating fan on his desk, but they were just stirring around hot air.

If you've never experienced July in Georgia, think back to the last time you were in a sauna. It's like that, but you have to leave your clothes on. Still, even the heat in the room wasn't going to dampen my spirits after what Peggy Sue had just done for me.

"Well hello," he said, mopping his forehead with a hankie. He glanced at the extra cup of coffee and the grease-stained bag. "Please God, tell me those are for me."

"I figured somebody over here could use an iced mocha latte and pastries. If that person happens to be you, then I guess it's your lucky day," I teased as he took the coffee and bag from me. "What's up with the AC?"

"I have no idea, but it must be the vents leading to here, because the rest of the building is fine. I can't even get anybody to come look at it until tomorrow. He turned the fan up a notch higher and set it to oscillate so that I got a burst of hot air every few seconds, too.

"I did want to bring you coffee, but that's not the main reason I stopped by. I was at the salon and they mentioned that Hank had a book containing the names of people he was blackmailing or otherwise ripping off. We figured maybe it was the target of the break-ins and that you should know about it."

He closed his eyes and pinched the bridge of his nose. "You gotta be kidding me. He was robbing so many people that he had to have a *book* to keep up with them all? I'm never going to find who murdered him. Hell, at this point, I'd like to kill him myself for disgracing the badge." He motioned with his chin toward a short filing cabinet to my right.

"The book could be why they broke in, I suppose. That's the locked filing cabinet I mentioned. I have no idea what was actually in there. It was open and empty, but they went through the other filing cabinets too."

I shrugged. "Well, take it to the basics. People almost always murder for either love or money. I'd bet dollars to donuts this was about money, because Hank's own mother didn't even like him, so love is out.

"I also guarantee it wasn't Anna Mae, regardless of what you found in her house. If I were you, I'd do my best to find that book. If it actually exists, there's a good chance whoever killed him is in there for one reason or another."

"Maybe so, but for now, the evidence still points to her. It's pretty hard to ignore the fact that a man turns up dead after his wife—who he's been cheating on—takes out a life insurance policy on him for half a million dollars."

He had a file open in front of him and I couldn't help but notice Hank's name on it.

I motioned toward it. "So that's his file, huh? Will you at least tell me what kind of poison was used?"

Hunter shook his head. "I can't. It's not that I don't trust you, but it's the only part of this investigation that isn't public knowledge. I'm having enough problems controlling this. Especially since Hank was so crooked, it would be too easy for people he was working with to set somebody up. Right now, there are exactly three people who know what killed him—me, the coroner, and the murderer. I intend to keep it that way, at least for now."

I saw his point, but if Anna Mae didn't kill Hank, and I was sure she didn't, then the method of poison could narrow the pool down considerably depending on what type it was. Considering Hunter didn't know much about the citizens of the town—especially that some of them were witches—he was playing with one hand tied behind his back and didn't even know it.

"Look, I understand, but there are things about this town that you don't know yet. You haven't been here long enough. I know you think of me as just a waitress, but I also have a degree in criminal justice and I know everybody in these parts. I may be able to help."

I could see his internal struggle. On one hand, he knew I had a point. On the other, it went against his training to breach protocol like that.

"Let me think about it. Don't take this the wrong way, but I have to keep in mind I just met you, too. I mean, I like you, but you have to admit I can't completely rule you out as a suspect. You were there and had motive."

That probably should have made me mad, but he was right. I shrugged. "Fair enough. Listen, there's something else I've been meaning to tell you about. Raeann insists it's important. I don't disagree with her, but I'm not sure what you can really do about it."

I filled him in on my experience with the real estate investor.

"The only thing that really bothers me is that he said this guy had a preliminary contract and applications for building and zoning permits. That's kinda creepy."

"And why would you think Hank had anything to do with it?"

"Well, he oversaw the permits, and just a few minutes before he died, he made an innuendo about my brakes."

He leaned forward and narrowed his eyes, his elbows resting on his desk. "Wait, you didn't tell me that."

I flushed. "I didn't really think it was a big deal. It's just how Hank was—he was always lording his power. He's dead, so whether or not he cut my brakes is basically a moot point."

"Actually, it's not moot at all—" One of the younger deputies came busting through the door without knocking. He skidded to a halt when he saw me and looked back and forth between us like he didn't know what to do. His face was beet red and he obviously had something on his mind.

"What can I do for you, JC?" Hunter asked.

The younger man looked at me and swallowed. His Adam's apple bobbed, and the look of indecision on his face was almost comical. "Well sir, can I see you in the hallway?"

Hunter stood up and followed him into the hallway, letting the door swing shut behind him. When it did, the open window and the fan combined to create a bit of a vacuum and blew the top paper in the folder off the pile and under the desk.

The edges of it slipped out from under the front of the desk and came to rest about two feet in front of me. The top of the paper read *Coroner's Report*.

I chewed my lip, looking back and forth between the paper and the door. I bent over to scoop it up to put it back on the desk, and I had the best of intentions to do just that, but the word 'belladonna' jumped out at me.

I sighed. There was no way to stuff that cat back in the bag, so I skimmed it quickly as I picked it up. The toxic plant was in the list of stomach contents.

I scanned through the rest of the list, picking out ingredients I recognized: raspberries, strawberries, blueberries, glucose, fructose, atropa belladonna berries, starch polymer, wheat proteins, lenoleic acid, lactones ... I didn't need to read anymore; I'm a witch and a dedicated baker; I know the chemical structures of my ingredients. Hank had eaten a poisoned piece of mixed-berry pie for breakfast.

Chapter 20

I slid the sheet of paper back onto the top of the pile and leaned back in my chair, thinking.

Poisoning somebody with belladonna was rockin' it old-school-witch style. That didn't make any sense. Anna Mae wasn't a witch and there was no other plausible reason she would just keep belladonna around. For that matter, most *witches* didn't even use it anymore because it was too easy to miscalculate the dose.

I flipped through my mental Rolodex and tried to think of any herbalists who might be able to point me in the right direction. There was one who lived about ten miles out of town, clear out in the sticks, but she was a few bricks shy of an outhouse. The problem now was that I knew what killed Hank, but I wasn't supposed to.

The fan swung around and puffed another burst of hot air in my face. I wrinkled my nose and turned my face away. I didn't know jack about air conditioning systems but fans were easy. I muttered a few words and sighed when the next blast of air that hit me in the face was cool.

Hunter said something from outside his door, then the latch clicked and he came back in looking flustered. I shot a guilty glance at the folder and debated whether or not I should come clean, then decided to hold off. I didn't want him to know I'd read his report, even though it had been an accident, and I couldn't exactly tell him he needed to start looking at witches anyway.

I decided to talk to Addy about it before I did anything. She'd lived here all her life and was a fair herbalist herself; it was a sure bet that she'd have some ideas about where it might have come from.

"Listen, I have a lot of baking to do so I need to go," I told Hunter, then remembered that J.C. had been pretty worked up. "But is everything okay?"

Hunter sighed and rubbed his hands over his face. "I may as well tell you. It's not like the entire town isn't going to know within the hour anyway. We just found a checkbook underneath a false bottom in Hank's desk drawer, and when we called to verify the account, we found out he had almost half a million dollars in it."

Color me surprised. "I told you Hank found a way to make being a sheriff in a backwoods town profitable. Though honestly, I figured there'd be way more than that."

He looked at me like I'd lost my mind. "More? I swear to God—up until this very minute, I thought everybody was exaggerating. We're going to have to do a complete audit of everything: tax records, fines, health department violations, code inspections."

I considered that for a minute. It would mean going through literally every record in the courthouse, and even then it would be in drops, not buckets. Lots of drops, for sure, but that didn't feel like the right trail to follow. "If I were you, I'd concentrate more on finding that little black book than combing through official records. Unless I miss my guess, that's where you'll find the big sources of that money."

Hunter drew his brows together and shook his head. "No wonder nobody wanted this job."

I rose to leave and patted him on his arm on the way out, adopting a blasé tone. "If it makes you feel any better, they just didn't want to get stuck with Hank's murder. Hurry up and solve that, and I'm sure there will be plenty of takers. As you can see, it can be quite the lucrative career."

I pressed my lips together and walked out, giving Hunter plenty to think about. When I passed Peggy Sue, she asked if everything was all right. I smiled and told her that, for the first time in a long time, I thought it was about to be. "And you may as well start going through the records tracking down all the other *errors*," I added, "because unless I miss my guess, that man's gonna end up keeping the sheriff's badge for good."

She smiled and winked at me as I stepped into the main lobby of the courthouse. "Sugar, I figured that out the minute the council appointed him interim."

I MADE A PIT-STOP AT the jail and visited with Anna Mae for a bit. It wasn't until I was on my way back to the truck that I remembered I'd left the fan in Hunter's office blowing cold. I gave myself a mental forehead slap, but there wasn't much I could do about it at that point. Let him wonder, and enjoy it.

I needed to restock my baking supplies and grab something for supper, so I stopped at the grocery store on the way home. As Hunter had predicted, the news about Hank's hidden account was running through the gossip mill like a hot knife through butter.

The cashier, Emma, was a short, squat woman wearing bottle-bottom glasses. As she ran my flour over the scanner, she asked, "You hear about Hank's secret account? I heard it has over a million dollars in it."

I gave her a good-natured half-smile. "I did hear about it, Emma. As a matter of fact, I was at the sheriff's office when they found it. It only had just under a half-million in it." I shook my head when I realized I'd said *only* like that kind of cash was chicken feed.

"Oh." She blinked at me and the glasses exaggerated the movement so much that she reminded me of an owl. I couldn't decide which was more comical—her expression or the fact that she looked so disappointed that I'd cut the value of the gossip in half.

I paid her and as I was headed back to the truck, Raeann texted me.

R: Thx for letting your best friend find out thru the grapevine about the acct!

Crap on a cracker. She was going to kill me, and I deserved it. I fired back a quick text.

N: OMG. I totally suck! Found out what killed Hank tho. Talk in a bit.

Of course, my phone rang two seconds later. I gave her the rundown and told her what I was doing, assuring her I'd keep her posted.

As soon as I got home, I hollered for Adelaide, who popped in and grouched, "No need to yell, girl. I'm dead, not deaf. And by the way, that worthless donkey is in my petunias."

I paused from putting the groceries away and stopped her before she could build a full head of steam. "Geez, what has your knickers in a twist?"

She heaved a sigh and floated to a chair. "I'm sorry, Noelle. It's just that I feel so out of the loop. All this excitement about Hank, and I have to wait around here to find out anything."

I'd never really thought about it, but I guess I'd probably get stir-crazy in her situation too. Belle and Angus popped to mind. They seemed to go wherever they wanted, but I assumed since Addy never left, maybe she was bound to the house or something. It never occurred to me to ask if she'd tried.

"Aunt Adelaide, have you even tried to go anywhere besides here since you came back? Belle goes pretty much wherever she wants, and so does Angus."

"Actually, I did. I tried to ride to town with you shortly after I died. You couldn't see me yet, but I was worried about you and just wanted to be with you. The truck just pulled out from underneath me, though."

Unbidden, tears popped into my eyes and I wished for the thousandth time that I could hug her. I sniffed and wiped them away before she could see them. There was no need to upset her too. Then I had an epiphany.

"Maybe it doesn't work that way. Maybe you just have to concentrate on a place, and you'll appear there."

I wasn't sure how this stuff worked, but it sounded logical.

Her face brightened. "I didn't even think of that—I'm going to try right now."

"No wait!" I reached out to grab her arm before I remembered she was incorporeal. I felt like I shoved my hand in an ice bucket. "First, I need to ask you something."

She turned back to me. "What?"

"I found out Hank was poisoned with belladonna. Specifically, the berries. I caught a peek of the autopsy report when Hunter was out of his office, and based on what they found in his stomach, my guess is they were baked into a mixed-berry pie." I sighed. "I doubt Anna Mae even knows what belladonna is, and I don't know where she would get it if she did. Do you know anybody?"

She hovered back over the chair again and rubbed her chin. "I can't think of anybody at all. Most of us stopped growing it decades ago. There's just no reason to use it, even in potions." She pursed her lips. "I'll think on it, but nothing comes to mind right off the bat. I'm sorry."

I felt like somebody let all the air out of me. "It's okay. I figured it was a long shot."

Aunt Adelaide gasped and popped up from her chair so quickly that if she'd been solid, it would have tipped over. "Wait—did you say it was *mixed-berry* pie?"

I glanced at her out of the corner of my eye as I put the groceries away. I didn't understand why the type of pie mattered. "Yeah. Strawberries, raspberries, and belladonna berries, which would have looked like blueberries. Why?"

She had a huge smile on her face. "Unless we have a bakery here that sells belladonna-berry pies, Anna Mae didn't kill Hank."

Chapter 21

I dropped the flour on the counter and spun to give her my full attention. "What? Why do you say that?"

She had her arms crossed and was shimmering with excitement. "Because," she said, "I know for a fact Anna Mae Doolittle is deathly allergic to strawberries."

"Are you absolutely sure?" I began to pace, trying to figure out a way to tell Hunter this without admitting I'd looked at the report.

"Positive," she declared. "I hosted the church summer camp out here a couple of times back when we had the boarding license. The kids always brought a packed lunch from home, and poor Anna Mae switched sandwiches with her friend once. It had strawberry jam on it."

She paused with a faraway look on her face. "Within just a few minutes, she couldn't breathe. Luckily, I kept an epi pen in the first aid kit or else I'm afraid she would have died before we could get her to the hospital. We found out later that she can't even touch them without getting a nasty rash."

My mind was going a mile a minute. I was going to have to come clean to Hunter so he could cut Anna Mae loose.

I picked up my phone and called him but it went straight to voicemail. Frustrated, I grabbed my keys and ran out the door. I'd just made it to the outskirts of town when my phone began playing "Kryptonite," the ringtone I used for Raeann.

I hated to blow her off, so I pulled over and answered. "Hey, I can't talk right now. I'm in the truck and I need to get to the courthouse to talk to Hunter."

"Oh. Well then, the courthouse isn't where you want to go; he's here. Want me to have him wait?"

"Absolutely. I'll be there in five. Bye."

It only took me four. I swung into a spot in front of the shop and jumped out of the truck almost before it came to a complete stop. The closed sign was already in the window, so when I burst through the door, the only two people there were Raeann and Hunter.

"Hey, Noelle. Raeann said you needed to talk to me."

I bit my lip and swallowed hard. How mad was he going to be when he found out that I'd looked at the file? It didn't matter; Anna Mae's freedom was on the line, so I'd just have to bite the bullet and let the chips fall where they may.

"Yeah. I uh ... you're probably not going to believe this, but when you left your office today while I was there, when you pushed the door shut, the top sheet of paper—the coroner's report—blew off your desk. When I went to pick it up, one specific item caught my eye, and I read part of the report."

I waited for him to blow up. He set his jaw and his expression turned stony. "I left the room for five minutes and you went through a confidential file? Even after I'd specifically told you I wasn't ready to share the information with you?"

I sighed and shifted my weight, fighting off my irritation. It wasn't like I'd picked it up and leafed through it.

He raked his hand through his hair and glared at me. "Okay, given the massive breach of trust here, I assume there's a reason you're confessing?"

"Yes. There is. I'm sorry if you feel like I breached your trust—I swear to God that wasn't my intent—but I'm not sorry I saw it, because you have evidence right in that report that proves Anna Mae is innocent. If not, she really reached around her elbow to scratch her butt in order to poison him."

Had the situation not been so serious, the look on his face would have been comical.

"Okay, I didn't understand half of that, but the half I did get is that you feel there's something there that would exonerate Anna Mae. May I ask what it is?"

I blew out a breath. I had a feeling that the issue of my nosiness was only tabled, not forgiven.

"The stomach contents listed ingredients that led me to believe the actual vehicle used to poison him was mixed berry pie. It had the chemical compounds for flour, cornstarch, butter, and then of course strawberries, raspberries, and belladonna berries, which, in case you don't know, look a lot like blueberries." I paused to take a breath.

"I'm listening." He was, but he didn't look happy about it. He had his arms crossed and was standing with his feet shoulder-width apart. And, of course, he was frowning and his eyes were practically shooting laser beams at me.

"So, if that's the case, then Anna Mae didn't do it. Obviously, the pie was homemade; you can't exactly swing by Walmart and pick up a belladonna fruit pie. But she's so allergic to strawberries that she can't even touch them. There's no way she made that pie."

"Maybe she wore gloves."

"That makes no sense. Why wouldn't she have just made a 'blueberry' pie with the belladonna berries? Sure, they're bitter, but he would have only have had to take a couple of bites for it to be lethal. And for Hank—pig that he was—a couple of bites would have been close to an entire piece."

He was relaxing his stance, but he was still suspicious. "Maybe she did, and he just ate some fresh strawberries and raspberries."

I rolled my eyes. "Hank never ate anything healthy unless it was covered in sugar, ranch dressing, or bacon. C'mon. What did the coroner postulate?"

He looked down at his feet and grumbled, "Mixed-berry pie."

"Okay, then. Combine her allergy with the fact that her house was ransacked and I think you pretty much have to admit she's looking less and less like a suspect."

Hunter ground his teeth together, but conceded. "All right. I'll follow up with her doctor to confirm the allergy, and if it's true, I'll release her."

He opened his mouth to say something else, but snapped it shut and stomped toward the door.

"Hunter, wait—"

He turned back toward me and the look on his face was thunderous. "No, Noelle. I'm not waiting. There's nothing to say. Just ... leave it." He stomped out the door and the little bell above the door jangled twice, then fell silent.

Well. That was that, then. Tears pricked the back of my eyes and I fought to swallow the lump in my throat.

Raeann rushed around the counter and pulled me into a hug. "Aww, honey, bless your heart; that was an impossible situation for you. He'll understand that and come around. Right now, he's just got a whole lot on his plate, and feels like the one person he was actually starting to trust in this town betrayed him. Once he calms down and has a chance to chew on things for a minute, he'll be fine. I know it."

I hugged her back. "I sure hope so. I honestly didn't mean to be nosy. It's just—it was there. When it slipped onto the floor face up, my eyes just scanned it. And what was I supposed to do? Nothing? I can't do that; belladonna is a witch thing, which puts him completely out of his element."

She pulled back from me. "No matter what, don't you feel bad for trying to help somebody. There's no such thing as a coincidence in a witch's life. That paper blew off the desk for a reason: you were meant to see it. You and I both know it, and for now, that's good enough."

She nodded her head once and handed me a tissue. "Now, help me close up and we'll go see if Anna Mae needs a ride home."

I WAITED IN THE CAR while Raeann went in to fetch Anna Mae. When they came out, she rushed over and hugged me.

"Oh Noelle—Raeann here was just telling me what you did. Thank you so much! And thank you for the ride, too. I was just fixin' to call Hank's folks, but I really don't think I could stand ridin' in a car with them right now. Those people wear me plumb out."

I hugged her back, then made a show of opening the passenger-side door and motioning her in. "I'll even give you shotgun to celebrate your newfound freedom. We were going to hire a limo but the only one available on such short notice was Ricky Holly's Just Married Love Limo, and we thought that might be a tad inappropriate given the circumstances."

She giggled. "Yeah, but it sure would have set tongues wagging." Her mood shifted, and she looked down at her hands. "Not that I'm not already the talk of the town, I'm sure."

Raeann reached over from the driver's side and squeezed her hand. "Aww, Anna Mae, everybody with a lick of sense knows you didn't do it."

She heaved a sigh. "I know that in my heart, but I can't help but feel like a bug under a microscope."

The ride to her house didn't take long and we made idle chit-chat, avoiding any mention of her current situation. When we pulled into her drive, I couldn't help but admire the view. It curved in such a way that the house wasn't visible from the road. Grand oaks lined the road and met overhead, forming a leafy canopy much like the one over my own driveway.

The ride was relaxing and by the time we pulled up to her front door, her mood was lighter. When she unlocked the door and let us in, I was a little surprised to see that it was pristine.

"Wasn't your house trashed, too?"

"Yeah, but Mama Doolittle called for a cleaning service. She said there wasn't much damage. I guess it just looked like somebody was lookin' for somethin'. They decided to stay at the Holiday Inn though, because she was afraid they'd come and molest her in her sleep."

I snorted at the visual. "I think she's probably safe."

For the first time, Anna Mae actually smiled. "Yeah. Me too, though I'd never say that to her. The woman is terrifying. I'm not gonna lie—I'll be glad when the funeral is over and they'll be out of my life. They're like a cross between the Gottis and the Addams family."

She dropped her purse on a marble entry table in the foyer and kicked off her shoes. Raeann and I toed ours off too and followed her through to the kitchen. Like the rest of her house, it was done in light colors with pops of color added strategically throughout.

"Do y'all want a glass of wine? I know I'm gonna have one. Or three."

After the day I'd had, wine sounded like a fabulous idea. She poured us each a glass and we headed out to the veranda to enjoy it. White wicker chairs with red-checkered cushions sat around a matching table.

She sat down, pulled a foot up underneath her, took a sip of wine, and sighed. "Wow. I was afraid I was never going to do this again. Thank you again, Noelle."

"It was my pleasure, Anna Mae. Now we just have to find out who really did it."

"Well tonight, all we have to do is drink a glass of wine or two and enjoy the air and the freedom," she said, raising her glass.

I shot Shelby a quick text to let her know where I was, then settled back into the chair. Anna Mae had a great garden in the back filled with a wide variety of plants and flowers that created a calliope of colors. She had a fountain right in the middle of it all and the sound of the water hitting the rocks was soothing.

We talked for a little bit about nothing, then after the first glass of wine, we started reminiscing about our high school days.

We'd already killed one bottle and were halfway through another when Raeann voiced the question everybody in Keyhole Lake had been wondering about for years.

"I don't mean to hurt your feelings, and I know you're probably grievin', but why on earth did you stay with him all these years?"

Her eyes misted a little. "I wasn't stayin' with him per se, Raeann. I was stayin' with all of this." She motioned to the house and the gardens.

"I built this into a home—my home. He wasn't even here most of the time, and when he was, we slept in different rooms. I was just an arm piece to him, but that's okay, because he was just a meal ticket to me. I figure after putting up with him for all these years, I wasn't gonna walk away from it without a pot to piss in."

She paused to empty her glass. "I knew just enough about him to have him where I wanted him. I told him he wasn't layin' a hand on me after he slept with that white-trash gypsy stripper, and we came to an arrangement."

Knowing all that, I suddenly understood. In a town like Keyhole, she really wouldn't have had anywhere to go. Most of Hank's money was off the books so she wouldn't get much of anything in a divorce, and he had enough power that she probably wouldn't have been able to find a place to live even if she did manage to get a job.

She found a way to make her situation work and I couldn't find it in me to look down my nose at her for it.

Out of nowhere, she giggled. "Are you girls willing to help me do somethin' I've been dying to do for ages?"

Raeann and I looked at each other and shrugged.

"Sure thing." Raeann answered. "What're we doing?"

"We're gonna take that god-awful moose head down. That thing's been uglyin' up my livin' room for almost a decade and I swore the day he took his dyin' breath, it was gonna be the first thing to go."

We set our glasses down and followed her inside. She had cathedral ceilings and the top of the beast was nine feet or so up the wall. We each grabbed a kitchen chair. Now that I was paying attention to it, I could see why she thought it was so creepy. The glassy eyes seemed to follow you wherever you moved, and the tongue was sticking out.

Rae and I situated our chairs on either side of it and Anna Mae stood front and center. We reached up and shoved it up a bit, expecting it to be hanging from screws or wires. Instead, I about fell off my chair when the thing finally gave and swung away from the wall like a door.

It swung so fast it darn near knocked Raeann off her chair. She squealed and found herself dangling from the antlers as she fought to regain her balance. I was too busy staring at what was on the wall behind it to even try to catch her.

The late afternoon sun glinted off the stainless-steel dial of a safe door that was about three feet wide by three feet tall.

Rae and I climbed down and looked at each other, then at Anna Mae.

She stared at it for a few seconds, then growled and threw her hands on her hips. "Leave it to that sumbitch to hide the money in the one place he knew for sure I wouldn't look. Well joke's on his carcass," she hiccupped. "I figured out his combinations years ago; he uses the same numbers—his birthday—for everything. A perfect combination of his stupidity and arrogance."

We moved her chair forward and steadied her so she could work the dial. Within just a few seconds, she grabbed the handle and gave a yank. When the door swung open, we just stood there with our chins on the floor. There were at least twenty bricks of money, and that was just what we could see. She reached up and grabbed a stack of hundreds, and a little black book slipped off the top.

It slid across the floor with a soft hiss and came to rest beside the couch, the worn black leather a stark contrast to the gleaming white tile beneath it.

"Well butter my butt and call me a biscuit," Raeann breathed. "It does exist."

Chapter 22

I was the first to recover. "We need to call Hunter and tell him about"—I made a circular motion with my pointer finger—"all that."

Raeann moved closer to the safe. "How much do you think is there?"

I walked around to the stand beside Anna Mae, who was still rooted to her spot in front of the safe, just staring at the bundle of hundred-dollar bills in her hand. I caught movement out of the corner of my eye and about jumped out of my skin. I admit, I squealed like a little girl.

When I pivoted to see what it was, the moose "door" was swinging a little bit. In profile, the creature looked even creepier, so I reached up and pushed the door a little wider so that most of it was completely hidden.

I was going to have nightmares about that thing eating me. Yes, I realized that moose—mooses? moosi?—don't eat people, but you would have had to see this thing to appreciate just how emotionally scarring stuffed antlered beings can be.

I touched her arm and she snapped out of her haze, though she was still staring at the safe like it was a combination of a brain-sucking alien and the pot of gold at the end of a rainbow.

"I don't know," she said. "I guess it depends on if all those stacks are hundreds."

She and Raeann pulled a chair closer so they could climb up and see, but I was more interested in the black book.

I leaned over to pick it up and was a little disgusted when I felt some sort of grease on the cover of it. Eww. The man was still managing to gross me out even after he'd been dead for several days.

I wiped my hand on my jeans, then flipped it open. Considering it had been locked in a safe full of cash, I was almost afraid to see what it contained.

It only took one glance at the first page to knock my idea that it might only be a book of contacts right out the window.

At the top of each page was a name—yes, he was stupid enough to use full names as well as contact info. Beneath the name was a brief description of how he was extorting them, then the rest of the page was divided in quarters, with two rows each of dates and amounts.

I flipped through the book, paying more attention to the reason and the dates and amounts than I did to the names. Some of these people had been paying him for years. I went back to the front and started focusing on the names.

Holy crap, was Hunter going to have his work cut out for him. There had to be at least forty names in the book—some I recognized, some I didn't. Hank's reasons for extortion ran from telling spouses about various nefarious activities to some real whoppers, such as some serious dirt on council members and even a couple of district judges. Embezzlement, fraud, drugs.

My, my, my. If the entries and the amounts they were paying Hank to keep his mouth shut were to be believed, some of them had been really naughty.

One name caught my eye, and my heart fell as I read the description. *Oh, Will ... no wonder you looked like seven miles of bad road.* I remembered how much better he'd looked this morning and, though I now understood the improvement, I couldn't forget his explanation. *I had a lot on my mind, but managed to work it out.*

Then my mind flicked back to that cryptic comment at the fair. What had he said? Something about holding a lot of power over good people. Now it all made sense.

Hank had been blackmailing him because apparently Cody was caught cheating on a final at the end of last year—giving answers to somebody sitting beside him. He was threatening to put it on his permanent record and make the principal include it in his letter of recommendation if Will didn't pay him. Most colleges would disqualify him out of hand at that point.

I thought about Mr. Larson, the principal. He was a fair man who wanted to see his students succeed. It didn't make sense that, if he had chosen to overlook it, he would be willing to sabotage Cody like that, unless ... I flipped through the book and confirmed my suspicions.

Apparently, Hank had caught him having an intimate dinner in Atlanta with another man. Keyhole was catching up to the twenty-first century, but it hadn't made it quite that far yet. It was fine for a gay man to sell fried baloney sandwiches, but it was another thing altogether, at least to many folks, for one to be a school principal.

I thought sadly of all the times Principal Larson had helped me with my trigonometry, patiently breaking it down into bits of information I could understand, and tears came to my eyes. Nobody deserved to live in fear like that. Mr. Larson and Will were both good people and a surge of pure hatred for Hank pulsed through my veins.

I understood how he was manipulating Will, but what evidence was he using to blackmail the others? I slapped the book closed; all of a sudden, I felt like a Peeping Tom. These people were paying Hank to keep secrets and it seemed somehow disrespectful to them to keep reading.

Raeann's voice brought me back to the here and now. "Noelle, there's a big fat accordion folder clear in the back and neither of us are tall enough to reach it. Come get it."

A binder? Oh, no. My heart sank as I realized the binder probably contained the answer to my question—Hank's dirt. I had no doubt that it exposed truly bad secrets, but it also contained information that good people had a right to keep private if they chose.

"I don't think we should open it. I'd rather we just call Hunter. It would be better if none of us touched it." It was true, but it was also an excuse to keep them from pulling out pictures and documents that had the potential to destroy people, good and bad. Hunter would make sure the bad was weeded out from the good; I didn't know him well, but what to do with information like that is so integral to a personality that I knew in my heart he wouldn't abuse it.

Mr. Larson's meal and Cody's singular fall from grace were private, and if I had my way, those secrets—and all the others the binder and book held—would stay that way, at least until criminal charges were filed on those who deserved it.

"Seriously. We've already tampered with evidence more than we should have. I'm calling him." I pulled out my cell and told it to call Hunter.

Both women were staring at me, and Raeann stepped forward and put her hands on my shoulders. "Noelle, what's wrong? You're white as a sheet. What's in that book?"

I just shook my head and wiped my eye with a knuckle. "Suffice it to say that if the good sheriff were still breathing, I'd beat him to death myself."

Too late, I realized his widow was standing right there. "Sorry Anna Mae. No disrespect meant to you, but what he got was too good for him."

"I thought I knew what he was, Noelle. That was bad enough, but I'm guessing now I didn't know the half of it. Call it the way you see it." She bit her lip and flicked her gaze to the book. "It's really that bad?"

"Worse."

As mad as Hunter had been earlier, I was a little surprised when he picked up, even though his voice was cold enough to freeze the flame off a match. I gave him a generic rundown of what we'd found; the safe, the money, the book, and the binder. I asked him to keep quiet and come alone because the book left no doubt Hank wasn't the only cop in the know.

"Thank you for calling. I'll be there in fifteen." His tone was abrupt and he hung up without saying goodbye.

I told the girls he was on the way, then called Shelby to let her know what the hold-up was and asked her to keep it to herself until the gossip wheel caught wind of it some other way or Hunter released the information.

Anna Mae wandered into the kitchen and we followed her. I was still clutching the book protectively.

"I wasn't going to suggest it earlier," she said, "but how about we open another bottle of wine while we wait for the deputy to get here? I suddenly find myself sober as a judge and believe I need another dash of liquid fortitude." I winced at the comment, remembering something about a not-so-sober judge that I'd seen in the book.

I nodded and went out to retrieve our glasses, though there wasn't enough alcohol on the planet to unsee the proof of what a douche Hank had really been. "You and me both, Anna Mae—you and me both."

TRUE TO HIS WORD, HUNTER was there in ten minutes, but he had to take a ton of pictures of the scene before he moved anything. By the time he was finished, he'd been there for an hour.

Raeann and I waited with Anna Mae until he finished up. He took the binder and the book but left the cash. Technically, it was in a private safe in a private home and no crime had been connected to it ... at least yet. By the time she closed the door behind him, she looked exhausted. "Are you sure you want to stay here by yourself tonight? Shelby and I have plenty of room at the farm. You're more than welcome."

"Or if you want, I'll stay out here with you," Raeann said. "Jake had to go out of town again, so I don't have anything else to do. We could have a girls' night."

"Nah, I'll be alright. Honestly, I just want to light some candles, take a hot bath, and sleep in my own bed. Hank's folks will surely come around tomorrow to fill me in on the funeral arrangements. I'll probably end up spending the day with Mama Doolittle, so I'm gonna take tonight to enjoy the peace, such that it is."

She did look exhausted. Her blue eyes were dull and had dark smudges, and her face was pinched. I tried to imagine how she must be feeling right now.

I took her by the shoulders and looked into her eyes. "You know none of this is your fault, right? Don't you dare go blaming yourself."

She looked away as a lone tear rolled down her cheek.

"That's sweet of you to say, sugar, but how can it not be at least a little bit my fault? I knew Hank was meaner than a rattlesnake and had an idea he was doin' some shady stuff, and I didn't say a word."

Raeann frowned at her. "Who on earth would you have told? For that matter, who in town didn't already know? He ran this town, for god's sake. Everybody knew Hank was crooked, but what were our options? We all lived right in the belly of the beast—there was nowhere to turn."

The problem was that nobody was willing to step forward and reveal their secret in order to bust him at it. It was a vicious circle—if they tried to take him down, then the skeleton was dragged out of their closet. If they didn't, they had to do what Hank said. It was a no-win situation if they wanted to preserve their lives and livelihoods.

Now mind you, a big percentage of them—the cheaters and thieves, and worse—deserved to be outed, but many of them, like Will and Principal Larson, were just doing what they had to do.

"Trust me, Anna Mae, even if you'd gone to the council, you'd have just been digging your own grave. I didn't take a close look at that book, but I saw enough to know he had some of them under his thumb, too."

I don't know if what we said made her feel any better but at least when we left, she wasn't crying. I guess that was a start.

By the time I made it home, it was almost eight o'clock. I was glad to see Shelby had brought the horses in by herself and fed them. We usually did the night chores together, but I was beat.

Before I even opened the front door, the smell of garlic, Italian seasonings, and baking bread wafted out to me. My mouth began watering and I realized I hadn't eaten anything except that pastry in Hunter's office early that morning.

I kicked off my shoes at the door and followed my nose to the kitchen, where Shelby was standing over the stove tasting a red sauce. I leaned against the door for a minute, just soaking in the scene.

Adelaide was floating beside her gazing into the pot and sniffing. "Does it taste bland? It smells a little bland. It may need a dab more salt and oregano. If it's sharp, add another pinch of sugar."

Shelby made to elbow her, but her arm, of course, passed right through and she shivered. "It's fine—delicious, even." Little sister sounded like she was at the end of her rope. "Stop already!"

Adelaide ignored her and pointed to the oven. "Check the bread. It's probably done."

I cleared my throat and both of them jumped.

"It smells amazing in here. I haven't had anything but a pastry all day." I walked over to the stove and dipped the spoon in the sauce, blowing on it to keep from burning my lips off. I was shocked when I slurped it off the spoon.

"Shel, this is really good—well done!"

She blushed with pride or embarrassment; sometimes it was hard to tell the difference. "I was going to just make plain old spaghetti with jar sauce because I figured you'd be hungry when you got home, but Aunt Adelaide decided to teach me how to make hers."

Adelaide made a show of clearing her throat and pointing to the oven again.

Shelby scowled at her. "I'm not gonna forget the danged bread!" She pulled the oven door open and grabbed a potholder. The rolls were perfect and my stomach growled when I saw the golden crowns on them.

She pulled them out of the oven and ran a stick of butter over the top, then followed that with a sprinkle each of Italian seasoning and Parmesan cheese.

I stepped in and helped her finish up by draining the spaghetti and grabbing plates.

We ate in silence for several minutes before their curiosity got the better of them. It was obvious by the palpable tension and frequent glances that they were doing their best to let me eat in peace, but Shelby caved first. "Do you think they'll be able to figure out who the people in the book are?" she blurted.

I rolled my eyes and took a drink of milk. "Oh, I'm sure they won't have any problems. Hank had first and last names written at the top of each page, along with contact information."

"You gotta be kidding—I knew he was dumber than a box of rocks but he *named names*?" The look on Aunt Adelaide's face was priceless.

I raised a brow and swallowed my spaghetti. "You *did* know him, right? Though to be honest, I don't think he was stupid. Crooked, mean, cocky? Yeah. Stupid? No. He had quite the scam going—I'm talking more than a million bucks, easy—and that's not something a stupid man could manage, at least not for so many years."

Shelby reached for another roll and dipped it in the seasoned olive oil. "Well, then that will make Hunter's job easier then, right?"

"It may seem so, but no. I mean, he now has a list of prime suspects, but there are so many that it's still a needle in a haystack. Plus, unless I miss my guess, he's going to be opening at least ten or fifteen new criminal investigations."

Addy, who had remained silent up to that point, finally chimed in. "Plus he can't just assume the killer is definitely one of the people in the book. Don't forget about the method of the murder—if he ate a piece of poisoned pie, it's likely it's a woman. Were there any women in the book?"

Huh. She was right. I'd lost sight of the method because I was concentrating on motive. I tried to remember if there were any women, but none popped to mind. Of course, that doesn't mean there weren't any; with the exception of Will and Principal Larson, I'd just skimmed through enough pages to realize I didn't want to read any more.

"None that I remember, but I didn't read through the whole book."

"That doesn't surprise me—Hank was a pig. Dealing with women would have been beneath him. In his eyes, the men were the sources of money in the house."

I reached for another piece of garlic bread and ran it through my sauce. "Yeah, I guess you're right."

Shelby took a drink of milk to chase down the huge forkful of spaghetti she'd just stuffed in her mouth. "So, who all was in the book?"

Unbidden, the names ran through my head—many of them men who were just trying to live their lives and protect themselves and those they cared about. I pushed my food around on my plate, my appetite gone. "Too many, Shel. Too many."

Chapter 23

I tossed and turned until five the next morning, then gave up any hope of sleep and padded to the kitchen. There were so many things running through my head that I didn't even know which end was up, so I did the one thing that always calmed my mind—I baked.

After I made a pot of coffee, I pulled out the ingredients for orange rolls and decided to skip the bread machine in favor of doing the work myself. The steady rhythm of turning the dough and kneading it in upon itself was comforting and was so ingrained in my muscle memory that my brain could work while my hands stayed busy. It was a good combination.

My mind sifted through all the events that had occurred over the past week. I was missing something. It had niggled at the back of my consciousness all night, but it was like trying to catch smoke. I'd catch a glimpse of it, but when I tried to grasp it, it just slipped away.

Knead, turn, flip. Knead, turn, flip. I lost myself in the repetition and the anxiety began to drain from my body. I felt my magic begin to flow, and the dough became pliable in my hands. Soon it was glossy and elastic, so I floured the butcher block and began to roll it out.

Names from the book swirled through my mind, along with the indiscretions attached to them. My thoughts drifted back to the previous afternoon at Anna Mae's and snippets of conversation flitted through my mind, like my brain was turning over the rocks searching for something.

I continued to work the dough—pushing the edges out, and giving it a little nudge of magic when it wouldn't cooperate. I was pushing out the edges and squaring them off so I could brush the butter over it when my brain finally slipped the puzzle piece into place.

I stopped what I was doing. "Aunt Adelaide!"

I paused for a moment and called her again.

She appeared, though she didn't look happy about it. I'd asked her once where she went when she popped in and out, and she'd told me that sometimes she was just somewhere else in the house or around the farm, and sometimes she just ... wasn't. She described it as feeling similar to a nap—so, for lack of a better term, that was what we called it.

"Holy moly, girl—stop yellin'. You'll have Shelby awake and you know what a bear she is. What's got you all fired up?"

I glanced at the clock on the stove as I rinsed the dough from my hands. It wasn't even six yet. "I'm sorry. Were you napping?"

"No. I was just down at the barn watching the horses sleep. I always did love being there in the middle of the night, when they're all soft-eyed and resting instead of pacing or rattling their feed buckets. Now, what's with the 911?"

"Anna Mae made a comment about Cheri Lynn yesterday, and it made me think."

Adelaide laughed. "I'll bet she has plenty to say about her, but what in particular has you in a dither?"

I brushed the butter onto the dough, then added the orange zest and sugar. "She called Cheri Lynn a gypsy, but I didn't know that about her. Do you know anything about her family? Because if that was accurate rather than just Anna Mae slinging slurs, it certainly would give her a reason to know about belladonna."

"Huh." Adelaide floated a little closer, rubbing her chin. "Now you mention it, her grandmammy was an herbalist. I'd forgot all about that. That was back in the day. Tryphena Hall was an odd woman, but I liked her. She had the sight, and I think that was why she tended to stay to herself.

"We got along well though. I could shield myself from her, so it made it easier for her to be around me. She was probably the best healer I've ever met—that woman knew what she was doing with plants."

"So you're saying she may have shared that knowledge with Cheri Lynn?"

Adelaide crinkled her forehead. "I don't know, sugar. Tryphena was old when Cheri Lynn was born. I suppose it's possible. She used to have one of the most extensive herb gardens around."

I covered the rolls and put them in the warmed oven to quick-proof. I'm too busy—and too impatient—to wait three or four hours for the traditional way.

"Where did they live? I know Hank owns the trailer she lives in now."

"Oh, that's where she grew up. That property used to be Cheri Lynn's, but Hank picked it up for taxes a few years back. I suspect it's why she was so ... accommodating, though I doubt that's the only reason." Adelaide shook her head and sighed. "Her poor grandmother has about rolled herself out of her grave over that girl, I suspect."

"So, you're saying it's possible remnants of Tryphena's old garden are still around the property?"

She snorted, an odd sound coming from a ghost. "With all the stuff that woman grew, I'd say it would be almost impossible for there not to be, but she kept it hidden and warded somewhere in the woods at the back of the property."

"Well, still. Belladonna's perennial, right? So that puts the murder weapon right in the hands of one of the prime suspects."

Adelaide shivered. "I know what I'd choose if my only options were sleepin' with him or killin' him."

I couldn't agree with her more.

"You gotta tell Hunter this, Noelle. If for no other reason than to clear Anna Mae once and for all. Besides, women can't just go around killin' men when they want; otherwise, the species would die clear out."

Fair point.

I rubbed my hand over my face. "It's not that simple. I can't hardly just call Hunter and say, 'Hey, by the way, I thought I should let you know Cheri Lynn's grandmother was a gypsy witch and had a garden out back where she grew plants for potions and spells. You should go check it out.'"

Addy scowled at me. "I don't need your sass, girl. You know good and well I didn't mean for you to do any such thing. But you need to get creative because he's going to go for the simple explanation—Anna Mae or the person in that book who had the most to lose."

I sighed. "That's the problem, Aunt. Everybody in there had reason, and Cheri Lynn doesn't appear to have any at all. Well, other than the fact that

Hank was gross and I can't imagine wanting to crawl into bed with him, but then again, Cheri Lynn's ... well, Cheri Lynn."

"You'll figure it out, Noelle. And I can just hear the wheels in your mind turnin' about the other stuff too. The book, and your argument with Hunter. You're all off kilter, but they'll work themselves out. The universe has a way of puttin' things right. You'll see."

I was measuring flour and cocoa into a bowl to make brownies, and it struck me that I hadn't told her about my fight with Hunter.

I narrowed my eyes at her. "Wait a minute. How did you know about my fight with Hunter?"

She had her chest puffed out like a banty rooster and was grinning from ear to ear. "I popped into the beauty shop today. I did just what you suggested. I imagined being there, then I was."

She frowned a little. "Though I need to practice my landing. I popped in right in full sight right in the sink while Coralee was washing Helga Anderson's hair." Adelaide snickered.

"She squealed and sprayed the old bat right in the face. I figure that was Karma's gift to me for the day."

Helga is Olivia's grandmother. We have a multi-generational disdain for each other. I wouldn't go so far as to say it's a feud; it's just that skanks beget skanks—proof that even evolution isn't a perfect process. We Flynns just feel it's our place to remind them of their true natures.

Just the visual of Coralee squirting the pretentious old bat right in her over-made-up face made me laugh until I cried. Addy was wiping ghostly tears from her eyes when Shelby came slinking into the room, blinking her eyes as they adjusted to the light. Her hair was standing on end, and she scratched her hip as she glared at us.

"What's wrong with you people? I heard you laughing like lunatics clear up in my bedroom. You woke me up."

While she poured a cup of juice and a bowl of cereal, we told her the story, which caused another round of hysteria. Shelby went to school with Olivia's youngest sister, Sarah, and proudly carried on the family tradition.

I explained the problem about Cheri Lynn.

Shelby thought for a minute. "Has he questioned her yet?"

"Yeah. The day after Hank was killed."

"Oh. Well that isn't helpful at all," she said around a mouthful of cereal. "I was going to suggest that you go with him and you could look for it, but I guess he probably wouldn't take you anyway."

"No. Especially not now. He's not exactly speaking to me."

"Well," Adelaide shrugged, "go to work. You'll figure something out."

While the rolls finished proofing, Shelby and I went and fed the horses and turned them out in the pasture.

We had a routine, so it didn't take long. She cleaned the stalls on one side of the barn and I cleaned the other, sharing a wheelbarrow that was in the aisle.

Once we finished the last stalls and emptied the wheelbarrow for a final time, we headed back to the house. Thinking about work reminded me of the property investor who had shown up the last time I worked, so I told Shelby about him.

"Has anybody ever came around asking any questions about the farm when I'm not here?"

"No. I mean, I'm not here much, but I would have told you if something like that happened."

"I figured, but I thought I'd better ask anyway. Are you and Cody doing anything today?"

"Yeah. He wants to take the horses out, so we'll probably just head to the lake again. Or he talked about maybe finding that place you talked about."

I thought about the privacy of the cabin and decided that might not be the best place for two handsy teenagers to go alone.

"I think the lake is a better idea. The cabin is a good place to think, but there's probably snakes and other creepy crawlies around there."

Her face blanched. She was deathly afraid of snakes, so unless I missed my guess, they'd head to the lake, where there were plenty of eyes to make sure they behaved themselves.

That was one worry off my plate, anyway.

Chapter 24

Throughout my shift, I tried to think of a realistic way to get Hunter to go to Cheri Lynn's place, but drew a blank. I finally just texted him and told him Cheri Lynn's grandmother was an herbalist so Cheri might have had access to belladonna. After almost an hour, my phone vibrated. I went to the waitress station and pulled it out of my pocket.

H: Believe it or not, I'm perfectly capable of doing my job. I now have an entire book full of better suspects. It's police business.

Well then. I guess that was that. I wanted to text back that he wouldn't have the book if it weren't for me, but I bit back the urge and stuffed my phone back in my pocket.

I talked to Bobbie Sue about it and she agreed with me; it had to be a female killer. "My Earl's one of the best cooks in the country and even makes a mean pie when he wants, but watch this."

She motioned my back to the kitchen.

"Hey, Earl. Name the top five ways you'd kill somebody, besides me that is."

"Shoot 'em, beat 'em, bash 'em in the head, cut 'em."

"That's only four," she pointed out.

"If none of those work, then I reckon I shouldn't be out killin' folks, then."

I figured I better ask directly, just in case. "You wouldn't poison them?"

He shook his head, appalled. "If I'm gonna kill somebody, I want 'em to see it comin' and know it's me."

Bobbie Sue looked at me with her I-told-you-so smirk. "Wasn't no man that killed Hank. Mark my words. That's the work of a woman. And a fed-up one, at that."

I sighed, at a loss. "I completely agree, and so does Adelaide. But obviously, Hunter doesn't. So now what?"

"Not that I'm sayin' it's a good idea, but it *is* Friday night." Bobbie Sue reminded me. "She'll be at Tassels all night. I reckon if you want to know for sure, your only option is to see for yourself. If you find anything, then figure out what to do from there."

Hmm. Sneaking into the bad part of town to search the woods for a dead gypsy's warded and spelled prize garden. That had bad horror movie written all over it, but she had a point. If I found something, then I'd figure out what to do next. If I didn't, then I'd quit worrying about it.

"I AM NOT SNEAKING OUT to East Keyhole to traipse around in the woods on a gypsy's property tonight—or any night for that matter—and neither are you!" Raeann shook her head so hard her ponytail brushed the sides of her face.

To be honest, it really was a bad idea, but now I'd gotten it in my head and I couldn't get it out.

She huffed, but lowered her tone. She knew by now she couldn't browbeat me into—or out of—anything, so she tried to be reasonable. "Why do you even care? He's dead. Frankly, that's a good thing. Let Hunter deal with the cleanup."

I scowled at her and held strong. "Hunter's got his head so far up his own behind he can't even see daylight right now. Besides, he's not speaking to me and he's determined to pin it on Anna Mae or somebody in that book."

"Well you have to come up with a better plan than this. There are seven ways to Sunday this can go wrong, and I can't see a single good thing coming from it even if you're right and we don't get hacked into little pieces by some cracked-out nutjob while we're there."

I rolled my eyes. "This is Keyhole. Nobody gets hacked into little pieces." Though to be fair, people didn't usually fall over dead in their coleslaw either, so maybe we were setting some new precedents here.

"Use your imagination. Play the damsel in distress or something. Hunter may be mad at you, but he likes you and if you need him, I have no doubt he'll help. If you call and tell him you need a ride home because something's wrong with the truck or something, he'll take you home and you can talk to him about this. He'll come up with something reasonable."

She took me by the shoulders and forced me to meet her eyes. "Promise me?"

"Fine. But if he won't listen and she goes and poisons somebody else, then it's all on you."

"I can live with that."

I picked up my phone and texted Hunter. "I'm not going to lie to him, though."

N: Hey. Can we please meet up for lunch? I'd like to apologize. I really didn't mean to invade your privacy or be nosy.

I didn't receive a response for nearly twenty minutes and I'd almost given up when my phone chimed.

H: I know you didn't. It's just been a rough week. I'll pick you up in 20 and we'll go for a drive.

Raeann read the text over my shoulder and elbowed me. "See! I told you he'd be reasonable. Now just explain what you know to him. No matter what he says, Cheri Lynn still has to be somewhere on the suspect list."

"Yeah, I guess," I grumbled. I couldn't grouch for more than a couple of seconds though; I was happy Hunter was willing to talk. I really did like him even if he did think I mighta killed Hank.

My biggest problem now though was that I'd have to convince him to search Cheri Lynn's property again. The sheriff's department had searched her house the same day they'd searched Anna Mae's, but I doubted they'd gone over the whole property.

True to his word, Hunter pulled up in front of the store twenty minutes later. I'd already made a couple of iced coffees and packed a few danishes as a peace offering, so I just met him out front.

As we drove away, I started to speak, but he held up his hand.

"You don't have to say anything. I know you didn't mean any harm. It's just that this whole thing is a mess, and what you did hit dangerously close to something that happened in Indy." He raked his hand through his hair and I noticed for the first time just how rough he looked. His eyes were bloodshot and he had at least a day's worth of beard growing.

"Have you slept?"

"Not much. I spent most of the night going through the books and the contents of the binder, comparing dates with deposit amounts." He shook his head. "I don't know which is worse; the good people he was torturing or the horrible people who were paying him to stay out of prison."

I nodded my head. "I know. I didn't really read what was in the book."

He looked at me with raised brows, skepticism clear in his eyes.

"Seriously! I didn't. I mean, I caught a peek at some of them, but once I read about Will and Principal Larson, I closed it. I felt like a voyeur. That's private stuff that nobody should be privy to."

I paused and looked at him, wondering how far I could push.

"But I do have one question."

He snorted. "I should have known it. What?"

"Were there any women in the book? Because I swear to you, Hunter, a woman killed Hank."

"I'm well aware of the statistics. And no, there aren't any women in the book."

I thought about how to approach the whole gypsy thing and decided to go with the "normal" world view instead of hitting him with the whole "magic is real" thing. Most people love the perceived mysticism, but believe that's all it is—smoke and mirrors and old wives' tales. I had no reason to think Hunter would be any different.

"About what I texted earlier ... I need you to hear me out for a minute, okay?" I paused, waiting until he agreed to continue. His jaw clenched, but he finally gave a curt nod. I took a deep breath. Here goes nothin'.

"Like I said, Cheri Lynn comes from a long line of ... herbalists ... and her grandmother grew an extensive garden right on that property. Belladonna is a perennial, so if she was growing it for medicinal purposes even thirty years ago, it's likely still growing out there. I think you should check the property."

"Thanks. Like I said, when I need you to do my job for me, I'll let you know. We already searched her house, the same as we did Anna Mae's."

That was it. I got it that he was mad at me, but choosing to ignore something that could solve a murder was ludicrous and I told him so.

He was clenching his jaw again; that seemed to be a habit that popped up when he was irritated. "What did she have to gain from killing him? He was keeping her—he paid her rent and utilities, he gave her spending money. She would have been cutting off her nose to spite her face."

"Who knows? You're asking me to explain crazy. From what I know about her, Cheri Lynn is about as self-absorbed as they come, so it wouldn't surprise me if she killed him for buying her the wrong shade of nail polish."

When he just kept staring straight ahead like he was afraid a little old lady was going to jump out in front of us at any time, I exploded.

"What's your problem, anyway? I've never done anything to you, and I've never intentionally done anything wrong. I thought we had fun during the barbeque, and then again that day on the bikes. I was looking forward to learning more about you. Then you turn into this knot-headed jerk, and I'm starting to question my own judgment."

After a few moments, his grip on the steering wheel relaxed and his shoulders slumped. He turned dull eyes to me and my stupid heart went out to him. He probably moved here to get away from the stress, not to become acting sheriff just in time to solve the previous one's murder.

"You're right. I'm being obnoxious. Part of it has to do with my past, and part of it has to do with the freak show this case is turning out to be. It seems like every time I turn over a rock, something big and nasty rolls out from underneath it."

His phone vibrated but he ignored it.

"May I ask what this has to do with your past? If it's too personal, I understand. But I sure would like to know why I keep winding you up so I can stop doing it."

He shrugged one shoulder. "I guess that's fair enough."

There was a small turnaround point in the road, and he swung over into it and put the truck in park.

"I was working a high-profile case and the suspect was a politician just as dirty as Hank was, except on a much grander scale. Money laundering, embezzlement, loan sharking, blackmailing ... the list goes on."

He adopted a faraway look, like he was back there again, experiencing it all.

"After investigating him for three months, I had him dead to rights on the embezzlement and money laundering, which would have cracked the whole thing open. I'd met a woman—a dental assistant of all things—who seemed wonderful. She had a great sense of humor and we had a ton in common.

"One night, after I'd gone to sleep, she slipped into my file drawer where I kept my personal files. Pretty much every cop has one. She went through my phone and found the numbers of my three star witnesses—women in accounting for his firm who were willing to testify that the books were cooked."

His eyes dropped to his lap. "The next morning, I knew she'd messed with my phone because my contacts page was open—I never do that, for obvious reasons. I have no idea how she got the password. Still, I thought she was just checking for other women. That made me mad, but I thought it was just a personal thing.

"By that evening, two of my witnesses were dead and the other recanted, then left town. Danny Bianchi is a free man to this day. Turns out she was the niece of one of his top men, and I hadn't even bothered to check."

I let that settle for a minute. "So, you drew a parallel between what she did and what I did?"

I began ticking points off on my fingers. "She slept with you to get on your good side, went through your files and contacts while you were asleep, then shared confidential information, knowing it would likely end in the death—or at the very least, the terrorizing—of three innocent women."

I had a head of steam going just thinking about what a deplorable human being he was comparing me to. "Yeah, that's totally the same as picking up a piece of paper from your floor that fell from a file which, I might add, was open on your desk. Yeah, I can definitely see why you'd think I'm just like her."

I knew I was reaching the point where my mouth was running faster than my brain, but I couldn't help it. I had to get out of the truck before I said something I'd regret later. "Let me out."

"What?"

"I said, stop the truck and let me out." By that time, we'd reached the outskirts of town and it would take me an hour to walk back, but there was a little diner a half-mile back. I'd call Raeann and have a cup of coffee while I waited on her.

"I'm not letting you out. We're practically in the middle of nowhere. I'll take you back to the shop."

He laid a hand on my arm, but I jerked away.

"Noelle, I—"

A piercing pain shot through my head; I can only describe it as sounding like a squealing microphone. I grasped my head with both hands and dropped my head between my knees.

Shelby's voice sounded in my thoughts, but it was like she was trying to speak underwater. Her voice was barely recognizable.

Noelle ...lp me ...

I tried to close out the background static and focus on her voice. I drew the blanket of my mental barrier in so that it was nearly closed. Then, like a photographer bringing a picture into focus, I concentrated solely on my sister's consciousness.

Shelby! Where are you?

Hit my head.

Okay, but where?

Hunter was shaking me. "Noelle! What's going on? Are you okay?"

I shrugged him off. "Stop! Be quiet for a minute."

He withdrew his hand, but I didn't open my eyes to see what his reaction was. I was too busy trying to pick up the scattered pieces of Shelby's thoughts.

Of all her gifts, telepathy was the one she had the most trouble with. We'd actually decided she could only grasp the occasional stray thread—kind of like being able to pick up a radio signal from two towns over. Sometimes she could get a little static or send a phrase or two short distances, but that was about it.

Sister, focus.

Trying. Floor.

Floor? What floor?

Barn.

Our barn?

Yeah.

I'm on my way. Hold on!

Hurryyy...

Shelby? Shelby!

She didn't respond.

I opened my eyes and looked at Hunter. "We have to get to my place. Now!"

"What? Why? Noelle, what's going on?"

"Shelby's hurt. I don't have time to explain. Just ... freakin' drive—fast!"

He was looking at me like I'd lost my mind, but he pointed the truck in the direction of the farm and gunned it while I called 911.

Chapter 25

We were a solid fifteen minutes from my place, but with my constant urging, we arrived in just under ten. I was out of the door and running toward the barn before the truck even came to a complete stop.

By the time I made it to the barn, I could hear the wail of the ambulance as it came up the driveway.

I yelled her name, but the only answer I got was a hungry nicker from one of the horses and an anxious kick to the stall wall from another. I ran down the aisle, looking in every stall.

Aunt Adelaide popped in, wringing her hands. "She's over at the foot of the ladder. One of the boards broke and she fell backwards and hit her head."

"How long ago?"

Hunter was running beside me. "How long ago, what?"

I ignored him, listening to Adelaide.

"Maybe twenty minutes ago? It's so hard for me to keep track of time. I heard her call out, and by the time I found her, she was already unconscious."

I was to the ladder in just a couple more steps, and my heart jumped into of my throat when I saw her lying on the floor with a pool of blood drying underneath her head. I knelt down beside her and felt for a pulse. It was there, but thready.

Her legs were tangled in the mess of broken boards. Her jeans were torn from where she'd tried to pull her legs free, and I could see more blood on her legs where she'd scraped them on the wood in the process.

I shook her while Adelaide hovered across from me, though I was afraid to move her much in case she'd hurt her back or neck. I pinched her cheeks and demanded she wake up, my voice choked and tears flowing freely down my cheeks. The medics had the gurney in the barn and I called out.

Once they bent over Shelby, Hunter pulled me back so they could work. They untangled her feet, then put the c-collar on her and rolled her onto the backboard, then lifted her to the gurney and rushed out of the barn.

While they worked, I concentrated on finding her mental threads.

Shelby! Shelby, we're here.

Nothing.

Shelby Kay! You answer me right now!

Nothing again, then I heard her. She was faint, but she was there.

'Mkay. Stop yelling.

I'd never been so glad to hear her voice in my entire life, even if it was just in my head.

We got you, sister. You're on your way to the hospital. You're going to be okay.

K. Sleepy. Love you.

Love you too. Rest, but come back to me, okay?

K

I collapsed onto a grooming stool in front of the nearest stall and dropped my head in my hands. I'd never been so scared in my life and, though I felt better since I found her and she was now in good hands, I knew she still wasn't out of the woods. Still, I needed just a minute to breathe before I followed the ambulance.

Hunter was just standing over me, and couldn't seem to decide what to do with himself. He was staring at me like I was a crazy lady, and I couldn't really blame him, but I didn't have it in me to give him the rundown right that second.

After a minute or two, I stopped shaking and felt collected enough to walk to the truck.

He seemed to be rooted to the spot, even when I was halfway to the truck, so I figured he might need a bit of a nudge. "Hunter! Are you coming?"

He seemed to realize he was standing there like a half-wit because he jumped to action and beat me to my door, which was still hanging open. He swung it closed after I was in and jogged around to the driver's side.

I was watching him out of the corner of my eye as we pulled out of my driveway, trying to figure out how I was going to answer the question that was inevitably coming. He was flexing his jaw again. The poor man was going to get TMJ. I figured he was mulling over the events of the last half-hour, trying to find a non-crazy, logical answer. Of course, he couldn't because there wasn't a realistic answer in his wheelhouse.

Three minutes later, he blurted, "What the—what just happened? How did you know she was hurt? Right in the middle of a conversation, you grab your head, look like you're in excruciating pain, then tell me to bring you here, doing everything but putting your own foot on the gas pedal. Oh, and you called an ambulance on the way, like you knew she was hurt."

His words were starting to jumble together and he was gesticulating like an Italian lady who just found out somebody switched her wine for water. As a matter of fact, that pretty much summed up his entire demeanor.

"Calm down. There's a logical explanation."

"Logical explanation?!" His voice jumped about three octaves.

"Hunter, that's the opposite of calming down." As mottled as his face was, I was beginning to fear he was going to have a heart attack. "Should I drive? You don't look so hot."

"No, you're not going to drive, dammit! You're going to tell me what just happened."

He closed his eyes and took a couple of deep breaths. I was down with the breathing, but I was pretty sure he should have his eyes on the road.

"Okay. But keep an open mind. And maybe look at the road."

At least he had to open his eyes to give me the stink eye. "I'm listening."

"I'm telepathic," I said, deciding to just rip the Band-Aid off. "And apparently so is Shelby, though we didn't think she was."

He looked like I'd hit him square in the forehead with an ax handle. It was so comical that, had the situation not been so dire, I would have laughed.

"Telepathic." His voice was flat.

"Yes. Telepathic." I rubbed my temples. "I read minds and can project my own, among other things."

"Other things?" He was starting to sound like a parrot I'd seen when I was on vacation in Key West.

"Yes. Other things. That's not really what's important right now, though. You asked what happened and I'm trying to tell you. When you and I were talking, this horrible screeching noise erupted in my head. Then Shelby asked for help and told me where she was."

He was silent for a few seconds, then nodded as if he were humoring me. "Of course she did. That's a perfectly logical answer, just like you promised."

For some reason, the snark really got my goat, and I did something I never did. I answered him in the only way that would shut him up.

Yes. It is a perfectly logical answer. Don't be an ass.

He snapped his gaze to me, then lowered his brows. "You didn't really just do that. That's not possible."

I sighed, weary, and leaned my head back against the headrest. "Yes, Hunter. I did just do that. I'm spent and don't have time to take the long route, trying to convince you of the existence of extraordinary cognitive functions, so I just skipped straight to the part where you'd tell me to prove it."

He started to say something, closed his mouth, then ended up with a lame, "Okay, then."

It was obviously not okay, given the only good way to describe his expression was *freaked out but faking it.* Still, he remained quiet for the rest of the trip to the hospital.

I texted Raeann and told her what had happened, and added a quick note about Hunter.

N: Hunter just found out the hard way that I'm not exactly his version of normal. Will explain later.

R: What? You can't just say that, then say you'll explain later.

N: Yes I can. Not now.

R: I'll meet you at the hospital.

Though I knew nothing would have kept her away from the hospital, I was grateful when she said she'd be there. I really didn't want to be alone, and I didn't want to answer a ton of questions from anybody or jump through hoops like a circus monkey.

When we pulled up in front of the hospital, Rae's car was already there. I turned to Hunter as I grabbed the door handle. "Thanks for helping me out. I've got to get in there and make sure she's okay. I'm sure you have some thinking to do, and I know you have a murder to investigate, so go do what you have to do. Call me later if you want."

That sounded kind of blasé, but I didn't have it in me to think of something better to say.

He surprised me by reaching out and squeezing my hand. "I'm sure she's going to be fine. I'll talk to you later."

I just nodded, not sure if I was looking forward to our next conversation or not.

RAEANN AND JAKE WERE waiting for me just inside the emergency room doors. She pulled me into a huge hug. "She's going to be okay, sugar. I just know it. She's as hard-headed as you are, so one little bump to her noggin isn't going to do her in." I gave her a half-smile, but my heart wasn't in it.

A nurse came out of the ER and I stopped her and asked for a progress report.

"She has a scalp wound on the back of her head that they're stitching up now, and then she'll go for an x-ray to make sure she doesn't have a skull fracture."

"But ... there was so much blood."

"I bet there was. She has a pretty good gash, and even small cuts to the scalp bleed like crazy." She smiled and laid her hand on my arm.

"If it makes you feel better, she's awake and lucid enough to threaten bodily harm to anybody who shaves her head. That's usually a pretty good sign."

I smiled. That sounded just like Shelby. I thanked her and she continued on her way. While I was filling out the registration information, a tall, dark-haired doctor in green scrubs emerged from the ER and approached me.

"Are you Shelby's sister?"

"I am. Is she all right? The nurse said she was going for x-rays but that she was awake."

"She is. I'm Doctor Adams, by the way. At this point, the x-ray is just a precaution, but I'd like to cover all the bases before I release her. Her pupils are responding equally and she's lucid, so I doubt she has any serious damage."

Relief swept over me.

Raeann was standing right beside me and his eyes shifted to her when she asked, "So she'll be able to go home as long as the x-rays are fine?"

He smiled at her and I'm almost positive his gaze flickered to her cleavage before he caught himself and made eye contact.

"Yes, as long as somebody will be there to watch her. Since she lost consciousness, she probably has a mild concussion and may be a little sleepy. There's no need to keep her awake, but it's a good idea to wake her every couple of hours for the next eight hours or so if she doesn't wake up on her own."

"Thank you so much, doctor. May we go see her?" My brain believed the doctor, but my heart needed me to see her for myself.

"Of course. The guy from x-ray will be here in just a few, but we're finished stitching her up."

We went in, and sure enough, she was sitting up with her cell phone in her hand, taking a selfie.

"Seriously, Shel?" Rae asked.

She quickly typed something and then looked up.

"I'm not posting it to Facebook," she said. "Cody was worried about me, so I sent him a pic. So, when can I leave? I'm starving. The doctor said to take it easy though, so I probably shouldn't strain myself by folding laundry."

Yep, she was going to be just fine.

Chapter 26

We went to Brew4U to pick up my truck and Raeann gave us both a hug before she went inside to finish closing up, assuring us she'd stop by later.

Cody was waiting on us when we got home. He was wearing a groove in the porch pacing and when we pulled up, he rushed around to Shelby's side and jerked her door open.

"I've been so freaked out since you texted. I know you said you were fine, but I had to come see for myself."

He looked her over like she was a calf at an auction when she climbed out of the truck and she laughed when he took her arm and tried to help her out.

"I wasn't lying. Here—look for yourself."

She turned around and pulled her hair to the side, showing off the row of neat stitches. He was both repulsed and intrigued. "Wow, that's sick. Do you like, have a concussion or anything?"

She nodded and gave him the doe eyes. "Yeah. The doctor said I had to stay under observation in case I have a brain bleed."

I rolled my eyes. "You're giving *me* a brain bleed. Cody, she's fine. The doc said she just needs to rest and that we should keep an eye on her."

"Phew. That's great! I have to go help Uncle Will, but if you need to go anywhere, Noelle, just give me a call and I'll come sit with her when I'm done."

It was nice to see somebody care about her. She didn't have many friends so I was glad they'd met, motorcycle and all.

"Thanks, Cody. I don't have anywhere I need to be, but I'll keep it in mind, just in case."

They said their goodbyes, then he pulled on his helmet and started his bike. I turned toward the house, but Shelby stopped.

"I want to see where I fell." Ugh. Morbid teenage curiosity.

"Okay, but then you're going in the house and finding something on Netflix."

As we made our way to the barn, Adelaide popped in and started fussing over her. We started to give her a rundown of what had happened, but she held up her hand. "I already know. I popped into the hospital right as they were stitchin' her up." She shuddered. "That's one of the few times since I died I've been glad I don't have an actual stomach. I only stayed long enough to see that she was all right, then left."

I was impressed. A week ago, she had no idea she could leave, and now she was just popping around wherever she wanted. "Wow, you're getting pretty good at the whole travel thing. Have you found anyplace you can't go yet?"

"I don't know. I haven't really tried anywhere besides the salon and the hospital. Both times, I just focused on the spot and I was there, though." She tilted her head to the side. "The hospital was easier, but I don't know whether that was because I was so worried, or because I've already done it once."

We reached the entrance to the loft and Shelby gasped. "Wow, it looks like somebody bled to death here."

I wrinkled my nose. "Yeah. Imagine how I felt when I found you here."

She gave me a squeeze and laid her head on my shoulder. "Thank you. I remember yelling for you, and when you answered, I thought I was dead. But then I woke up in the ambulance."

Adelaide's forehead crinkled. "You didn't yell. You called out to her telepathically. You didn't know that?"

"What? No. I just remember falling, and this really sick feeling—and a sort of mushy, crunchy sound—when my head hit the concrete. I tried to untangle my legs so I could catch myself, but they were caught in the wood. Next thing I know, Noelle was yelling at me in my head."

I didn't know what to make of that. I'd assumed she'd called out on purpose. And I didn't yell at her. Not on purpose, anyway.

"Well, you may not have meant to yell, but you did."

I was confused.

She gave me the 'duh' look. "You just said you didn't yell at me, at least not on purpose."

Adelaide looked back and forth between us like she was missing something. She could join the crowd on that one.

"Shelby, I didn't say that; I thought it."

She looked at me suspiciously. "Think something else."

You still have to fold the laundry tonight. It's only towels.

She scowled. *That's so not fair. I almost died; I shouldn't have to do laundry, even if it is towels.*"

I don't know which of us was more stunned.

"Oh my god," we said at the same time.

Now Addy was just irritated. "One of you two better start talking right now, before I find a way to take a broom handle to your backsides!" She'd never laid a hand on either one of us, but if the look on her face was any indication, she was ready to break the streak.

"Apparently Shelby's telepathy has manifested in its full glory."

She snickered. "Now I'll know what you really think."

"Shelby, that's not how it works. You have to respect people's privacy, plus the noise will drive you nuts if you leave your mind wide open."

I crossed my arms. "And by the way, you *can't* read me. I've had years to practice closing my mind and I doubt you'll find a chink in my armor anytime soon."

"Ugh," she said, turning back to the house. "If I can't hear you, and it's rude to listen to others, then what good is it?"

"Well, it just saved your bacon, for one. I'm not saying you can't use it—you just have to be judicious. We'll work on it. Did you hear anybody at the hospital, or Cody?"

"Maybe. It's hard to separate out the voices in the hospital. As far as I know, everybody was talking out loud. As for Cody, his voice had kind of an echo."

I nodded. "That's because he was just saying what he was thinking. We need to start practicing now or you're going to want to slap half the people you run across and hug the rest. Knowing what people really think isn't what it's cracked up to be—trust me. That can wait a few hours, though. For now, I've got to cook supper and you've got a date with Netflix and a basket of towels."

While I was cooking, I thought about why a knock to the head could cause her powers to manifest. For people with latent powers, that was a semi-normal phenomenon, but not for witches. Though I was glad she had her power—at least that one—I now knew Camille was right. There was something wrong with my little sister and we needed to find out what.

I DIDN'T HAVE TO BE to work until eleven the next morning, so I let Shelby sleep in while I made her favorite breakfast—homemade blueberry Belgian waffles with mixed-berry syrup, bacon, and dippy eggs.

Raeann and Jake had shown up the night before and we'd cooked out before playing a game of darts on the veranda. Shelby and I beat them fair and square—mostly—then we made an early night of it and went to bed.

I heard Shelby shuffling around upstairs, and just as I was finishing up, she stumbled into the kitchen wearing a tank top, sleep shorts, and Cat Woman slippers. Her hair was standing up in the back and mashed flat to one side of her head and her eyes were ringed in mascara she'd forgotten to take off the night before.

After rooting around in the fridge for the OJ, she squinted against the sunlight and peered over my shoulder as I poured more mix into the waffle iron.

Her voice was raspy, but I wasn't surprised; the kid snored like a lumberjack. "Did you make me blueberry Belgian waffles?"

I reached around and gave her a hug. "I did. As a thank-you for not dying yesterday. I would have bought whipped cream, but you lost some points for breaking the steps and getting the concrete all messy."

She tried to elbow me, but groaned. "Crap. I feel like I got ran over by a truck."

"Don't exaggerate. You just got slapped by a thousand-pound slab of concrete. Seriously though, eat some breakfast and you can have something for the pain. The doctor figured you'd be sore, but didn't want you to have anything last evening."

Addy popped in behind us and gasped. "Oh, sweet baby Jesus! Shelby Kay, your whole shoulder is black and blue! Oh, sweetie, I am so sorry I never got around to replacing that stupid ladder!" She had that anguished look on her face that every mother adopts when she fails to keep her kids safe.

"Addy, you can't blame yourself. It was an accident. No permanent harm done, and we'll replace them now."

Shelby tried to crane her head around to see it but winced. "I guess I'll have to take y'all's word for it. My head is pounding and my neck hurts."

I pulled her hair to the side and checked her stitches while Adelaide hovered beside me. She shrugged away and swatted at my hand. "Stop! I just told you it hurts."

"I know, but I had to make sure you didn't pop any stitches loose or anything."

While I fried our eggs and plated our breakfast, I let my mind wander back to the conversation with Hunter. I remembered the look on his face when I projected to him.

Shelby sat straight up in her chair. "You did what?"

It took me a minute to realize she'd picked my thoughts out of the ether. "Stop that. And yes, I projected to Hunter. I was with him when you fell, and I had to tell him to get me to the farm, and I called the ambulance on the way, so he was understandably confused."

I slid her plate in front of her and slumped into my chair. "I had to tell him something, so I decided the truth was the best option. I really like him, and if things are going to move forward, I'd have to tell him eventually, anyway."

I poured syrup over my waffle, then dragged a slice of bacon through it and popped it into my mouth. Even the divine burst of sweet, salty, and smoky wasn't enough to make me feel better, though it didn't hurt.

"When I just explained it to him, he got snarky. So, I projected and told him not to be an ass."

She whistled. "Well, probably not the best communication to start with, but at least he knows. How did he take it?"

"Not so great. As a matter of fact, after he realized what I did, he didn't say another word all the way to the hospital. He did say he'd call me later, but his tail's still in a knot about the file thing."

"Aww. He'll come around; you're obviously the best sister ever, and you're smokin' hot, too. If he doesn't get his head out of his butt, then he's an idiot and doesn't deserve you."

Sometimes I wanted to wring her neck, but then she'd go and say something like that.

"Shelby's right, sugar. I have a good feeling about that boy. You haven't seen the last of him; he seems to be level-headed, and he's sweet on you. That won't hurt matters none."

"Thank you both. But for now, it's just a waiting game. What can't wait, however, is teaching Shelby how to block the free flow of others' thoughts into her brain. Seriously, sister, it'll make you crazy if you don't learn."

We practiced while we ate, then some more while I got ready for work. Thankfully, one of our boarders took care of the horses and cleaned the stalls on the weekends in exchange for her board, so we didn't have to worry about that.

By the time I left, she had a pretty decent handle on blocking me out as long as she concentrated, which was impressive. It would take some serious practice to turn it into an automatic response, but she was on the right track.

My thoughts turned again to Camille, and I checked my phone for any missed voicemails. Still nothing. It might be time to call the council.

Chapter 27

I didn't even get a chance to get my purse stashed behind the coffee filters in the waitress station before Bobbie Sue was bee-lining it toward me. Her red hair was tied up in its usual messy knot and she had a pencil sticking out of it. She tilted and bobbed her head as she talked and I wondered how it stayed put.

"What, you can't pick up the phone long enough to tell me Shelby had to go to the hospital?"

I sighed. "I'm sorry. You're right, but in all the hubbub, I never even thought."

She huffed. "Just don't do it again. You know I worry about you girls. I heard she rung her bell pretty good. You sure you don't need the day off to take care of her? Me and Sarah can run things today."

"Nah, I'm good. She's at the house taking it easy. Raeann's gonna stop and check on her later and she promised to call if she starts feeling weird."

I thought she was going to argue, but after a few seconds, she said, "Alrighty, then. If she calls, let me know, then hightail it out of here. Nobody's gonna die because it takes me an extra minute to refill their tea in case I need to cover for you. Family first."

"And that right there is why I'll probably work here forever, even if I win the lottery," I told her.

She snorted. "You win the lotto and me, you, Shelby, Raeann, and Sarah are gonna be loungin' on a beach somewhere where it never snows, sipping drinks out of coconuts while somebody else runs this dump!"

She wasn't wrong.

The door swung open, ushering in a rush of hot air along with Gary Wilkenson, the real estate investor. He smiled at me as I led him to a booth.

"I'm going to eat, naturally, but I just wanted to tell you I saw the man who told me about your farm day before yesterday. I'm afraid I lost the slip of paper with your number. He was coming out of the coffee shop right down the street."

"What? Are you sure it was him?" I craned my neck toward the window facing Brew like he was going to be standing there, waiting to be pointed out.

"Quite sure, Ms. Flynn. I even tried to approach him, but he was in such a hurry that by the time I managed to cross the street, he was gone. He disappeared around the corner and that was the last I saw of him. I wish I would have caught him; my time isn't cheap, and if I hadn't already been on vacation here, I would've made a trip to the backwoods of Georgia for nothing. No offense."

I waved him off. "None taken. Trust me, I've called it much worse myself. Recently, even. Do you remember what he was wearing?"

"Yeah, though it's not going to help much. He was wearing a tropical shirt and khaki shorts."

Of course he was. Because he couldn't wear something different than every other tourist and half the residents in town.

"Well, thanks for the effort, at any rate."

"No problem. I wish I could have done more. My offer stands on your land, by the way. Next week or next decade. If you decide you want to develop it, I'll make you a rich woman."

I looked over at Bobbie Sue and thought of Raeann and Shelby, then smiled at him. "I'm already rich in all the ways that count, Mr. Wilkenson, but thank you for your generous offer."

A half-hour before I was due to leave, Coralee came in with Marge, who appeared to have been crying. I told them to sit wherever they wanted, then grabbed a couple of teas along with some extra napkins and headed their way.

When I approached, Marge was sobbing and Coralee was comforting her.

I bent down next to her and placed my hand on her back. "Marge, are you okay? Is it Will or Bob? Is somebody hurt?"

"Of course she's not okay," Coralee snapped, grabbing the stack of napkins and handing a couple of them to Marge.

The poor soul did her best to pull herself together, dabbing the corners of her eyes in an attempt to save her makeup. Coralee brushed her hand away from her face and handed her a menu.

"Oh, honey, that ship done sailed. Your mascara is halfway to your cheeks; it's not going anywhere. Let's grab a bite to eat then we'll go over to the shop and I'll do your hair and makeup for you."

I sat the teas on the table. "What's going on, Marge? You never get rattled."

Coralee answered for her. "That danged black book has this entire town turned upside down. Apparently, Hank was blackmailing or railroading dozens of folks, and Will happened to be one of them."

"Okay, but what does that have to do with anything, really? Like you said, there were dozens of people in that book."

"That's what we thought too," Marge said. "Then Hunter started asking Will how close he and Peggy Sue are." Peggy Sue, the clerk at the courthouse, was Marge's sister, and had doted on Will since the day he was born. "Now she's done gone and lost her job because of us!"

She devolved into near-wails again, and Coralee attempted to comfort her.

"She didn't lose her job. Everything's going to be just fine." I gave her the WTH look and she said, "Peggy Sue's been suspended because she won the pie contest at the Fourth of July celebration."

I must have looked as confused as I felt because Coralee glowered at me then looked at me like I was an idiot. "It proves she can bake, and Hank stopped at the office right before he met Anna Mae at Bobbie Sue's. Apparently knowing how to bake and hatin' Hank are all it takes to go to jail for murder around here."

"That job's all the money she's got. She'll lose her house for sure, and now people are gonna be whisperin' about her behind her back, all because that nitwit city slicker can't find his butt with his hands in his back pockets!"

I had no idea how to deal with them other than to offer the traditional but generic, *there, there.*

Bobbie Sue had heard the commotion but wasn't the type of woman who was comfortable around tears. Instead, she waited to ambush me at the waitress station.

"What in blue blazes is wrong with her? The last time I saw her like that was the night before her weddin', when that catty sister of hers told her Bob had been over at Tassels for his bachelor party and had got himself a lap dance."

I explained the problem and she pursed her lips. "What a crock. Hell, just about every woman in this town bakes pies and every man in that book knows at least one woman who'd consider baking a poison one for him if she knew it was for Hank. If he's trying to get to the bottom of this by going that route, the killer will die of natural causes before your boy catches her."

I agreed, ignoring the fact that—once again—she'd referred to him as my boy. Adelaide chose that moment to pop in near the soda machine beside us and Bobbie Sue about jumped out of her skin.

"Holy hoecakes, Adelaide! It's good to see you, but you about gave me a heart attack. No offense, but I'd rather not be joinin' ya anytime soon, so give a girl some notice!"

Adelaide had the grace to blush. "Sorry Bobbie Sue. How ya been? No wait—time to chat later, now that I figured out how to leave the house. Noelle, I just popped in over at the coffee shop to let Raeann know Shelby baked some chocolate tarts for her. While I was there, I overheard some crazy stuff about that boy of yours."

"Oh my god!" Why did everybody insist we were a thing? It was enough to make me snap. "Will both of you please stop calling him my boy? We haven't even been on an official date and he's not even speaking to me because he thinks I'm a freak. And besides that, he's turning out to be kind of a douche. Adelaide, what's he doing now?"

"Well you know how Bonnie and Jim who run the lakeside cottages there have been having some financial problems and we all thought it was because Jim had a gamblin' problem? Well, it turns out Jim's name musta been in that book, because Hunter was out there questionin' them. Bonnie's just beside herself and the rumor mills are grindin' her and hers to a fine meal!"

"Oh, lord love a duck, Noelle, you gotta go muzzle that boy before he turns this whole town upside down. Poor Bonnie hasn't been well since her mama died and she don't need this hassle. They're barely scrapin' by as it is and if their business dries up ..."

I pulled my phone from my apron and dialed Hunter's number. It rang twice, then he swiped me, so I texted him and asked him to call me immediately. While I waited, I took Coralee and Marge their lunch and refilled their teas.

Marge had calmed down marginally, but the more I thought about it, the madder I got. I called him again and he still didn't answer, so I pulled up the number for the sheriff's office. It rang forever before somebody finally answered. Of course it did—because Peggy Sue wasn't there.

I asked to speak to the sheriff and was placed on hold.

A minute later, the man who'd answered asked for my name and I gave it.

"Uh, Ms. Flynn ... the sheriff's in a meeting and can't take your call right now."

"But he's in?"

"Yes, ma'am, but like I said, he's in a meeting."

I thanked him and hung up. Meeting my ass. I yanked off my apron and handed Bobbie Sue my check presenter.

"I'm going to the sheriff's office. He's got it in his head I'll go away if he avoids my calls. I need to go set him straight." I shot all three of them a dirty look and added, "I hope one of y'all picked *never* in that pool because I may just kill him before this day's out and I'd hate for *all* of you to lose your money."

Bobbie Sue waved me toward the door. "That's my girl. Take him to the woodshed!"

BY THE TIME I PULLED in front of the courthouse and made my way to the sheriff's office, I had a full head of steam going. Obviously, there was nobody at Peggy Sue's desk, so I just headed straight to his office. The door was ajar and Hunter was sitting at his desk looking through a file. I didn't bother to knock before walking right in.

He looked up from the folder and his eyes turned stormy. "What are you doing here? This is my office and I'm the sheriff. If you want to see me, make an appointment. Unless, of course, you'd rather just control my mind and make me see you."

The barb was meant to be hurtful but was so outlandish it just pushed me over the edge. "Trust me—I have no desire to crawl around inside your empty head looking for the controls, though lord knows somebody needs to. And as you can see, I don't need superpowers to make you see me. What do you think you're doing, chasing down the people in that stupid book and questioning them publicly?"

He looked baffled. "I'm not questioning anybody publicly."

"You don't have to, you big idiot. This is Keyhole Lake, not Indianapolis. People here aren't anonymous. They have neighbors who have nothing better to do than look out the windows and watch who comes and goes, then call the other neighbors and speculate. Before you know it, they're running a grow house, or having an affair, or sacrificing virgins.

"Everybody in town knows you have that book, so when you show up on somebody's doorstep, you may just as well scream it from the rooftops that their name is in there. You're messing with peoples' lives!"

He looked back down at the file in front of him and started shuffling papers, trying to dismiss me. "That's not true."

"Really? Then how is it that I've been stuck at work all day, but know you've suspended Peggy Sue and questioned Marge because Will's name was in that book? And that you went out and questioned Bonnie and Jim at the lake?

"Bonnie's mama just died after being sick for a long time and they're swamped in medical bills," I continued. "Now people are wondering what Jim was doing that landed him in that book. That lake is their livelihood and if they land on the wrong side of the gossip mill, they'll lose everything. You've placed them in a position where they either have to keep quiet and let folks speculate—and believe me, people can come up with some pretty horrible scenarios—or they have to admit why their name is in there."

Hunter closed the file and met my eyes, his face pale. "I didn't realize. I thought I was being discreet."

I put my hands in my pockets so I wouldn't reach out and choke him. "I've tried to tell you—this isn't like the big city. There is no discretion here. It's a freakin' fishbowl. How do you think Hank had the leverage to squeeze those poor folks to begin with? Fear!"

I took a deep breath and tried to gain control of myself. "Folks have long memories here and once you've been judged, that doesn't go away. I did see why Will was in there, but he's not going to defend himself because he wasn't protecting himself. I don't know what Bonnie or Jim did, but whatever it was, you've made sure they'll keep paying for it as sure as Hank did, just in another way. Will, too."

"But Bonnie and Jim didn't do anything. Hank was making them pay him half what they made off jet ski rentals or he was going to pull their permits and report them to the IRS for tax evasion because they don't claim the income from the food stand or jet skis. How the heck he even knew that is beyond me."

"Well congratulations on that one. Because half the town probably has Bonnie dancing in disguise at Tassels, and the other half has Jim pegged as a philanderer with a gambling problem." All the fight suddenly went out of me. "Just ... stop before you ruin anybody else."

I turned to leave his office.

"Noelle, wait."

"What Hunter? I've been trying to tell you Keyhole's different than your big fancy anonymous city but you just wouldn't listen. You've been like a bull in a china shop, and you can't work like that around here. I even offered my help, but you obviously have something to prove. Well, go prove it. You may even be on the right track, but try not to catch any more good people in the crossfire."

I climbed in my truck and pointed her toward home, disgusted and a little heartsick at the same time.

Chapter 28

I didn't have to work Sunday morning, so I made it a point to sleep in. Hank's funeral was at two and I debated whether or not to go. Honestly, I just wanted to laze around the house and do various forms of nothing, but then I felt bad for Anna Mae so I hauled myself off the couch and dusted off my multi-purpose black dress.

I tossed it in the dryer with a dryer sheet for a few minutes to shake out any wrinkles and make it smell fresh while I put my face on. I was letting Shelby off the hook because she didn't want to go and I didn't blame her. If I didn't feel obligated, I wouldn't go either.

Sometimes I really missed the days when I was living in Atlanta and could fake a sick day just to go shopping.

I pulled up to Blake's Funeral Home and Monuments—which was Blake's Counter Tops on the other side of the building—and found a place to park. The hearse was already parked outside and I wondered for the thousandth time why on earth there were curtains in the back window. It wasn't like they were closed to keep people from staring in.

There was a respectable amount of people there, but I noticed they were all there for Anna. Hank's goons weren't present.

I walked up to the receiving line and offered my condolences once again to Mr. and Mrs. Doolittle, then gave Anna Mae a hug.

When I pulled her in, I whispered, "Did your house escape the Great Cabbage Rose Infestation?"

Surprised, she snorted.

Mrs. Doolittle, maintaining her mask of sorrow, leaned over and used her mad-mama church whisper to say, "I'm glad to see you have so many friends here for you. Lord knows if it weren't for you, the place would be empty because they sure aren't here to pay their respects to the dead. But for the sake of propriety, pretend for three more hours that you're actually grieving."

Anna Mae straightened. Freedom was within her grasp. She'd do whatever she had to for the next few hours to get away from this particular box of Fruit Loops forever. Her mouth twitched but she solemnly bowed her head, took my hand in both of hers, and thanked me for coming.

The rest of the service went on pretty much like you'd expect for a man who was despised by all. The Doolittles had arranged a caterer for the lounge and most folks came, ate, and left after telling the family how sorry they were.

I knew what they really meant, though. They meant they were sorry there wasn't any booze or take-away boxes. I knew that because after an hour of listening to false platitudes about how great Hank was, *I* was sorry there wasn't any booze.

Hunter showed up, and though I thought he was going to head my direction a few times, he kept his distance. So be it. I made a circuit of the room, stopping to talk to folks I hadn't seen in a while, and paused by the coffin.

I know it's a huge deal for somebody to look good in the coffin, but every time I hear somebody say, "Oh, she looked so nice; they really did a great job with her," I don't get it. They don't look good. They invariably look dead. That's the opposite of good as far as I'm concerned.

I was studying the waxy complexion of a man who I was actually glad to see in a coffin when I heard gum snap. A voice beside me declared, "Wow, he looks like shit. Even worse than when he was alive."

I turned to find Cheri Lynn standing beside me wearing what must have been her Tassels costume—a black pleather bustier and matching short shorts, fishnet stockings, and red, four-inch stilettos.

I couldn't decide which was tackier—her wardrobe choice or her decision to show up to begin with. I lowered my voice and adopted the same tone Mrs. Doolittle had used earlier. "Jesus H. Cheri Lynn! What are you doing here? And, for the love of God, what are you wearing?"

I placed my body between her and Anna Mae, who was speaking to the reverend with her back to us, in an attempt to block her from view, then reached out to take her arm, hoping she'd follow my lead and peacefully exit the room.

Don't get me wrong—I've never had anything against Cheri Lynn per se. She wasn't dealt much of a hand in life, but she played it the best she could. Years of being under the thumb of one man or another hardened her.

Her choices, if you can call them that, placed her on the fringe of Keyhole society. The "good Christian folk" looked down their noses at her and locked her out of polite society, which made her an easy target for the less savory citizens. It was a vicious cycle.

She learned to survive though. She'd been branded as trashy, and she sorta was, but her propensity to give most of the world the finger was a defensive reaction to being rejected by the "good" people who could have helped her instead of slinging rocks at her from the porches of their glass houses.

Still, she couldn't stand there half-naked in the middle of a funeral, even if it was Hank's. When I looked closer, I realized what should have been obvious from the beginning if I'd been paying more attention to her and less to the situation.

When my hand passed right through her arm, she jerked back and flickered a little. "Stop that. It freaks me out. And I'm not going outside with you. I haven't even read the flower cards yet."

Freaks *her* out? Houston, we have a much bigger problem than figuring out who sent the flowers.

CORALEE WAS STANDING across the room from us talking to Ms. Bloom, our former English teacher. She was listening with one ear, no doubt learning way more than she wanted to know about corns or body hair, while perusing the room in search of an escape route.

Her gaze wandered over and past us, then jerked back as her brain belatedly processed what she was seeing. Coralee wasn't exactly a medium; she preferred to say she was unbiased toward her friends' existential statuses, which allowed her to see more than other people could.

Of course, there weren't many people she didn't consider at least a distant friend, and so far the few who didn't make the cut hadn't shown up as ghosts.

Thus, Coralee and her unbiased brain understood exactly why I was standing there, probably looking like I had to pass gas but couldn't find the exit sign.

I breathed a sigh of relief when she excused herself and made her way toward us. If there was one thing Coralee was good at, it was whipping ducks into a row, and I was desperately in need of that skill right now.

As she approached, she plastered on her funeral smile and gave me a hug, then drew back. "I believe I need some air. Would you care to join me, sugar?" She looked at Cheri Lynn, daring her to refuse. I was all for the idea.

"I think that's a wonderful idea. It's a little crowded in here."

We made our way around small clusters of people who were standing around chatting and eating finger foods, then pushed through the back door, with Cheri Lynn floating along beside us, pouting. Thankfully, the parking lot was empty.

As soon as the door closed, Coralee rounded on Cheri Lynn. "What in the name of little red wagons have you gotten yourself into now?"

Cheri Lynn was outraged. "How on earth is this my fault? Somebody up and kilt me. I'm the *victim* here."

I looked heavenward and would have prayed for patience, except I knew better. This situation was likely a result of the last time I made that mistake.

Instead, I ran my tongue over my front teeth and changed tacks. "Cheri Lynn, back up. How long have you been ... like this?"

She puckered her mouth and twisted it to the side. "I don't know for sure. I remember getting home from work Friday, which would have been early Saturday morning. I remember my key wouldn't work for some reason, so I went around to the back door. I saw a shadow come up behind me in the slider. When I turned around, there was a guy swingin' a shovel at my head."

Her eyes were fixed on some point over my head, staring at something only she could see. "I was so scared. I felt the crunch when it hit me. I saw stars. It sounded weird—kinda like when you bite into an M&M. Then everything went black.

"I woke up on my back porch where I'd fallen. I don't know how much later, but the sun was comin' up; I could see its reflection in the glass. I couldn't move, and was so cold, but the colors of that Georgia sunrise comin' up over the mountains ..."

She shivered, then turned her attention back to me. "You! They were talkin' about you, Noelle."

I swallowed around the lump in my throat and swiped a tear from my cheek. "Me? Who was?"

"Jim and the guy who killed me."

Jim Simpson was the guy who owned Tassels and several of the other businesses over in East Keyhole. He was also my closest neighbor. He lived on fifty acres or so that butted up to the east corner of the farm. Adelaide used to joke that he wanted his house set up on the mountain so he could look down over his kingdom.

Coralee chewed her lip for a minute. "Okay, back up a minute. What did the other guy look like? Had you ever seen him before?"

"Yeah. He'd been in a couple of times, but both times I seen him, he came through the back door into Jim's office and left the same way. He never went out into the bar. He was a looker—a tall drink of water with dark hair. He kinda had that hot military thing going on."

The hair on my arms stood up. Even though it was pretty general, it was the same description Gary Wilkenson gave of the guy trying to get him to invest in my farm.

"You said they were talking about me?"

"Oh yeah. I went back to get change for the bartender and stopped when I heard your name. They were talkin' about your farm."

"What about my farm?"

"About how much money they were gonna make when they developed it, which didn't make no sense to me because I knew you wasn't gonna sell that place. That was when Jim noticed me and asked what I wanted. I got the change and left, but I heard that guy ask if I'd heard anything."

She cast her eyes down. "Jim told him not to worry about me. That I was nobody."

Coralee tried to touch her, but of course her hand passed right through. "Oh, sugar. Don't you believe that. Jim Simpson is a waste of good air."

"Well, apparently the other guy didn't believe him, either. Because he showed up at my house and bashed me in the head with a shovel."

What do you even say to something like that? Again, not a topic Miss Manners even came close to touching on. "Cheri Lynn, you didn't happen to hear the name of this guy, did you?"

She thought for a minute, doing that sideways pucker thing with her mouth again.

"No. I'm sorry, sugar. I sure didn't."

The wind had picked up a bit and the entire top of Coralee's hairdo flipped up at once. She smoothed it back down and it fell obediently right back where it belonged.

"Okay, we gotta get back inside. The service is about to start. Cheri Lynn, you can stay if you want, but you have to behave yourself. I know you have some decency in ya, so, considering the circumstances, show some respect for Anna Mae, regardless of what you may think of her. Then we need to get you taken care of."

"Oh, I don't have nuthin' against Anna Mae, 'cept she wanted to throw me outta my house. She woulda come around, though. Actually, I kilt Hank as much for her as I did for everybody else."

Wait, what?

Chapter 29

"Come again?" Coralee was looking a little faint. I, on the other hand, didn't bat an eye at her confession. As a matter of fact, I crowed a little bit inside for figuring it out.

She popped her gum. "Yeah. I offed Hank. I baked him up a mixed-berry pie, 'cept I used belladonna berries from Bebee's garden instead of blueberries. I remembered from summer camp Anna Mae was allergic to berries, so they'd have to clear her. And I'm used to bein' underestimated. Throw in all the other people Hank was robbin', and the water would be so muddy that by the time it cleared, all anybody would see was what a better place the planet was without him on it."

That still didn't answer my question. "I can't argue with your logic, but why kill him now?"

"Things had gone on long enough. He was suckin' the life outta this town. Outta me, and Anna Mae. I heard him talkin' to Will on the phone about that nephew of his, Cody. I realized what he was doin' and went to see Will, usin' the excuse that my cat was sick. He looked awful," she said.

"I've run into Cody a few times in town. Once he opened the door for me when I was comin' outta Raeann's shop, and another time, he helped me load my groceries in the car."

She shrugged. "He's a good kid and deserves a shot. A coupla days after that, Hank left his shirt on the bed while he took a call," she shuddered. There was this black book in there, just full of awful things he was doin'. I thought long and hard about how to get rid of him legally, but y'all know that wasn't gonna happen. So," she shrugged, "I baked him a pie."

We stood there for a few seconds, each of us lost in our own thoughts. Cheri Lynn broke the silence.

"Alrighty, then," she said, changing her tone as if she hadn't just confessed to murder. Or euthanization, whichever. The line in this case was kinda blurry. "Let's get in there and get this over with so we can plant the no-good sumbitch and figure out who kilt me and wants to steal Noelle's farm."

Just as we were reaching for the door handle, Hunter stepped around the corner.

"I didn't hear you answer her question, Coralee. And I'd sure like to know the answer. Why *did* you decide to kill him now, or at all for that matter?"

Coralee realized the conclusion he was making at the same time I did, and her face paled a bit underneath her foundation. She fell back on the timeless defense of last resort; charm. Like I said, she was good at gettin' ducks into a row.

Cheri Lynn floated over so that she was standing between the three of us. "Just blame it on me. Tell him the berries are still growing at the back of my property."

Yeah, because I hadn't already tried to do that.

"Sheriff. We were just speculating as to why somebody had decided to kill Hank now, when he's been terrorizing the town for the last two decades. Longer, actually, if you count the bullying he did as a kid."

Hunter didn't look convinced. "But the way she phrased it ..."

I stepped in. "Exactly how did I phrase it?" Honestly, I wasn't sure exactly what I'd said, and I was hoping he wasn't either. From the look on his face, my dog was hunting.

"You said, 'I can't argue with your logic, so why kill him now?'"

She turned back to Hunter. "I didn't answer because I haven't the foggiest. Frankly, I thought he'd manage to keep bullyin' folks until his ticker gave out. As a matter of fact, I had money on it and lost."

Poor Hunter. He had no idea what to think; I had to cough to cover my laugh because the expression on his face was just off the chain. "You what?"

Coralee looked him in the eye and spoke clearly and slowly. "I lost money on it. We run little pools at the salon. You know—a way to pass the time and keep things interesting. Just ladies' bets. Twenty-dollar buy-in most of the time. We had one on how and when Hank was gonna die. I woulda won it except I went with natural causes. Roberta from the church auxiliary beat me out because she bet on murder."

It was too much for him; he was developing a nervous twitch at the corner of his eye. Storm clouds had gathered overhead while we'd been talking. The wind had picked up and a fat raindrop landed right on my cheek.

"Let's get back inside. The service is starting. I assure you, Hunter, Coralee didn't kill Hank, and if you want to question her afterward, I'll be one of the first in line to attest that she's a lot of things, but a baker's not one of 'em. As a matter of fact, I need to talk to you anyway, and it's important." I studied his thoughtful expression and narrowed my eyes. "And don't go thinking Roberta had motive, either, though that woman *can* bake."

Coralee and I headed back inside and Hunter trailed behind, still trying to make sense of what had just happened.

AFTER THE SERVICE, I told Hunter I had reason to believe something bad had happened to Cheri Lynn, but he wasn't in the mood to be accommodating. As a matter of fact, he was a jerk.

"What, did you have a vision?"

I glanced at Cheri Lynn, who was hovering right beside him. "You might say that, yeah."

"Well I deal in facts, not carnival ju-ju and mysticism."

Cheri Lynn smacked him in the back of the head, though her hand passed right through. "Hey! Tell him to take that back. My Bebee was a gifted carnival mystic!"

I didn't know what else to do; he wasn't budging an inch and frankly, he was starting to make me mad.

"Tell him to call Tassels. I didn't show up for work last night."

I relayed the suggestion and was surprised when, after staring me down for a good two minutes, he picked up his phone and searched for the number. I'm pretty sure he was doing it out of spite though, so he could gloat when I was wrong.

It only took him a minute to confirm she hadn't shown for her shift last night and he frowned.

I tapped my foot, about to my breaking point. "Now can we go to her place?"

"No. Now you can go home. I'll go to her house and check on her." He stood and opened the door to his office, an obvious hint for me to leave.

"Hunter ... I'm sorry you found out about me the way you did. I was hoping to get to know you a bit and tell you when we were both ready, but that's not how it panned out. You're a real knot-head, and you're kinda riding roughshod right now because you're in a new arena, but aside from that, I like what I know about you and would like to get to know you better."

His jaw twitched in the way I'd learned to associate with irritation, but I think part of it was that he liked me, too. I know I wasn't the only one to feel that spark between us the day we went for the ride, or when we cooked out before that.

"I just can't do it right now, Noelle. That's a huge chunk of information for a person to process, and I just don't think I can do it. I'm sorry."

I hung my head and stood to leave. "I'm sorry, too."

Peggy Sue was back to work and stopped me before I passed her desk. "You're a good person, Noelle, and he knows that. He likes you. Just give him some time."

I nodded, but didn't trust myself to speak.

I thought about what she said as I headed back to the farm. I knew she was right, but part of me just wanted to say to heck with it. Though if he decided he could live with the telepathy, the rest of it would be a breeze. After all, knowing somebody can read your mind but trusting them not to do so opens a pretty big door.

Shelby's car wasn't there when I got home and I found a note on the kitchen table letting me know she was at the clinic helping Cody and Will. That was good for her; she was considering a career as a vet, so a little hands-on experience might help her decide.

I kicked off my heels and headed to my room to lose the dress and pantyhose. Once I'd traded them for gym shorts and a tank, I pulled out the ingredients for a seven-layer cake. I decided to go with one of Shelby's favorites; chocolate cake and peanut butter frosting.

I decided to whip up some homemade peanut butter cups to decorate it with while it was baking—nothing like losing yourself in details to take your mind off your troubles.

Aunt Adelaide popped in while I was mixing the cake batter and asked how the funeral had gone. She'd decided not to go since she couldn't stand him in life and wasn't obligated to pay her respects to anybody now that she was dead. I filled her in on everything that had happened.

"Wow. Well, I gotta say, the girl did always have that streak in her. Mama always said not to get on the bad side of a gypsy. They live by their own rules and have their own ideas about right and wrong."

"So is there any way to follow up on this guy?"

"If there is, I haven't thought of it. I haven't had a lot of time to think about it, you know, with Cheri Lynn being dead and admitting to killing Hank and all."

She narrowed her eyes at me. "Don't sass me, young lady. I know you've had a long day, but you need to find him before he comes after you."

She was right, but I had no idea where to start. I decided to contact Mr. Wilkerson to see if maybe he'd remembered the guy's name.

I'd just finished creaming the butter and peanut butter for the peanut butter cups when Cheri Lynn popped in. I don't know who was more startled—me when she arrived, or her when she saw Adelaide.

"Ms. Adelaide! But ... you're dead."

Aunt Adelaide raised a brow. "I guess that gives us something in common, then."

She wrinkled her nose. "Oh yeah. Right. Anyway, I popped to my place and waited on that sheriff to get there, and you're not going to believe it—my body was gone! Along with my clothes. And that's not all—there were belladonna berries in my fridge."

I dropped my wooden spoon. "Say what? Your body couldn't just be gone."

"I know, right? Now I'm a lot of things, but stupid's not one of them. Once I baked that pie, I made sure all the berries were gone. Bebee made her garden so that you have to know the exact entry spot. Otherwise, it just looks like a big patch of briars from the outside. When she was alive she had it warded, but since I'm not good with herbs, I didn't bother settin' another one when she passed."

Adelaide was shaking her head. "This isn't good, girls. Somebody's cleaning up their mess. They made it look like Cheri Lynn killed Hank and then took off. They tied it all up in a neat little bow."

"So?"

"So why bother setting her up for Hank's death? They could have gotten rid of her body, which they obviously did, then just let everybody assume she left town. There might have been speculation, but nobody would have ever known for sure unless they found Tryphena's garden."

She was right. It didn't make sense.

My phone dinged with an incoming text. It was Mr. Wilkerson, returning my text from earlier. He apologized but said he still didn't remember the name.

Cheri Lynn and Adelaide hovered over my shoulder and read the text with me. Both of them started nagging me to call Hunter.

"Have you both forgotten that my name is now mud with him? Not only am I a freak who can read his mind and talk to him without moving my lips, but now I'm also Chicken Little. I told him I thought something had happened to Cheri Lynn when all he found was proof she left town."

"Well, to be fair, the first part is his problem. And something did happen to me—he just doesn't know the truth. Neither of those changes the fact that you were right."

"He has a history of not wanting to see the truth unless he's the one who finds it, especially if I'm the one pointing it out."

Aunt Adelaide sighed. "Pride goeth before the fall."

"Yeah," I muttered. "Let's just hope it's not *my* fall."

Still, I pulled up his number, steeled myself, and hit call. It rang four times and I thought it was going to go to voicemail, but he answered.

"What, Noelle? Do you have another theory, or has somebody else killed someone, then packed up and left town?"

"Look. I'm sorry I called. I get that you're freaked out, but you're also being a real jerk. I called because I'm actually worried about myself and Shelby this time. I have a bad feeling about the guy who was trying to round up investors for this place. Did you find any permit applications or anything?"

"Why are you worried? Have you heard from him, or caught anybody out on the property?"

I wanted to scream, "No, I hadn't heard from him, but my ghostly friend overheard him talking about my place before he followed her home, murdered her, then hid her body." Yeah, I should just tell him that.

"No, but it worries me that he had papers drawn up and had applied for permits."

"I checked, Noelle. There are no permits pending to do anything on your place. As a matter of fact, the last time one was even requested was when your aunt replaced some of the gas lines. I'm sure it was probably just a scam artist. If you hear anything else, let me know."

He hung up without saying goodbye.

I finished making the peanut butter cups, but my heart wasn't in it. The oven timer dinged at the same time my phone did. I pulled the cakes out, then checked my phone, hoping it was Hunter. It wasn't—it was Mr. Wilkerson again.

W: Was just thinking. My wife took pics at the party. I'll go through when I get home and see if there are any of him or his wife.

N: That's so kind! Thank you.

Wife? He hadn't mentioned a wife before.

Of course, Adelaide and Cheri Lynn were hovering right over my shoulder, reading the text.

I tried to elbow them back, but it's kind of hard to do when the people creeping on you are incorporeal. "Sheesh! What if it had been naked pics or something? Boundaries, y'all!"

Cheri Lynn laughed. "You gotta be kiddin' me. He's not even speakin' to you. I'm pretty sure nekkid pics aren't somethin' we gotta worry about right now, or ever, unless I miss my guess. He's not the type and neither are you."

Sadly, she had a point. The closest I'd ever come to a naked pic was when I sent beach pictures to my college boyfriend. And even those had made me blush because of the bikini.

I really did need to get a life.

Chapter 30

An hour or so later, a silver Audi drove around the bend and up to the house. Shelby climbed out, along with Cody and Violet. I met them on the porch.

"Hey, guys! Come on in. What's up?"

Shelby and Cody bounded up the stairs, and Violet followed along behind.

"Shelby's tire was flat when she went to leave the clinic," Violet said. "She invited me over to see that new foal she's been telling us about. Plus, to be honest, I needed a change of scenery. I love working at the clinic but the last few days have been hellish, with all the Hank garbage coming to light. I'm glad it's over. As bad as I hate to say it, whoever killed him did this town a favor."

Cheri Lynn had followed me to the porch and puffed out her chest. "Tell her I said 'you're welcome.'"

I rolled my eyes at her, but decided to give her the victory. To say she'd had a rough few days would be the understatement of the year, and she was taking it all much better than I think I would have.

"Come on in. Would you like a glass of tea?"

"That would be great."

I led her to the kitchen, where Shelby had already found the cake and was slicing into it.

Violet sat down at the table and looked around. "Wow, I knew Ms. Adelaide had remodeled, but I haven't been here since she did. It looks great in here!"

"Thanks. This is my favorite room in the house. Cake?"

She nodded, and I cut us both a slice and joined her at the table. I asked her about the clinic and we talked animals for a little while.

"So, did you hear anything else from that real estate investor? I know you were worried about it."

"Nope. No such luck. Mr. Wilkerson said he may have some pictures of the man or his wife that were taken at the party. He's going to check and send them to me."

"Well, if not, I'm sure he's probably moved on. A lot of big buyers keep an eye on properties like this and try to buy them when the owners pass because the kids would rather have the money than the property. They have to find the investors in order to come up with the initial capital, so they start scouting in advance. I wouldn't worry too much about it since you've made it clear you're not selling."

"I'm sure you're right." Oh, how I wished it were so!

"I'm sorry. I didn't mean to bring it up. It's just that sometimes I really miss the business. I used to love buying and selling houses. Commercial stuff wasn't fun for me, but I loved showing a family a blank slate that they could carve into their own home."

"Oh, I get it, totally. When I was in college, I missed the horses and the farm so much I came home practically every weekend. I always knew this is what I wanted to do. I can't imagine giving it up."

We moved on to other topics and just chatted a bit, then went to the barn. I showed her the new foal, and Shelby, being the drama queen that she is, had to show off where she'd fallen.

"Wow! That's quite a fall! You're lucky," she said, then looked at her phone. "I need to get back to the clinic and help Will close up. I think Cody's going to fix Shelby's tire tomorrow so she'll have her car back. They'll work it out."

After she and Cody left, I called Raeann and brought her up to speed on the day. She'd skipped the funeral because it was her mom's birthday, so she was completely out of the loop.

I'd just finished supper dishes while Shelby did the outside chores. Cheri Lynn was floating around checking out our family pictures when she froze, then swept over so she was face to face with me.

"Noelle! That's the guy! Come see." She was pointing wildly in the direction of the mantle and I couldn't for the life of me think of a single picture on there that wasn't of direct family, and most of them were dead. The rest were of me, Shelby, and Raeann.

"What? Which one?"

"The guy with Raeann! That's the guy who was in Jim's office! That's the guy who kilt me!" She tried to pick up the picture but growled when she couldn't.

I scrambled to the mantle and picked up the picture she was pointing at. It was taken the day Raeann did that stupid bungee jump. She was standing beside Jake, flushed and grinning to beat the band.

"You're absolutely sure?"

"Uh yeah. Pretty sure," she said, sarcasm dripping off her words. "A girl's not likely to forget the face of a guy who whacks her in the gourd with a shovel. Who is he? Why is he with Raeann? Last I talked to her, she wasn't seeing anybody."

"Yeah, they're pretty new. She met him at the bungee jump."

"You gotta call her. Right now. Make sure she's safe, then call that sheriff of yours. Make him find out who that guy really is."

"Just hold up for a minute." I needed time to think. It wouldn't do any good to go to Hunter now. I had zero cred with him. Think, think, think. I grabbed for my phone, nearly knocking it to the floor, and snapped a picture of the picture.

I pulled up Mr. Wilkenson's name and attached the picture, asking if that was the guy.

It took less than a minute for him to answer me back. Yes, it was him, and he also had a picture of him with his wife he would be sending from his wife's number.

While I was waiting, I called Raeann, but she didn't pick up. I sent her a simple 911 text and waited.

I also sent a psychic shout-out to Shelby and told her to get to the house immediately. She usually listens to music while she cleans stalls, so yelling for her the old-fashioned way wouldn't work.

Raeann still wasn't answering and I didn't know what else to do. I tried to call Hunter but he kept swiping me. I texted him and told him what was going on but he didn't reply. To be fair, all that I could really tell him was that Jake was the one who had spoken to the investor, so I guess in his mind that probably didn't rate a Code Red. My only other option was to tell him the guy killed Cheri Lynn, but brute honesty hadn't worked with him so far, plus there was no body.

Cheri Lynn was hovering and pacing as much as I was, except she wasn't wearing a path in the carpet. Adelaide was wringing her hands. None of us were used to doing nothing—we were all *doers*, and the lack of options was killing us. Okay, maybe that wasn't the best choice of words, but whatever.

My phone binged and I snatched it up, opening the text from a number with an Atlanta area code. It was a picture of a smiling Jake, and standing beside him was—

Cheri Lynn squealed in my ear. "Is that freakin' Violet Newsome? The Violet Newsome that was just here?"

I felt like I'd stepped on a rake and taken the handle to the face. All this time, I'd been asking her about the mystery real estate guy and it had been her. Or at least her partner. And she'd just been on the property.

It occurred to me that Shelby hadn't answered me. We had an unbreakable code: texts, or in this case psychic phone calls, always get answered. If not, I know to panic. She's never broken it before, so the fact that she was then, when all the crap was hitting the fan, was enough to send me over the edge.

I bolted through the door and made tracks for the barn with Addy and Cheri Lynn right behind me. The wheelbarrow was sitting in the middle of the aisle and her blue manure rake was on the floor beside it. I yelled her name, but the only responses I got were anxious nickers. I heard something scrape on the concrete behind me and Addy hollered for me to watch out. I didn't have time to turn around before somebody grabbed me and jabbed a needle into my neck. Then I knew what *fade to black* really meant.

I REGAINED CONSCIOUSNESS in stages. The first thing I noticed was that somebody was kicking my ankle and making weird noises. The second thing I noticed was that I was lying on a floor. My head was pounding, but when I went to feel the back of my head, I realized I was trussed like a Thanksgiving turkey.

I opened my eyes and saw my kitchen floor about two inches from my eye. Raeann was the one kicking me and trying to yell at me through her own gag. Shelby was tied up a couple of feet from me and still unconscious. The rotten-egg smell of gas was faint, but there.

I'd like to tell you I kept a cool head and immediately came up with a plan to save us using only the roach trap pushed underneath the cabinet in front of me, a paper clip, and some of the cake crumbs scattered on the floor, but that would be a lie.

I panicked. I've always had an irrational fear of constraint, probably from where Bobby Rae Casto held me down in the fifth grade and put his stupid pet tarantula on me. Regardless, when I realized my hands and feet were tied, I freaked out, struggling against the bindings.

Raeann kicked me again, this time harder, and brought me back to the present.

I pulled in a deep breath through my nose and almost gagged when I sucked in a lungful of gas; it was getting stronger. I concentrated on the rope. I tried to work my magic through the fibers so I could untie it, but my head was fuzzy and I couldn't focus. Instead, I turned and started kicking Shelby like Raeann had kicked me.

She started to come around, and I closed my eyes and tried to clear the fog. *Scoot toward me and put your back against mine,* I told Raeann, and she nodded. I sat up and pushed myself backward toward her. We met in the middle and began working on each other's ropes. No luck. I spied the knife caddy sitting on the counter and pushed my back against hers, hoping she understood what I was trying to do and pushed back. I could float one toward us, but as fuzzy as I was, I was just as likely to drop it mid-air and stab one of us as I was to get it to where we could use it.

Luckily, we'd played so many field-day games together throughout school that we were pretty synched and we pushed against each other until we were both standing.

It struck me as funny that it was quite possibly going to be the stuff I learned during field day that saved my life rather than magic or any the techniques I picked up in my criminal justice courses in college.

I clumsily hopped to the counter, teetering to the point of catastrophe several times because my ankles were tied together. I wasn't the most graceful on the best of days, so give me a concussion and limited use of my feet and I was definitely off my game. I scanned the surface for anything that would help, but everything remotely sharp was in the block, shoved too far back to reach.

I wondered where Adelaide and Cheri Lynn were. I was shocked they weren't both floating over us trying to tell us how important it was for us to get out. Stating the obvious seemed to be a superpower they shared.

When I caught movement out of the corner of my eye, I was sure it would be one of them. Instead, it was Violet. She walked over to the mantle and started picking up the pictures of Raeann and Jake.

"I'm pretty sure there's not going to be much left after this place blows, but I'm gonna take these just in case. It wouldn't do to have any pictures of the guy y'all know as Jake turn up."

I looked at her like she'd lost her mind because, obviously, she had. I tried to ask her what was wrong with her, but couldn't speak around the gag in my mouth.

Shelby was moaning. I was relieved she was coming around. I worked the rag with my tongue until I'd stretched it enough to push it out of my mouth, though my head still felt like it was full of cotton.

"What in the name of God is wrong with you? You can't just blow people up, then walk away."

"Oh, I have no intention of walking away. I'm going to work from my office in the Bahamas to develop this place and make enough money that I can go anywhere and do anything I want for the rest of my life. If I never see another dog thermometer, it'll be too soon."

Jake chose that minute to enter, dressed like he'd just come from a business meeting. If Raeann wasn't tied, he would have been a dead man. As it was, all she could do was scream muffled invectives at him, though most of them weren't hard to decipher, especially the ones involving his mother and suggestions to do the anatomically impossible, but those were the mild ones. She's creative when she's got a mood on, and this definitely qualified. He walked around her, careful not to get within kicking range. That was smart of him because if she got a shot, he'd be spitting out his nuts.

"We're going to have to tie them to the chairs. Otherwise, they might get loose. They shouldn't have come to this soon. We'll have to give them another shot before we leave." Violet was digging for something in her purse and Jake was messing with the stove.

My head was starting to clear and I focused on a large pottery vase that was only a few feet from where Violet was picking through the pictures. Shelby nudged me with her foot.

The vase? She motioned toward it with her eyes.

I tried to remain passive and keep my eyes straight ahead so they didn't notice anything strange. *Yeah. Her, then him. I can't do it by myself. My head's too fuzzy.*

Me neither, but together?

I drew in a deep breath, struggling to shake the fog from my head. *Okay. On three.*

One ... two ... three!

We managed to get the vase just a few feet above her before both of us gave out, but it did the trick. It crashed onto her head and she dropped like a sack of potatoes.

The crash startled Jake and he rushed to Violet's side, unable to understand what he was seeing.

"Ah. The town gossips weren't lying when they said you two could do freaky hoo-doo stuff. I thought it was just redneck superstition. Well how about this?"

In three strides, he was beside Shelby. He reached under his suit jacket, withdrew a gun, and pointed it directly at her head. With his other hand, he pulled a full syringe from his outside pocket, pulled the cap off with his teeth, and plunged it into her neck. She collapsed against him.

I tried to summon enough energy to do something, but the gas was getting thicker and making me light-headed. He shoved another needle in Rae, then me.

The last things I remembered were the smell of eggs, a pleasant floating sensation, and seeing Adelaide and Cheri Lynn yelling at each other and working to raise the kitchen window even though their hands kept passing through. Silly girls. Why didn't they just pass through the walls like they always did? Of all the final hallucinations I could have had, my messed-up brain chose that one.

Chapter 31

I found myself floating back to consciousness yet again, except this time I wasn't tied up and I wasn't greeted by the smell of rotten eggs. I peeped one eye open to see whether I was dead or not.

I could see the sky through a canopy of pecan leaves, and a cool breeze was tickling across my body, but there was an absolute absence of noise. Not like silence, but a total vacuum. Nothing. Okay, so the hearing thing was a little freaky, but none of the points were a dead giveaway—pardon the pun—one way or another. Seeing as how I'd never asked Addy if she could feel the breeze, I could be a ghost.

Next, I tried moving my head and it felt like somebody was driving a railroad spike through my temple. I cringed. Okay, so not dead. I shut my eyes again and let my brain and body assimilate before I tried opening them up again. This time, I felt more aware and was able to turn my head a little *sans* railroad spike.

Raeann was on one side of me and Shelby was on the other and we were in my front yard. There was an ambulance parked several feet away, alongside a police cruiser. Sound started to filter back in. My vision was suddenly blocked by a giant, semi-translucent head—Cheri Lynn's to be exact. Except blocked wasn't quite the right word. Shaded, maybe.

"She's awake, Ms. Adelaide!" No sooner had she uttered the words than Adelaide was hovering over me, too. Their individual transparencies kind ran together, like those tissue-paper projects you make as a kid. Blue and pink make purple. That struck me as hilarious for some reason, and I giggled.

"And I think she's stoned from the drugs and the gas," Cheri Lynn said. "Either that or the knock to the noggin rattled something loose." She furrowed her brow as I giggled again. A bird flew above us, seeming to go in one of her ears and out the other. "Either way, I don't think she's quite right just yet."

"Well, leave her to it, then. Lord knows she's earned a few minutes of vacation without leaving the farm. Raeann's stirring, too."

Their voices drifted away and blended in with the other sounds. I caught bits and pieces of conversations from cops and medics, and I even thought I heard Cody's voice at one point, but it was all a distant buzz.

After a few minutes, a medic knelt beside me. "Ms. Flynn, we're going to load you up and take you to the hospital for observation. We're pretty sure you're going to be okay, but we want to make sure, because you inhaled quite a bit of gas fumes, and that lump on your head should be looked at."

"Okay," I sing-songed. Right then, whatever they decided to do was fine with me as long as I was left to float. A brief flash of clarity revealed that if I was okay with going to the hospital, I probably needed to go—but the thought drifted away as the incredible fluffiness of the clouds caught my attention. They lifted me onto a gurney and tucked a blanket around me, and I drifted back to sleep.

When I woke up the next time, I was in a hospital bed. Oddly enough, Will was sitting beside me looking anxious and guilty.

"Noelle, I'm so sorry!" he said as soon as he realized I was awake.

"Why?" He hadn't had any part in this had he?

"I should have seen this coming. She'd made comments about being unhappy, and about wanting to move back to Atlanta, especially after Hank started pinching me and money got tight. She even talked about what a goldmine your farm was, but I never thought she'd do something like this."

"Well, to be fair, most people wouldn't suspect that the person they love is a homicidal sociopath, so I think I'm willing to forgive you. But I do expect some free vet services. You can float Max's teeth if you want to. That would be a serious win-win for me."

The corner of his mouth lifted. "You always did have that funky sense of humor. Thank you."

"She said the same things to me about my house. I thought she was just being a friend and educating me. I never thought she was going to do something like this either, so if you're guilty, so am I."

He rose to leave, but I reached out to him.

"Don't go yet. I know it's probably hard to go through again, but two of the four people in my life who would visit me in a hospital are, I assume, in the hospital with me." When I spoke, my throat felt raw and scratchy and dry. I reached for my water with the standard-issue hospital bendy straw, but Will grabbed it and handed it to me before I could pull the stand toward me.

"Well, from what we can gather, Violet met Frank—Jake—at a restaurant in Atlanta." He flinched when he said that, and I know it had to hurt. "He was there for a real estate convention and she was visiting her folks. We'd been having problems for a few months at that point. Somewhere along the line, they ended up ... sleeping together ... and then it became a relationship.

"When Adelaide died, they saw the perfect opportunity to make a fortune. They figured you'd sell at least most of it to them, but when you turned Jim down and wanted to keep the whole thing intact, they went to Hank. Well, Jake did. Violet stayed behind the scenes."

Huh. That explained why Hank had cut my brake lines. He really did want me dead. Man, death by pie poisoning couldn't have happened to a nicer guy. I had to remember to thank Cheri Lynn again the next time I saw her.

"I guess, in a nutshell, the grand plan was to get rid of you and get your place. But then they found out Raeann becomes Shelby's guardian and trustee, so they had to factor that in." He scrubbed a hand over his face.

"Our guess is that they planned for you to die in the wreck, and Shelby to die in the barn—or maybe that part really was an accident or intended for you—then Jake was taking Raeann skydiving. The chute wouldn't have opened. When plan A didn't work, they planned the explosion. You know the rest."

I examined all the facets of their plan. They pretty much covered everything. The sad part of it was that it likely would have worked. Hunter had recently mentioned that an application had been filed for gas line repairs, and that was what Hank seized on. The house could have blown up. It happens enough in old houses that nobody would have been the wiser.

The only loose end would have been Gary Wilkenson, but thanks to me, he probably would have been taking a dirt nap too if Hunter hadn't stopped them when he did.

"So, the only question left then, is how did we get out of the house?"

"Addy and Cheri Lynn popped straight over to the Clip N Curl and told Coralee what was going on. She called 911 and raced straight out to your place herself. By the time she got there, Max had dragged you and Shelby out by the ropes tied around your feet, and almost had Rae out."

I heaved a sigh. Not that I wasn't extremely grateful to the lop-eared pain in the ass, and I would definitely be showing it, but it was going to cost me a fortune in scotch and butter mints, and I had no doubt I'd hear about it every time he wanted something for the next eighty years or so.

We sat in silence for a few minutes while I digested all the information he'd just doled out. Will looked absolutely tragic sitting there hanging his head, but he looked much better than he had the day of the fair.

"Hey!" I said, flicking his arm. "This is *not* your fault."

He just gave me a lost little smile and patted my hand. "Is it horrible that, aside from what happened to you and Cheri Lynn, I feel better than I have in months? Violet and I fought all the time, the books weren't adding up at the clinic and somehow we were in the red, and I had Hank bleeding me dry." He paused and shook his head.

"I found a savings book for an account at an Atlanta bank with almost a hundred grand in it," he said, grinning. That was the first real smile I'd seen from him in months. "She was considerate enough to use the same password for that account as she does for all the others, so online banking was extremely convenient. Then I changed all the passwords, just in case."

I smiled and squeezed his hand. "Good. Do something for yourself. You and Cody go on a fishing trip or something. You've earned it."

He took a deep breath and nodded. "That's not a bad idea at all."

"And you may want to use some of it to file for divorce, too. Just sayin'."

He laughed and rolled his eyes, then waved goodbye as he headed out the door.

Shelby, Raeann, and I were released the next morning and I took a few days of much-needed sick time to get my poop back in a group.

Rae came over the night we got out of the hospital and we'd gone through the whole post-breakup, man-hating routine, complete with wine, ice cream, and Netflix. Since this one took bad luck in men to a whole new level, we sprung for the good stuff and bought a bag of truffles, too.

The one good thing that had come of it was that she no longer had any interest in jumping off bridges or out of airplanes. She finally had to agree with me that folks who do that are crazy. The proof was in the pudding with that one. She ran into the doctor who had taken care of Shelby when she'd fallen off the ladder and they were having coffee, though she'd placed a strict moratorium on personal relationships for at least six months, or until she could do a full background check.

Anna Mae showed up at my front door a few days later.

I'd been baking, so I wiped my hands on my apron as I motioned her in.

"Hey, you! You look amazing!" Her color was back and her eyes had regained their gleam. That haunted look was gone.

"Oh, I feel a hundred percent better, all right. I'm getting my half a mil from his life insurance policy today."

"Well, well! Then I assume the wine is on you tonight? And not that cheap stuff, either."

"Actually, I come bearing a little better gift than wine."

"Sweetie, I'm not sure that's possible after the week I've had."

She was practically vibrating with excitement, so I decided to quit messing with her and let her spill it. She handed me a pink-camouflaged envelope with my name on it. I had no idea what it was, but I'd once gotten one just like it with a wedding invitation in it. Surely she hadn't gone and done that again already. Her taste in men was equal only to Raeann's.

"Well go ahead—open it!" She was bouncing on her toes and grinning like a five-year-old on Christmas morning.

I slipped my finger under the flap and pulled out a fancy thank-you card. When I opened it, a check fell out. I understood my name and the amount separately, but didn't know what to think about them being side by side on the same check. I closed my eyes and popped one open to check it again.

"Mama Doolittle says no matter what kind of rabbit trail you went down to do it, you found Hank's murderer and she never goes back on her word. There's your fifty grand." She jumped up and down—hats off to her surgeon because her boobs didn't move an inch—and squealed the last few words. I have to say, I was feeling pretty school-girly myself.

I looked at the check again just to make sure it was still there, then leaned against the table to keep from falling over. "Holy crap, Anna Mae. I don't even know what to say!"

She stepped up to me and brushed that stupid curl out of my face, then looked me in the eye. The laughter didn't entirely fade from her pixie face, but she did look a bit more somber. "You don't have to say anything, sugar. You earned every penny of it and then some. Just do with it what you want, and be happy."

I pulled her into a hug. "Thank you, Anna Mae."

I still couldn't hardly believe it. I had fifty grand, and my taxes were paid for another whole year, so it was free and clear. I was so discombobulated that I sank into a chair and flicked a wrist to turn off the oven without even thinking about what I was doing. She just arched a brow when my gaze shot to her, then moved to stand beside me so she could sneak a couple of Snickerdoodles off the cooling rack.

"Ain't nuthin' I didn't already know, sugar." She winked and closed her eyes as the cookie melted in her mouth. "'Sides, anybody who's ever tasted your baking has to know there's magic involved."

We just stood and enjoyed not worrying about things for a few minutes as I poured us a glass of wine. The topic of insane amounts of money made me think of Hank's secret bank accounts and that giant stack of cash in the safe. I hip-checked her and grinned. "So, what are you going to do now that you're a free and independently wealthy woman?"

"Well, I've decided to give back a lot of it. I don't want to know what was in that black book of Hank's, but I do want to make things as right as I can. Between me, you, and the fencepost, there was almost three million dollars, countin' the bank and the safe."

I whistled. Even though I knew there was quite a bit of money in the safe, I never suspected there was that much.

"I've asked the sheriff to go through the book and figure out which of the people in there were good folks that Hank was stickin' it to. I'm not talkin' about crooked judges and paid-for cops—far as I'm concerned, they don't get squat. I mean folks like Will and Bonnie and Jim—good people.

"I want him to give me an amount, and I'm going to give him the cash so he can make sure it makes it back into the right hands. Through the mail, so that they remain anonymous. He said he was doing a full tax audit and notifying folks who've paid too much, so Benny down at the post office won't know one city hall envelope from another. Their secrets are theirs and died with Hank."

"Anna Mae! That's perfect!" I wiped a tear off my lashes with my knuckle. I'd been so worried about what would happen to those poor people.

She shrugged. "Well, like I said, I'm not givin' it all back—just the part that he skinned good folks for. I'm gonna let that tight-wadded SOB pay for something nice for us, too, because I've earned it and because it'd really get his goat. He never wanted me to have friends." She took a sip of her wine and grinned like she was up to no good.

"I'd like for you, Raeann, Bobbie Sue, and Coralee to go on a cruise with me. I've always wanted to try one of those drinks in a coconut with the little umbrellas, and I can't imagine doin' it without the four women who stuck by me through this whole mess! Plus, poor Raeann! That girl just can't catch a break with men!"

I barked out a laugh at the irony. Anna Mae stuck around for a few more minutes and we chatted about what kind of car she was going to trade Hank's fancy, pride-and-joy pickup for, then made plans for the five of us to get together to plan the cruise the following day.

After she'd gone, I sat at the kitchen table and pulled out the check, unable to believe something with that many zeros attached was actually going into my bank account.

I sensed I wasn't alone a second before Cheri Lynn popped in beside me. She whistled when she saw the check.

"Yeah, I know," I told her, shaking my head. "Can you believe it?"

"Actually, Noelle, I can. It's Karma. Good people like you deserve a good turn."

She was hovering over a chair with her hands clasped on the table in front of us, her eyes sad. They still hadn't found her body.

"Cheri Lynn, you weren't a bad person. You just did what you had to do to survive. You didn't deserve what you got, honey. Not by a long shot."

Her lips tipped up a bit, but her smile was wistful. "I was always jealous of you, ya know. I always wondered what it would have been like to have been born you instead of me. I thought that was what made us different." She bit her lip.

"But then I saw you go through your mama dyin' and your daddy leavin', and then you lost Calvin and Adelaide and took on the responsibility of raisin' Shelby. You've been through a lot, too, and you didn't make the choices I did though you could have. That's what got me where I am, but honestly, it's almost nicer now. I have more friends now that I'm dead than I ever had when I was alive. I even went over and smoothed things out with Anna Mae."

I didn't know what to say to that, so I kept my mouth shut. Instead, I asked, "Have you decided what to do yet?"

She'd seen the light, and the choice whether to stay or go was hers.

"I haven't decided yet. I have the feeling I don't have to decide immediately. It feels more like an open-ended invitation, so if it's okay with you, I'd like to hang around for a while."

"That's just fine with me. Take your time, sugar. I'm sure Addy would be glad to show you the ropes."

She nodded and congratulated me on the money again, then left.

After she faded out, I took a few more minutes to admire the check, then tucked it into my birdhouse cookie jar on top of the fridge.

I took my glass of wine out to the porch and settled in the swing. I sipped and watched the horses stand side by side, nose-to-tail, swishing flies for each other. Hunter had already made several arrests, starting with Hank's two goons, Butch Davies and Ronnie Dean.

Rumor had it they'd flipped on each other before Hunter even offered them a deal, which meant that in addition to providing lots of dirt on each other and Hank, they also confessed to some crimes themselves. I knew neither of their elevators went all the way to the top, but I didn't think they were that dense.

Sadly, their crimes didn't add up to much, so they'd likely only get a few months' jail time, but it was better than nothing.

Camille had finally called me back. In typical council fashion, she didn't explain herself. When I told her what happened, she surprised me by insisting on conducting the test to see why that had happened. That was scheduled for the following week.

Hunter had stopped by the hospital to check on me, but I hadn't heard from him since. That was why, when my phone dinged with an incoming text, I was a little surprised to see it was from him.

H: I'm going for a ride around the lake if you'd like to go.

I paused, considering what to say. I ended up going with the ever-brilliant, loquacious, "Okay."

While I was waiting, I stuffed a couple of bottles of water and some bear claws into a small backpack.

He pulled up a few minutes later and shut the bike off.

"Hey, Noelle."

"Hey, Hunter."

He seemed to be searching for the right words, looking everywhere but at me.

"I'm not going to say I understand all this," he said, "but I do know I like you. And I like Keyhole Lake. I'm going to stick around, and I'd like to get to know you better. I guess I'll figure out the rest as we go."

"Well, isn't that how most relationships go? At least you know straight out of the gate that you're getting a certain level of crazy with me. When it comes down to it, I'm just a regular girl. My gifts aren't like superpowers. Look how much good they did me when a couple of nutjobs tried to blow me up."

His eyes crinkled and he gave me the first genuine smile I'd seen from him since the night we rode the bikes.

"Fair point, though I think calling you a regular girl is a bit of a stretch. Now, just one more thing," he said as he climbed off the bike.

"What?"

He came so close I could smell that clean cologne that reminded me of the ocean, or maybe the woods after it rains. He looked into my eyes and my heart stuttered a little, then he laid his hand on the side of my face.

"This," he said, as he brushed his lips over mine.

It only lasted an instant before he stepped back and handed me my helmet, but wow—what an instant.

I strapped it on and swung my leg over the bike, then wrapped my arms around him and hoped like crazy there was another one of those in my near future.

Thank you!

Thank you for reading Sweet Murder. I hope you enjoyed reading it as much as I enjoyed writing it. Reviews are the lifeblood of an indie author's career, so if you would take just one more minute to share your opinion and insights, I would greatly appreciate it!

In case you're wondering what's next for Noelle and crew, here's an **unedited sneak peek at Murder to the Max[1], Book 2** in The Witches of Keyhole Lake Series. I hope to see you there.

Happy Reading,

Tegan

1.   https://www.amazon.com/Murder-Max-Witches-Southern-Mysteries-ebook/dp/B076RT73W7

Sneak Peek of Murder to the Max

"That should do it." Hunter pulled the last tie-down strap tight and climbed up on the trailer to give the motorcycle a firm shake. When it didn't budge, he jumped down and double-checked the hitch.

I took one final, longing look at the log cabin we'd enjoyed for the last week. I closed my eyes and inhaled, relishing the last few minutes of peace and quiet before we headed back to Keyhole Lake.

"You know, it's not like we can't come back," Hunter called. "We're only an hour from home."

I heaved a regretful sigh. "I know, but everything is just so ... perfect. As much as I miss everyone, I hate to leave."

"Well, at least everything will be back to normal—as normal as Keyhole Lake gets, anyway—when we get back."

"I don't know whether to be happy or depressed about that." Our little burg in the middle of Georgia gave new meaning to "sleepy little town." At least it did until recently.

He leaned down and gave me a kiss on the forehead. "Ready to head back?"

I scrunched my nose. "Not really, but we don't have much choice. At least not until one of us wins the lottery or finds a random bag full of hundred-dollar bills."

"Well, I'll be sure to keep my eyes open, but with our luck, it'll be sitting beside a dead body."

"Don't even joke about that!" Hunter and I had met over the body of Hank Doolittle, the biggest crook in town, when he'd keeled over dead in his plate of barbecue, but that's another story that, hopefully, you've already read about.

Anyway, the hubbub from Hank's murder had died down and all of the loose ends had been tied up. When it was all said and done, Hank Doolittle ended up doin' way more good by dyin' than he ever did by livin'.

After the murder, Hank's widow Anna Mae had taken me and the other three women in our little group, who you'll meet in a bit, on a week-long Caribbean cruise. Adelaide, my ghostly aunt, and Cheri Lynn, a recently deceased exotic dancer (we don't say 'stripper' because it hurts her feelings) had also tagged along.

Cheri had met a really nice, extremely attractive living-impaired man and had opted to stay for an extra week on the ship to get to know him better. The rest of us, however, had to get back to reality.

After a couple of months living under the watchful eyes of the local gossip mill, Hunter and I had decided that we needed some time away from it all to focus on each other.

On a whim, we'd rented this cabin, loaded his motorcycle onto a trailer so that we could take advantage of the great back roads and scenery, and headed out without so much as a by-your-leave to anybody other than my family and his closest deputy.

I glanced at the cabin one more time before heaving my duffel bag onto my shoulder and heading for the truck. Hunter took it from me and tossed it into the bed, along with his bag and our riding gear. It would have been so much easier just to magic it to the truck, but I was trying to break him in gradually to the concept.

He opened the driver's side door and climbed in, leaving the door open. "I need you to stand behind the trailer and tell me if the lights are working, please."

I walked around behind the truck and waited for him to hit the brakes. When he did, nothing happened, so he got out of the truck and came around to check the wiring. Just as he was kneeling down, an older, grizzled man wearing jeans and a blue Dickies work shirt appeared beside the trailer. Well, more accurately, the ghost of the man appeared.

My eyes about popped out of my head and my heart started to race. Hunter had accepted that I was a witch, but I'd been trying to ease him into it by keeping things as normal as possible around him. New relationships were hard enough without the additional burden of, oh, I don't know ... say, ghosts appearing randomly.

I checked to make sure Hunter's back was still turned before I made a frantic throat-sawing gesture and mouthed the words *not now* to the ghost. He just looked at me, then at Hunter, who was on one knee with his head under the truck checking the wiring.

The ghost turned to look at the trailer, wrinkling his forehead. "That tie strap ain't gonna hold," he said. I pinched my lips together and glared at the man. "What? It's not. Look." He pointed to the strap, but I was too busy trying to shoo him away to look where he was pointing.

"Did you say something, Noe?" Hunter's voice was muffled as he was still fiddling with the wires.

"Uh ... no?" I hadn't said a word, which means that he shouldn't have heard a word.

The ghost stepped closer to him and spoke a little louder, becoming more corporeal as he did. "She didn't say anything; I did. I said your tie strap isn't going to hold."

Hunter pulled his head from under the truck but remained kneeling. He looked puzzled, and when his gaze drifted in the direction of the specter, he fell backward onto his butt and the color drained from his face. I groaned and pinched the bridge of my nose. Somehow, he could see him.

Just lovely; this is *so* not how I wanted to do this.

Hunter was still wrapping his head around the fact that magic existed, so we were letting him dip his toes into the pond before we took him to the middle and threw him overboard. We hadn't exactly introduced him to the local ghost community. Or told him there was one.

"Noelle, do you see a man standing there?"

With a resigned sigh, I said, "Yes, Hunter. There's a man standing there."

"A transparent man?" he was on his feet gripping the tailgate so hard that his knuckles were white. I couldn't tell if he was going to bolt or pass out.

I stepped to his side, watching him carefully. His eyes were glued to the guy, but there was some color coming back into his cheeks. "He's a ghost," he announced. Well, when all the possible options are gone ...

"Yes. He's a ghost. Breathe."

Hunter took three or four deep breaths and then nodded, though he was still a bit pale.

After a few awkward seconds, the ghost lost his patience. "What's the matter with him?" He jabbed a thumb in Hunter's direction. "Don't tell me Numbnuts here is the only one in town who doesn't know you're a witch." He put the word 'witch' in air quotes.

The rudeness snapped Hunter out of his daze. "Hey! Don't call her a witch like that!"

"Oh, but you're okay with Numbnuts?" The ghost rolled his eyes and Hunter opened his mouth to retort.

Ugh. I decided to step in before it got ugly. "Okay, first, don't call him Numbnuts. I assume that since you're here, you need our help with something and being rude isn't the way to get it. Let's start with your name. You look familiar, but I can't place you."

"Max Wheeler." He started to put his hand out to shake, but realized the futility of the gesture and withdrew his hand. Now I knew why he looked familiar; he owned the company that was building my pool and patio. Fabulous. Now my pool was never going to get done. Before the thought was even fully formed, I felt bad for being so selfish.

"All right, Max. Now I know who you are, and as far as I know, you were alive and kicking when we left town. It would seem that's no longer the case. Is there some reason in particular that you popped in on the tail end of our vacation, or did you just happen to be floating by on your way to the great hereafter? Obviously, you know who I am. This is Hunter Woods. He's the new sheriff of Keyhole Lake."

"I know who he is. He's the reason I'm here. Well, that and I didn't expect him to be able to see me so I was trying to catch him when he was with you."

Hunter finally found his voice. "Me? Why are you looking for me?"

Max flickered in and out for a few seconds, sort of like bad reception on a TV. When he stopped fizzling, he looked around as if he had no idea where he was.

His eyes roamed over the bike strapped down in the trailer. "That tie strap isn't going to hold," he repeated in a way that made me believe he didn't know he'd already said it.

Hunter looked at me, asking what to do. I tilted my head toward Max and he nodded.

"Why do you say that, Max?"

The ghost's gaze bounced from the tie strap to Hunter and his brow furrowed. "How do you know my name?" His gaze strayed to the bike again. "It's not going to hold because it's about worn clean through right there." He pointed to a frayed spot on the tie down.

Hunter looked closer and whistled. "You're right, man. I didn't even see that. Thanks." He loosened the tie strap and opened his toolbox to get another, almost as if there wasn't a ghost standing right beside him. I had to hand it to him; he'd taken rolling with the punches to an art form.

I eased closer to the trailer, afraid that if I moved suddenly, our visitor would pop out of sight again before we figured out why he was there. Or that Hunter would suddenly realize what a nutjob he was dating, and leave like his hair was on fire. "Max, you said you were looking for Hunter. Can you remember why?"

Max looked at me for a few seconds, then the haze lifted from his eyes and he stopped flickering. "Of course I can remember why. I'm dead, not senile. I need Numbnuts here to go find my body. Otherwise, I'm going to be lying there until the cows come home."

Hunter stopped fidgeting with the straps and snapped his gaze to him, incredulous. "Say what?"

Max rolled his eyes and scratched his whiskers as if he were gathering what little patience he had. He leaned closer to Hunter and spoke slowly, enunciating each word. "Go. Find. My. Body. I'm speakin' English."

That irritated me. "There's no need for snark. It's not like this happens to him every day."

He crossed his arms. "Well, for a sheriff, he seems a bit dense. My body's at my shop. Some meathead bashed my skull in with a toilet tank lid."

His eyes glazed over again and he drew his brows together, confused, then glanced at his watch. He muttered something about having to meet Darlin', then flickered out.

Well alrighty then. It looked like we had a body to find.

Ready to read the rest? Then pick up Murder to the Max here[1].

---

1. https://www.amazon.com/gp/product/B076RT73W7/ref=series_rw_dp_sw

Connect with Me

Join my readers club here[1] to be the first to hear about new releases, giveaways, contests, and special deals. I'm a reader too, so if I come across a good deal by a great author, I may share in the weekly update, but I won't spam you with salesy BS. I may include obscure trivia, though; you'd be amazed what I learn while researching!

If you're not an email-list person, keep track of new releases by following me:

ON BookBub[2]

On Facebook[3]

On Amazon[4]

Or at Teganmaher.com

Email me – I always love hearing thoughts and feedback, or just drop me a line to say hi!

Happy Reading, and thank you for your time. ☺

---

1. http://eepurl.com/c0MFc5

2. https://www.bookbub.com/authors/tegan-maher

3.   https://www.facebook.com/AuthorTeganMaher/

4.   https://www.amazon.com/Tegan-Maher/e/B0759XYYZD/

Other Books by Tegan Maher

Witches of Keyhole Lake Series

Book 1: Sweet Murder[1]
Book 2: Murder to the Max[2]
Book 3: Murder so Magical[3]
Book 4: Mayhem and Murder[4]
Book 5: Murder and Marinade[5]
Book 6: Hook, Line, and Murder[6]
Book 7: Murder of the Month[7]

Witches of Keyhole Lake Shorts

Bubble, Bubble, Here Comes Trouble[8]
Witching for a Miracle[9]
Moonshine Valentine[10]

---

1. https://www.amazon.com/Sweet-Murder-Witches-Keyhole-Mysteries-ebook/dp/B075BR5L45/

2. https://www.amazon.com/Murder-Max-Witches-Keyhole-Mysteries-ebook/dp/B076RT73W7/

3. https://www.amazon.com/gp/product/B0786WP84L

4. http://www.amazon.com/Mayhem-Murder-Witches-Keyhole-Mysteries-ebook/dp/B078P9D318

5. https://www.amazon.com/Murder-Marinade-Witches-Keyhole-Mysteries-ebook/dp/B079GB3L4B/

6. https://www.amazon.com/Hook-Line-Murder-Witches-Mysteries-ebook/dp/B07B6QR17H

7. https://www.amazon.com/Murder-Month-Witches-Keyhole-Mysteries-ebook/dp/B07DB33Q8H

8. https://www.amazon.com/Bubble-Here-Comes-Trouble-Witches-ebook/dp/B0782X67ZC/
   ref=la_B0759XYYZD_1_7?s=books&ie=UTF8&qid=1518635101&sr=1-7

9. https://www.amazon.com/Witching-Miracle-Witches-Keyhole-Mysteries-ebook/dp/B079VKXD9P/
   ref=la_B0759XYYZD_1_12?s=books&ie=UTF8&qid=1526530253&sr=1-12

10. https://www.amazon.com/Moonshine-Valentine-Witches-Keyhole-Mysteries-ebook/dp/B07C89K8TY

Cori Sloane Witchy Werewolf Mysteries

Howling for Revenge[11]
Dead Man's Hand[12]
Bad Moon Rising[13]

Enchanted Coast Magical Mystery Series

Deadly Daiquiri[14]
Surfboard Slaying[15]

11. https://www.amazon.com/Howling-Revenge-Werewolf-Mystery-Mysteries-ebook/dp/B079R911ZW/

12. https://www.amazon.com/Dead-Mans-Hand-Werewolf-Mysteries-ebook/dp/B07C7KKF8W

13. https://www.amazon.com/gp/product/B07FD3QFBB

14. https://www.amazon.com/Deadly-Daiquiri-Enchanted-Magical-Mystery-ebook/dp/B07CBCY1LQ

15. https://www.amazon.com/Surfboard-Slaying-Enchanted-Magical-Mysteries-ebook/dp/B07DF5KCH3

About Tegan

I was born and raised in the South and even hung my motorcycle helmet in Colorado for a few months. I've always had a touch of wanderlust and have never feared just packing up and going on new adventures, whether in real life or via the pages of a great book.

When I was a little girl, I didn't want to grow up to be a writer—I wanted to raise unicorns and be a superhero. When those gigs fell through, I chose the next best thing: creating my own magical lands filled with adventure, magic, humor, and romance.

I live in Florida with my two dogs. When I'm not writing or reading, I'm riding motorcycles or binge-watching anything magical on Netflix.

I'm eternally grateful for all the people who help make my life what is today - friends, readers, family. No woman is an island.

37774002R00134

Printed in Poland
by Amazon Fulfillment
Poland Sp. z o.o., Wrocław